Return of the

Return of the

Book 2 in
Border Knight Series
By
Griff Hosker

i

Return of the Knight

Return of the Knight

SWORD
BOOKS

Contents

Prologue

The circumstances of our departure from Sweden were not the ones I would have chosen. We had been virtually thrown out of the country by Bishop Albert. We had served his purpose and helped him to create an Empire. We had defeated the barbarians and brought Christianity to the Estonians. I had left behind friends I had had since that day at Arsuf when my father had died and my world had changed. However, for all of that, I could not have been happier as we sailed south through ever warmer waters. I had saved and married Lady Margaret, the widow of a German knight who had been duped out of her fortune by an unscrupulous knight. I had challenged him to combat but he had been a knight without honour. He had refused and Bishop Albert had ejected us from Sweden. My wife was penniless but I was not. I was a sword for hire and my men and I had made coin in the wars against the pagans in the cold Baltic.

Now we were heading south. Sir Philip of La Flèche was the grandson of the man who had followed my great grandfather, the first Earl of Cleveland. King John might have taken all of my lands in the valley of the Tees but La Flèche was still mine. We had no idea what we would find there. All that I knew was that Sir Philip was loyal to me and my family and for that I was grateful. My aunt had sent me a letter, shortly before we had left Sweden, in which she told me that King John had lost Anjou, Maine and Brittany. Poitou still belonged to his mother, Eleanor of Aquitaine. His young nephew, Arthur, Duke of Brittany had claimed the estates his Uncle Richard had left him. King Richard's death had now given my most implacable enemy great power. I had decided to serve this twelve-year-old who had the backing of Philip of France. As old Edward, one of my father's faithful warriors had said once, '*You roll the dice Master Thomas and make the best of what they show. You do not make your world, it makes you. That is how you become a man.*'

I was now that man. I had hardened warriors with me, I had my squire from the Holy land, William, now knighted, ten men at arms and ten archers. We were not a large number but there were no finer warriors anywhere. As the mouth of the Loire hove into view I knew that I was throwing the dice. I had a manor and, one day, I would sit in a castle in Stockton. That was some way off but I was determined. John Lackland would not defeat me.

Chapter 1

I had had word that Sir Philip held La Flèche for me. How would the young Duke of Brittany view me? The nearer we came to La Flèche the more worried I became. I was now a married man. I had a wife and her women to consider. If it was just my men that I had to worry about then I would not be concerned. While King Richard had been alive then I had had hope that he would return and undo the wrongs done by his brother. Now that John was King my hopes were undone. My fate lay in the hands of a twelve-year-old boy.

On the last part of the voyage south, I had written a letter to my aunt who still lived in Stockton with her husband Sir Richard. He had proved an unlikely benefactor. He had been appointed by Prince John but had sympathised with me. The castle was gone. It had been destroyed on the orders of John Lackland. The hall remained and so long as it stood I still had a home to which I could return. I told my aunt my news and where I was. It did not matter if others knew. I was hiding no longer. For the first time in my young life, I would be fighting for a cause in which I believed, the restoration of my family's lands.

La Flèche had grown since Empress Matilda had first given it to my great grandfather, the Warlord. Much of that was to do with Sir Leofric who had been the first castellan. His son and his grandson had served us well. I knew little about Sir Philip. He had been an ocean away when I was growing up. When we tied up I took Fótr and Robert of La Flèche with me. My man at arms had come to me from this manor and would be my guide.

"Sir William, have the chests and horses landed while I go to the castle. Captain, I have a letter for you to take to Stockton. When I return, I will pay you for your troubles."

They both gave a slight bow. My wife and her ladies came on deck, "Do we not go with you, too, husband?"

"I believe that we will be welcome here but, until I am certain, I would not risk my most precious possession, and that is you."

"Husband, I am made of sterner stuff than you imagine."

I smiled, "Then supervise Sir William so that our goods are landed safely."

She nodded and Robert led me through the small town to the castle. There had been a gate from the quay into the town. Now we crossed a large and spacious square to a gate in the curtain wall of the castle. This was well designed. An ancient sentry stood on guard there. My livery made him wrinkle his brow. He did not recognise it. My great grandfather and grandfather had ridden beneath the wolf standard. I rode with the yellow gryphon. I was not

Return of the Knight

certain if my father had ever visited here. He did, however, recognise Robert. He grinned, "My old friend! I thought you long dead."

"No, although I have travelled far and seen many dead I have survived. This is Sir Thomas of…" He hesitated.

I smiled, "I know, Robert, this is hard for us all. I am Sir Thomas formerly of Stockton. I am the heir of the Warlord. Is Sir Philip at home? I would speak with him."

"Of course, my lord. Now I recognise the surcoat. Forgive me. When I saw Robert, I should have known. I will take you to him." He led us into the gatehouse and then the inner ward. The keep was a solidly built square one. It was at the far end of this triangular castle. The outer wall joined the town wall. La Flèche had a wall on three sides and a river on the fourth. The sentry banged on the door of the great hall and then opened it.

He did not get the chance to speak for Sir Philip recognised my livery, "You must be Sir Thomas! Welcome to your home! Lady Ruth wrote to me and told me of your troubles. Know that I am aware of my duties. This castle and the manor are yours."

I clasped his arm. Sir Philip was not just an old man, he was an old and sick man. He was grey. I suddenly realised that I knew next to nothing about him. "I hope that we will not inconvenience your wife and family."

He shook his head, "I have no family. My wife died in childbirth twenty years ago and… well I am content to live alone for the time the good lord allows me. I confess that I was pleased to hear that you were coming …" he looked at Fótr and Robert. He wished to speak to me privately.

I nodded, "Fótr, take Robert and have our goods fetched from the ship." As they left I smiled sadly at the knight, "I fear your quiet little world will be upset. There are half a dozen women with us."

He closed the door, "I am happy that this old castle will have a woman's touch. My wife only lived here a year. This is furnished for my mother. I am dying, lord. That is why I was happy to hear of your arrival. This belongs to your family. Since the death of King Richard, I have feared for our security. This is a rich manor. It is a jewel. Young Arthur is well-advised but he has allied with the French and we have never trusted them. King John wishes this land to be returned to him. He holds onto Normandy and his other domain Aquitaine but betwixt lies Brittany, Anjou and Maine. There will be war and…" he shook his head, "I will fight but I fear that my sickness will not give me a noble end such as your father's."

My father's death had been glorious but it had cost us all. "What is the sickness, my lord? Cannot it be cured by the healers?"

He shook his head, "It is something within me which eats at me. The healers have told me they can do nothing. I have some aqua vita which the monks make and that helps me to sleep." He looked at me and smiled. It was a sad smile,

5

"You will be happy here, lord. It is a good castle and a comfortable home. I will move to the west tower, with your permission."

"I would not put you from your quarters."

"My chambers are too big and I like the west tower. It looks to the sea and I often go there to watch the sunset. That is where I shall die. And now I will fetch my steward. Sorry, your steward." He went to the door and shouted, "Geoffrey!"

A neat little man appeared. He was in his thirties and looked a little young to be a steward, "Yes my lord?"

"This is Sir Thomas of La Flèche. He is the lord of the manor. Have my things moved to the west tower?"

"Yes lord. You are most welcome, Sir Thomas."

"There will be myself and another knight. We have wives and there are four women with us. Some of my men at arms and archers are wed. Are there rooms for them?"

Geoffrey beamed, "We can do better than rooms, my lord. We have a row of small houses just inside the wall of the inner ward. We keep them for the workers who come in the summer to pick the grapes. They stand empty for most of the year. There are six of them. Will that suffice?"

"It will indeed!"

For the first time in a long time, it looked like things were going my way and the next few days were hectic as we all adjusted to our new life. We had a home and for most of us, that was the first time.

I rode, at the end of that first week, with Sir Philip and Sir William to Anjou. Arthur, Duke of Brittany was there and we had to ensure that my title was approved. I did not want a repetition of Stockton. As we rode Sir Philip told me what he knew of the young Duke.

"He was King Richard's choice of heir. The King neither liked nor trusted his brother. You, of all people, knew that. His mother, Constance, was and is his adviser. She ruled with him in Brittany until she was abducted by the Earl of Chester. He has an elder sister, Eleanor the Maid of Brittany. She is much sought after for if anything happens to the Duke then Brittany is hers. The Prince's advisers are now French. I do not like that but it protects him from John Lackland." I smiled for the knight could not bring himself to accord John his title. "There are some good men. William des Roches of Le Mans was trusted by King Richard and there are others. I would think that your counsel would be appreciated."

"Mine?"

Any man who has advised the King of Jerusalem and the King of Sweden is a man who can be trusted."

As luck would have it we had arrived at a most propitious time. The Duke had summoned his barons to a council of war. Before we had left part of me

6

Return of the Knight

wondered why he had not sent for Sir Philip but the journey to Angers had shown me why. He was a sick man and the Duke's advisers must have known that. Sir Philip's name gained us entry. There would not be enough room in the castle for us to stay there but Sir Philip had enough contacts in the busy port to get us good rooms at an inn.

The Duke was holding court in a small chamber off the main hall. The three of us joined the barons, earls and counts who milled around the Great Hall. We stood apart. A clerk came over to us. He had the tonsure of a monk. "The Duke has asked me to make a record of those who are here."

"I am Sir Thomas of La Flèche, this is Sir Philip, my castellan and Sir William. He is my household knight."

He scribbled something on the wax tablet. I guessed it was our names. Then he looked up, "Were you Sir Thomas from Stockton?" He took a step back. "Did you not kill the Bishop of Durham?"

I nodded, "I did and I have been absolved by Bishop Albert of Uppsala. I have sinned but I am now forgiven. I have done my penance and helped to bring God to the godless."

Although he looked relieved he still looked at me warily. "I will tell his grace that you are here."

"I heard you had killed the Bishop but not that you have been absolved." Sir Philip chuckled, "I thought that one was going to make a puddle." He began coughing and I saw flecks of blood in the cloth he held in his hand. "My lord, I shall sit down. I do not think that the Duke will need my advice. My time is past."

Other knights came and went and then I was summoned. Sir William said, "I will wait with Sir Philip. He does not look well." My old squire was a thoughtful man.

When I was admitted there were four men in the room. One was a scribe and I recognised the Duke by his youth. He had no beard. He was a boy. The other two were knights, one looked to be older than I was but not by much. The other was much older and, I know not why, but he looked French. It was the older man who spoke, "I am Raymond, the Comte de Senonche. I am the adviser to the Duke. This is William des Roches, lord of Le Mans." William de Roches nodded. I got the impression that he was scrutinising me. I did not like it.

I bowed, "I am here, Prince Arthur, to claim back the manor which belonged to my father." I was aware that I could be given the same reception as I had received from Prince John.

Instead of dismissing me, Arthur, Duke of Brittany smiled and stood. He held out his hand, "It is yours and glad am I that I can give it to you. Both of us have had something taken away from them which was theirs by right. Yours was the County of Cleveland and mine was England and Normandy! Before these two august nobles, I say that when I attain the throne of England you shall

7

have Cleveland returned to you." He sat down and gave a self-deprecating smile. "Of course, first I have to defeat my enemies closer to home."

I liked the young man immediately. He was innocent and untutored.

The Comte de Senonche did not like the answer, "Quite, your grace. My liege, Philip, King of France has promised his full support to the Duke and you have come at a propitious moment. We are about to retake those parts of Anjou and Maine which foolish supporters of my Uncle have declared are not part of the Duke's land!"

"I will serve in any capacity I can, your grace."

William des Roches spoke for the first time. He was most definitely Norman. "You do not do yourself justice, my lord. Your name and reputation precede you. Was not the King of Jerusalem just a little older than his Grace when you helped him? From what I hear it was others who lost the kingdom and your name, along with the Master of the Hospitallers were the only two to emerge with any honour. And now you have returned, successfully, from the Baltic Crusade. His Grace would do well to have you as a leader."

The Frenchman shifted uneasily in his seat, "Let us not be hasty des Roches."

Prince Arthur was not yet a lord who played games. He was honest and spoke from the heart. "I agree with the lord of Le Mans. We need a leader like Sir Thomas. We all heard of his heroics at Arsuf. His name alone will strike fear into our foes. I leave you and Sir William to work out our strategy. I thank you again, my lord."

We were dismissed and the two of us left. Sir William put his arm around my shoulder. I felt uncomfortable but I decided to say nothing. I was in foreign waters. When we were safely out of earshot he said, "The Prince is right. There are many enemies here and some feign friendship. I do not trust the French. Philip sees this as a way to increase his kingdom at England's expense."

"And yet you work with them."

"You will discover in this land of intrigue that you have to play the game of kings and princes. The trick is to keep one step ahead."

"You have a plan?"

He nodded, "Saint-Suzanne lies to the north-west of Le Mans. The lord of the manor is Godfrey de Clairmont and he has declared for John. We could take that and then move onto Ballon which is to the northeast of Le Mans and guards the border. With those secure then we would have a ring of castles which would protect the northeast of Anjou."

It made sense but I did not know what sort of distances were involved. I needed to see a map. "Have you maps?"

"You can read them?"

"I can read them."

"Then come to my chambers I will show you them."

8

Return of the Knight

"First I need to see my knights."

When we reached the Great Hall Sir Philip had returned to our rooms and so William accompanied us. He laid out the maps and then explained his strategy. The Lord of Le Mans knew his business and all was carefully planned. I saw that we could meet at Le Mans and that was a day's ride from La Flèche. Le Mans was the perfect base from which to launch our attack. We left feeling satisfied.

As we headed back to our rooms William said, "Sir Philip has worsened. We should take him back to La Flèche as soon as possible. I am no healer but he is close to death. He should have the dignity of dying in his own bed."

"We will leave in the morning. We have no need to stay here." While we had been waiting in the Great Hall the three of us had noticed the huddles of men speaking in hushed tones. To me, it had all the marks of a conspiracy. I did not like it. I had had enough of that in the Holy Land. I knew that I would have to make compromises. I had a wife now and men to lead. My aim was to regain my valley. To do that I would sleep with the devil if I had to.

All the way back to La Flèche I worried about Sir Philip. It was as though whatever was eating him had suddenly begun to devour him even faster. As we rode he spoke of his father and the grandfather he had known all too briefly. Sir Leofric was something of a legend. My father had been in awe of him and his father had spoken at great length of how Sir Leofric had helped to make him the knight he had become. He had had humble beginnings and yet had achieved greatness. Sir Philip felt that he had let his blood down. He had done nothing of note.

As we neared La Flèche I told him, "You are wrong. You have done that which your grandfather would have wished. You have kept your lands for the family of the Warlord. You have no children but I will have and your grandfather's story will be told to them. I swear, Sir Philip, that my children and their children will know your story and that of your family."

He nodded. I could see that he was too distraught to speak. He knew his end was close and like all men who face such moments he looked at his life and wondered if he had done all that he could. Perhaps my father had had a good death. It was over in an instant and there was no chance to regret decisions made.

Margaret noticed my mood. When we lay, later that night, in the bed in which Sir Philip had slept, alone, for so many years she said, "Some men have poor luck. The lord I was to marry was such a one. Men do not choose their luck. It chooses them. I thought that I would end up miserable and yet I have found the man that I might have searched the world to find. I am lucky. Embrace that luck, my love and celebrate life. It is too short for anything else." I am lucky I had married a beautiful woman who was also wise.

9

Return of the Knight

We had much to do. We had only brought a few horses. I used some of my coins to buy good horses for all of my men and remounts too. It was an investment. We had good swords, shields and armour. What I needed was more men at arms. I was not foolish enough to think I could find archers here in Anjou. They would have to wait until I could return to England. There were three good archers at the garrison. They were descended from the archers Sir Leofric had brought with him: Griff of Gwent. James the Short and Robert of Derby. Sir Philip's men at arms were, by and large, as old as he was. There were just six I could take with me. The rest would guard my new home. While my men prepared I went with Robert, Sir William and my squires to find more men at arms.

There had been war, off and on for more than twenty years in this land. There were many men at arms who had chosen a life of peace. There were others who had lost a lord and become lost. We searched every village and hamlet for twenty miles around seeking men who wished to earn gold. The Baltic Crusade had rewarded me. I was happy to invest in swords. In all, we acquired ten men and that doubled my retinue.

Sir Philip had taken to his bed. The old servants from the castle doted on him and it was touching to see the way they attended to him. "My lord," he said, "it is knights you need."

I shook my head, "I will have knights I can trust. Sir William will do for now and my men at arms are the equal of a knight. They can fight and they are loyal. They know that they will not be ransomed. If they are taken then they will die. Such men are like gold dust. But enough of our preparations, how are you?"

"I sleep more than I wake and when I sleep I see my mother, father and grandfather. My dead wife has spoken to me. My lord, I do not have long." He took a small chest and handed it to me. "When I die then here is my will and the last of my valuables. I pray that you will honour my wishes."

"You know that I shall."

"Then I can die content. Send Father Michel to me, lord. I would be shriven for I am content."

He died the next day. I opened the chest and found a document which told me his wishes. The money he had accrued was to be divided between the garrison and the servants. His mail and weapons he left to me to give to a deserving warrior. He asked to be buried in the church yard close to Sir Leofric. We honoured all of his wishes. When we left four days later all of my men were silent for although we had known him briefly, Sir Philip had been an example of a man who had been true to his vows, his lord and his liege. He had never fought in a major battle. I doubted that he had slain anyone and yet he had done his duty and what man could do more? I obeyed his wishes and he was buried by Sir Leofric and his wife. As I turned away my thoughts went back to my grandmother. I prayed that this grave would never be desecrated.

La Flèche

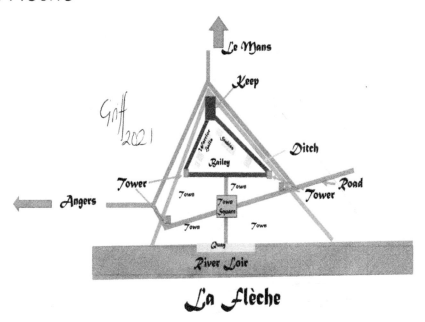

Chapter 2

My wife was a strong woman but, as I prepared for war and the ride north, I detected anxiety. She was fussing around me more than usual. I sat her down, "This is my life, my love. I am a warrior. I know nothing else. I am not a farmer. The only crops I reap are my foes. We go to fight John Lackland. The end is a long way away but the valley of the Tees is worth fighting for." I waved a hand around the chamber, "This castle is now yours. Make it the way you would wish it. Sir Philip would be happy. There are chests of coins. Geoffrey will know where to find anything that you wish."

She nodded and, taking my hand, kissed it, "I care nothing for possessions. I owe you so much that I am afraid to lose you."

"I have the best of men. You will not lose me."

William and his squire, Johann, had as yet no men at arms. Nor did he have his own surcoat and livery. Before we left he had a local seamstress make a pair of surcoats for him and his squire. It was the same as mine but there was a sword in the right-hand corner and the gryphon was smaller. We looked a fine sight as we left for Le Mans. We had two banners now and my men led ten sumpters with our war gear and spare arrows. We had learned many lessons in the Holy Land and the Baltic. We now put them to good use. For the first time, we would be both travelling and fighting in a land that was more familiar to us. This would not be the heat of the desert nor the snow of the frozen north. This would be a green and verdant land filled with forests, rivers and fields.

The scouts we used were two of the garrison and were led by Robert of La Flèche. Michael of Anjou and Phillippe of Poitou were both young men but they knew the land. With them rode two archers: Griff Jameson and Tom Robertson. Both were able to use their bows whilst mounted. I had seen the Seljuk Turks do so and I was pleased that at least two of my archers were able to try to master that skill.

Our caution was unnecessary. We were in friendly land all the way to Le Mans and we entered that mighty fortress at the end of a long hard day of riding. William des Roches greeted us warmly. I still found much in the man I did not like and yet I could not think of a reason for my dislike. He was over-familiar but other men were like that. It was something in his eyes that I did not trust. There were many other knights there. William des Roches had gathered all of the barons who were loyal to the Duke of Brittany. We would be taking fifty banners with us. As we ate William des Roches discussed his plans with us. There were five of us seated at the head of the table with him and we would be his lieutenants.

The next day I rode with William des Roches and the four other lieutenants to view the road which led to the castle of Saint-Suzanne. We rode with helmets hung from our saddles but we wore our arming caps and carried our shields over our left legs. We were prepared. We had our squires with us but, alarmingly, we took neither archers nor men at arms with us. I thought that was a mistake but William des Roches seemed confident. "Sir Thomas, I would have you become familiar with the land. I have heard you have a good eye for terrain. The castle is thirty miles from Le Mans. I would have you look at the first twenty miles and see if there are problems you envisage which I do not see. There are still five knights who are yet to arrive. Let us enjoy the ride."

I did enjoy the ride. What surprised me was the lack of any large village. Once we left Le Mans we passed nothing larger than a large hamlet. There were no castles, not even a fortified hall. I mentioned this to William. He nodded, "That is why I devised this strategy. Saint-Suzanne is the nearest castle. It is in Maine and guards the border. With that in our hands, we can make inroads to the north and east."

It seemed a good plan. It was coming onto noon. We had stopped to water our horses a couple of times and I could feel the first pangs of hunger. The road was approaching a wood and I was just about to ask if we should stop when Fótr said, "Lord! There are men ahead!"

From what William des Roches had told me there were few friends ahead. I guessed that we were about fourteen miles from Saint-Suzanne. I drew my sword and said, "Ware enemies!"

Suddenly a conroi of knights and squires burst from the woods. There were twelve of them. We were outnumbered two to one. This was when I would see the mettle of William des Roches.

"Ambush! Squires protect the rear." He donned his helmet and hefted his shield, as we all did. He turned to see that we were ready and, drawing his sword, shouted, "Charge!"

The six of us were armed with swords and the enemy with lances. That did not worry me but I wondered about the Angevins. One thing in our favour was the enemy formation. They had burst from the woods, realising that their ambush had been spotted and they came at us loosely. I was riding boot to boot with William des Roches and Guy de Changé. I pulled my shield a little tighter to me and, as we approached them tried to work out whom I would be striking.

The knights were, like us, ahead of their squires. In the centre was a knight with alternate yellow and red stripes. Next to him was a warrior with a green shield and three yellow birds. I would be striking him. I saw the tip of his lance wavering up and down as he charged. They were riding war horses. They had come prepared. We were riding palfreys. Mine was Skuld and was a better horse than might be expected. Skuld could turn quickly and was a clever horse. When the mêlée began I would have the advantage.

I braced myself for the blow from the wooden tipped lance. He pulled his arm back for the punch. I do not think either of us knew the exact place he would hit for the end of the long lance was wavering up and down. The ploughed field over which we were moving was far from level. When his horse's foreleg found the hole, the lance dipped and it was just when he was striking. The lance's tip glanced off the mail protecting my right knee. It was a painful blow but that was all. I swung my sword backhand. I hit him squarely in the back. Already off-balance from the mistake his horse had made he toppled from his mount and landed heavily.

As soon as he fell I wheeled. There was no honour in fighting squires and Skuld's fast hooves had taken me behind their knights. With my left protected with my shield, I rode for the two knights who were engaged with Roger d'Aubrey. All rules of combat had been abandoned and so I felt no shame in attacking one of them from the rear. I did shout as I charged close to him, "Turn and fight, traitor!"

The warrior with the red shield and yellow fess turned. His lance was the wrong weapon. He should have discarded it but, instead, he swung it at me hitting his companion's mount in the process. I stood in my stirrups and brought my sword down hard onto his right hand. He was wearing mail mittens but years of wielding the blade had made my right arm like a young oak. I broke the bones in his hand and he dropped his lance. He cried, "I yield!"

The blow from the lance to his horse, my attack and Roger d'Aubrey's own efforts forced the second knight to yield. I turned to look for more enemies but saw that the survivors had sped off. The knight I had unhorsed was not moving and there were two other knights nursing wounds. Four had yielded. I feared one lay dead. There would be no ransom from him. I turned and saw that Fótr alone out of the squires had slain a squire. From the livery, I saw that it was the squire of the knight who had fallen to me.

"Well done, Fótr, gather their horses." I sheathed my sword and said to the knight nursing the broken hand, "Who was the knight who could not keep his saddle?"

"That was Hugo de Ferrers. His family have estates in Derbyshire. You have made a mistake, gryphon knight, for he is a close confederate of King John."

I nodded, "And your name?"

"Hugh de Clare from Pembroke."

"Well, Hugh de Clare from Pembroke, two things you should know about me, I hate King John more than any man alive and my name was Sir Thomas of Stockton. You may have heard of me. Now I am lord of La Flèche."

Return of the Knight

His hand went to his crucifix, "The priest killer! If I had known it was you..."

William des Roches came over. He had with him the two squires who had stayed with their knights. "You two ride to your lords' families. They may have their knights returned when the ransom is paid." He looked at the dead knight and squire. Fótr had taken their mail and swords. They were now draped over their horses. "Put these bodies on your horses. I daresay you would give them a better burial than we would."

I saw the horror and distaste as the bloody bodies were slung across their horses' rumps. We waited until they were out of sight before we turned to return to Le Mans. "That is a pair of fine war horses you now have."

I was distracted. "What?"

"The horses, you have two fine horses."

I nodded and looked over my shoulder. The four knights were being watched by our squires and Roger d'Aubrey and the other three were behind us. "Tell me, when did you come up with this plan to scout out the road? It was not just a whim when we spoke last night was it?"

"Why no. When I rode north from our meeting with the Duke, Sir Ranulf Avenel suggested it. He said it would familiarise you and the others to the land hereabouts."

"And he is not with us, is he?"

"What are you implying?"

"I am not implying anything I am stating plainly. That was an ambush. Twelve knights waiting in a wood. Had Fótr not spotted them they would have had us and this expedition would have been the end of the Duke's attempts to regain his lands."

"But Ranulf is loyal!"

"How else do you explain the ambush? If I am wrong I will apologise to him."

We were some way from Le Mans when we were spotted from the gates. When we reached the inner ward William des Roches asked, "Where is Sir Ranulf Avenel? I need to speak with him."

The sergeant at arms at the gate smiled, "You just missed him, my lord. When you were spotted approaching he and his squire rode out. We thought they went to meet with you."

I gave William a knowing look. He said, "It may be innocent."

I laughed, "You like the warhorses I have won? I wager the better of them that when you search his chambers you find he has fled and that nothing of his remains. And if there is one traitor then there may be others. I will sleep with a dagger 'neath my pillow."

"You are safe in my home, Sir Thomas."

15

Return of the Knight

I said nothing. I was used to the treachery of my fellow knights. I was proved to be right. It was not only the knight and his squire who had fled but his four men at arms and two servants. I sent for Sir William, Harry Longsword and David of Wales. I told them of the ambush and the treachery. "Keep your ears open and keep your counsel… Until we know more then we just trust our own men."

Harry said, "And that includes our new men?"

I had not thought of that. "You have heard something?"

He shook his head, "So far as I can tell they are what they say they are but we have yet to fight alongside them lord and we both know that is when you see the true worth of a warrior."

"We will be fighting soon enough." I handed the mail hauberks and chausses I had taken from the two knights. "See if these are the right size for any of our men. I would have us all mailed."

"Lord. these are valuable. The coin for them should be yours."

"No Harry. I learned in the Holy Land that my fate is bound inextricably with the men I lead. I would rather be protected than rich! Besides, there will be coin enough in this war. I have ransom coming from de Clare. There will be profit enough for me."

Fótr had gained a horse and he and Johann examined and then groomed the new horses. I could see the envy on Sir William's squire's face. I was not certain that the attack on Sainte-Suzanne would result in horses. The only way would be if Gilbert, lord of Gilsland, decided to meet us horse to horse. William des Roches was not certain how many knights would be in the castle. His intelligence was not what it should be. I had learned that the more information you have the better. I wondered why he had only sent twelve knights to take us. Perhaps he was short of knights.

Keen to strike as quickly as possible, we left two days after the ambush. Hurdles and ladders had been prepared. We had wagons to carry them. There were still knights to arrive, Juhel of Mayenne was a powerful lord and he had promised us, thirty knights. We left without them. Even so, we were a powerful battle. We had seventy banners. With two hundred men at arms, archers and crossbows we were a threat to be reckoned with. What I worried about was the lack of archers. Mine were the only ones. I knew the value of them but the rest of the knights did not seem to even consider them.

William des Roches had learned from the ambush. He had his own men ahead of us. These were not men at arms nor were they archers. They were his eight foresters. It was a wise decision. They would not have to fight, they merely had to sniff out the enemy. This time the men who supported King John had remained behind their walls. We reached Sainte-Suzanne in the late afternoon. Our approach had not been secret and the gates were barred We saw that the walls were manned as we set up our camp. Sainte-Suzanne was a

16

simple castle. There was a curtain wall and a good gatehouse behind a ditch. The keep was a large square one and there were two towers at the other corners of this triangular castle. In normal times it might have had a garrison of perhaps twenty knights. From the banners on the walls, there were many more. William took myself, Guy de Changé and Roger d'Aubrey to speak with the castellan.

We had our helmets in our hands and our palms open. It was the sign of peace. We halted at the ditch and while William spoke I examined the ditch. There was water at the bottom and that might have hidden all kinds of dangers and traps. We had used enough in our castles in the Baltic for me to be keenly aware of the dangers.

"The true ruler of this land is Duke Arthur of Brittany. I am his representative and I demand that you yield this castle to me."

I recognised Sir Ranulf Avenal who was standing next to an older warrior. It was the older knight who spoke but I watched Sir Ranulf. He was a knight, I could see now, who had seen service in the Holy Land. He had the cropped beard of a seasoned warrior. Back in Le Mans, I had barely noticed him but now I saw how dangerous he looked.

The older knight spoke, "King John was given this land when his brother died. It is you who are the traitors. Begone."

William had expected this. "We outnumber you and your castle is not a large one. If we invest it then there will be much slaughter. This is not a tourney. We are warriors fighting for a just cause. Think hard before you reject our offer."

Both men knew that there would be no surrender. The war was just beginning. When you defended walls then you expected to be able to defeat an enemy. What they did not know was that we had another thirty knights on their way. We would be reinforced. They would not.

"I reject your offer. The next time you come then we will greet you a little more warmly."

As we rode back William des Roches showed why he was the commander of this army. He had his plans already. "We divide the battle into three. I will lead one group of men tomorrow at dawn. We will attack the southwest wall. You, Sir Thomas, will lead another third and attack the southeast wall. Sir Guy de Changé will have the other third as a reserve. Sir Guy, you will follow up whichever of us succeeds in gaining their walls. If we can take the gatehouse then you can use that as a means of gaining entry to the castle." We both nodded. "I will select the knights for each of us."

While I waited for my knights to come and have their counsel of war with me I had my men at arms and archers collect our ladders and hurdles. I spoke first to Edward. He was my sergeant at arms, "The ditch is waterfilled. I am certain that they will have put traps in there. David of Wales, your task is to keep the walls close to us free of our enemies. You have enough arrows?"

17

Return of the Knight

"We have enough arrows, lord." We had learned in the Holy Land and in the Baltic that a good supply of arrows was essential.

When my knights arrived, I found myself commanding the largest number of knights since the Crusade. I had thirty knights who would follow my gryphon banner. "I know not if you have attacked a castle before. I have and it is never easy. I will lead my men and Sir William of La Flèche. We will have one ladder. The rest of you will have the other eight ladders. You choose your own men to ascend. We use hurdles to cover the ditch and to cross. Have your archers and men at arms keep the heads of the defenders down. We spread the ladders out evenly. I will be taking the corner close to the gatehouse. Whoever leads up the ladder must be prepared to endure stones, rocks, arrows and, perhaps, boiling water and burning fat. When we attain the wall walk, the fighting platform, the first ones up will hold and clear to allow the rest to follow. Before we can advance we need our men up the ladders and in the castle."

They seemed happy enough but I was pleased when they asked questions. I answered them as well as I could.

That night as we sat around our fire Fótr asked me of my own plan. "Will you send Ridley the Giant up first, lord? He would be strong enough to endure whatever they throw at him."

"No, Fótr, I lead this battle and I will be the first up the ladder."

Does that mean I will be second, lord?"

I looked at my former squire, "No, William. I will have Harry Longsword and Ridley behind me. Then Godwin of Battle. You will come next." The two squires looked at each other. "And before you ask you two will be at the rear. We need you to see how the attack is going. You will have to direct the archers and ensure that the men at arms ascend regularly. When you do join us, you will be able to tell me how many of our ladders have succeeded."

"Surely all of them lord."

"In a perfect world that would be true. Here," I shrugged, "I know not. I believe that our ladder will achieve what I intend but I have yet to see these other knights fight. That is another reason why you two will watch. You are my eyes tomorrow. Now make sure the swords are all sharpened and that our mail is oiled."

The mail and weapons were all prepared but I wanted the two squires occupied. Death could be around the corner and I wanted them to be too busy to dwell on such thoughts. After I had prayed to God to bring us all through the next day I retired but I found sleep elusive. If I had been Gilbert of Gilsland I would have sortied and tried to disrupt our plans. When I woke after a short sleep I realised he had not and I had a better idea about our foe. He did not take risks and that gave us hope. My restless sleep meant I was the first up. The night guards had built up the fire to prepare some porridge. Jack son of Harold knew the value of a full stomach. Other conroi might not eat but mine would.

We walked to just beyond crossbow range. My men at arms would use the hurdles like giant shields to get us close to the ditch. Once there we would use just two of them as a bridge and the other four would be propped as defences for our archers. An arrow does not need a flat trajectory; a crossbow does. My archers could send arrows over the hurdles and into the men standing on the fighting platform. That was how I knew that we would succeed when the others might fail.

When we were assembled William des Roches raised his standard along with that of Prince Arthur and we marched in a long narrow column behind the six hurdles. We marched obliquely so that our shields on our left arms protected us. Slingshot and crossbow bolts thudded into the willow hurdles but none of us was hurt. The ladder was carried in the middle. I was taking a risk just using one but sometimes risks paid off. When we reached the ditch, we allowed the archers to get behind the hurdles and then they began to nock, draw and release.

There were thirteen archers. Many people thought that an unlucky number. It was, for the defenders! David of Wales and my other archers were well trained. They knew exactly how far they could send an arrow. While we had negotiated they had been estimating distances. The result was that their first five flights caused deaths amongst the most irreplaceable of defenders, crossbowmen. They had been ready to send bolts at us when we could be seen. My archers did not need to see the target to kill. Harry and his men ran out with the hurdles and dropped them into the ditch. They returned to the safety of the hurdle wall.

I made certain that my helmet was on tightly. I might have to endure blows from above. I said, "Are we ready?"

They all roared, "Aye lord."

We made a shield wall with three of us at the front and the rest behind us. The ladder was carried by the men on the right. Once again, we approached obliquely so that our shields faced the walls and protected all but our legs. When we reached the ditch, we would have to break formation. This was the most hazardous part of it. I moved to the right and took the ladder, Harry and Ridley also held it.

"Ready?"

"Aye lord."

I stepped out with my shield held before me. Immediately a bolt thudded into it and a heartbeat later I heard a scream and then a double thud. I jumped down onto the hurdle. Although it lurched it held. Harry dropped onto it as I was nearing the other side. I had just stepped onto the slippery, grassy bank when Ridley landed on the hurdle. I heard it creak and crack ominously but it held. As I ran to the wall, still holding the ladder, stones hit my shield. I saw the crossbow and the crossbowman lying before me on the grass close to the wall. He had an arrow in his head. We began to lift the ladder into place. I risked looking up. There were two men standing there and they were trying to push the ladder away. Three arrows ended their efforts and I quickly stepped onto it. I would not need my sword until I reached the top.

I held my shield over my helmet and climbed. I used my right hand for support. Stones, both large and small, crashed down on me but I had archers who were protecting me. I was tempted to see how the other ladders fared but that would have been foolish. I had to concentrate on my job. I knew I was getting close as I looked at the ground below me. It took all of my willpower to resist grabbing my sword. I had to hang on until I saw the crenulations. Only then would I be able to draw my sword.

As soon as I saw the stones standing proud I drew my sword. When I did so my shield was rocked by a defender with an axe. The shield cracked alarmingly. An arrow whizzed over my shoulder and I heard a cry. It was my chance. I quickly clambered up the last two steps and pushed my shield between the crenulations. One of my archers had cleared the way for me.

As I stepped down I sensed, rather than saw the spear man lunge at me. He was on my right and so I used my sword to flick the head away. It scraped along my surcoat making a tear. Keeping my shield behind me I did that which he did not expect. Keeping the wall to my right I ran at him. The wall walk was two paces wide but the spearman's lunge had unbalanced him and I used the side of my sword to push him from the wall walk. He tumbled, screaming, to the outer ward. I turned and saw two men with raised axes. Harry Longsword was there. I just ran at them. Once again, their raised arms unbalanced them and I knocked them to the ground. I swung my left leg between the legs of one of them and then, as I lunged forward, I skewered the other one.

Behind me, I heard, "Thank you, lord! I have your back."

I did not reply. I brought down the edge of my shield across the throat of the second man at arms and he lay still. I left the two bodies there. They would be a barrier until my other men arrived. When Ridley the Giant stepped behind me I shouted, "You two clear that side. Sir William and I will deal with this side."

Two more men approached me. I was now better placed to fight. I held my shield before me. The wall protected my left. They had spears which they held two handed. They had no shields. Both lunged at the same time. They were veterans. They hoped that one would break my defence. I raised my shield and flicked with my sword at the same time. I had been taught the trick by my father. At the same time, I placed my foot on one of the bodies and, bringing my head back, butted the defender to my right. He had a bascinet helmet and my full-face helmet smashed his face to a pulp. I grabbed his shoulder and threw him over the wall walk. I brought my sword around and it hacked across the upper arm of the second spearman. It cut through to the bone. He grabbed his left arm with his right and I ended his life.

Behind me, I felt a shield in my back. "It is William, lord!"

"Take the wall side. We will head for the gatehouse. Harry and Ridley hold here and send the rest behind us. We take the gatehouse!"

Already knights were pouring from the gatehouse to deal with this incursion. Numbers did not matter. The wall walk would only allow two men at a time to fight. If they wished to risk pushing then so be it. The one advantage they had was that their shields protected one of their sides and the wall the other. I was also worried about my shield. The blow from the axe had done it no good whatsoever.

William knew me well. He knew my strokes and he knew my pace. We walked together in perfect time towards the two knights. We were equally matched and the victor would be the most cunning or the one who wanted it the most. I raised my sword above my head. That way the knight did not know which stroke I would use. Would I swing from the side? Would I make a backhand strike or simply bring it down from above? Neither of us could see the other's eyes. He was watching my sword hand and so, when I punched with a weakened shield, he was taken by surprise. He had on a great helm. It gives good protection but it limits the view. He did not see the shield and he began to topple backwards. That was when I brought my sword over. I caught his helmet square on. He lay prone. I put my sword at his throat and simply leaned in. Blood spurted.

The blow had all but destroyed my shield and so I threw it at the knight fighting William and picked up the dead knight's shield. The flying shield distracted the knight and William ended his life. Our steps had taken us closer to the gatehouse which was now just four paces away. Behind me, I heard the voices of my men as they joined us.

"On my shout, we charge!"

"Aye, lord!" It was not simply shouted, it was roared.

I felt a shield in my back and with a new, solid shield before me, I shouted, "Charge!" There was neither skill nor subtlety in our attack. William and I just led half a dozen warriors in mail. The defenders should have retired to the gatehouse and barred the door. They did not. The two knights who stood there backed by their squires and a crossbowman thought they could beat us. We did not give the crossbow the opportunity to release. We hit them hard. The crossbowman, the squires and one knight were bundled backwards through the door and into the gatehouse. The other knight lost his balance and fell to the outer ward.

The gatehouse was dark. There was a stair that led to the fighting platform above us and one which led down to the gate itself. There were two other crossbowmen at the slits. All were surprised. The knight and the two squires shouted, "Ransom!"

"Lower your swords."

Fótr and Johann ran in through the door. We looked to see who it was. The crossbowmen made the mistake of lifting their crossbows. Edward son of Edgar and Jack son of Harold were upon them and slew them before the machines were halfway up. I heard the rattle of swords being dropped.

"Sir William, take Johann and two men at arms. Clear the fighting platform above. Fótr, bar the door to the other wall walk and stay here with Jack. Guard our prisoners. The rest of you, we will descend to the gate when I have seen how the day goes."

Fótr said, "Not well, lord. Sir Robert de Rumilly and his men have made the wall walk but that was because they were next to the breach made by Ridley and Harry."

I opened the door and went back outside. I saw that Ridley and Harry were supported by James and John, two of my recently recruited men at arms. They had proved their loyalty. The four of them were fighting to reach the beleaguered men to Sir Robert. I leaned over the wall and shouted, "David of Wales, bring the archers up the ladder. Tell the other knights to use this way in. We have the gatehouse!" He waved his arm in acknowledgement. As I turned I saw a movement and I instinctively raised my shield. A crossbowman on the fighting platform of the gatehouse had seen his opportunity. The bolt's tip came through the shield. I lowered it in time to see the crossbow tumble as Johann rammed his sword into the man's back.

I had no time to waste. With just two ladders that we could use the attack was in danger of stalling. I ran into the gatehouse. I led my men down the stone staircase. As I turned the corner a spear was thrust up at me. It ripped through my chausses and sliced into my calf. I ignored the pain and the blood which seeped down to my feet. If the spearman was close enough to thrust then I was close enough to attack. I jumped. The man was not expecting that and I landed on him. I heard ribs crack. I barely had time to regain my own feet when two men at arms ran at me. They had swords. Both were short swords. I blocked one with my shield and used my longer weapon to riposte and disarm the other. I lunged and my sword ripped across his neck. I heard a cry as Michael of Anjou ended the life of the man with the broken ribs. My men at arms quickly despatched the other men who were guarding the gate.

"Get it open, Michael. The rest of you with me." I heard the bar being lifted. I went to the gate which led to the outer ward and opened it. I saw more men running from the keep towards the stairs which led to the walls. Behind me, the gate was opened and the gloomy gatehouse was suddenly brighter. "Right, men, let us get amongst them!"

Return of the Knight

I threw open the door and we ran through. I could feel the blood in my left chausse. I knew that I would become weaker.

"Lord, you are leaving a trail of blood."

"I know Edward."

I looked around and saw that our sudden arrival had caused panic. Some of those who had been racing to the walls now stopped, wondering what to do. As David of Wales and my archers, now on the wall walk began to slay them with arrows that indecision turned to panic. The door to the keep remained invitingly open.

"To the keep!"

I had twelve men with me. My archers could see what we intended and arrows cleared our path. Those inside the keep had yet to see the danger. Gilbert of Gilsland was still trying to clear his walls of the men who had gained entry. There was a roar as Sir Guy de Changé led over thirty knights and squires supported by forty men at arms through the recently opened gate. They burst into the outer ward. As we neared the door I saw a knight appear. It was Sir Ranulf Avenel. I levelled my sword at him, "Treacherous knight!"

He should have turned and entered the keep. They had lost the outer ward but the keep was a different matter. I think that he was swayed by the fact that I was bloody and carrying another's shield. He saw both as weaknesses. He regarded my men at arms as a ragtag mob who were beneath contempt. Both judgements were misguided. He came towards me.

Aware that I was weakening I took the offensive. I gritted my teeth and stepped onto my stronger, right leg. He had not fought that day. He had a sharp sword and he was fresh and he was a battle-hardened warrior. He made the predictable strike at my head. I did two things at the same time. I blocked the blow with my shield and then hacked at his knee with my sword. I had space to swing and I put all of the power at my disposal into the blow. I saw him buckle. I pulled back my arm and punched with my shield. The bolt was still embedded in the shield and the feathered flights went through the eye hole and into his eye. He began to tumble over.

"Yield!" His helmet nodded and I shouted, "Edward! Take the keep!"

"Aye, lord! Come on lads."

In that moment of distraction, Sir Ranulf raised his sword to swipe at me. Peter, son of Richard, shouted, "Watch out, my lord."

I glanced down and saw the sword swinging towards my right leg. I stabbed down with my sword and it went through the treacherous knight's throat before the blade could reach me. I contemplated following my men into the keep but as Sir Guy de Changé led his knights towards me I decided to let them have the glory of taking the keep.

"Are you all right, lord?"

"Just a slight wound, Sir Guy. I will wait for my squire."

Return of the Knight

He nodded and led his men into the keep. We had slain enough men already to make the capture of the keep a certainty. I sheathed my sword and knelt next to the body of Sir Ranulf. I took off his helmet. As I did so I noticed a chain around his neck. I pulled it out. I recognised it immediately. It was the seal of Templar. Two knights riding one horse on one side and the cupola of the dome of the Holy Sepulchre in Jerusalem. I had not known he was a Templar. His skin was not burned by the sun. He had not been on Crusade. I did not like this. The Templars were a law unto themselves. I slipped the seal into my tunic.

Fótr, Sir William and Johann ran up, "My lord you are wounded! Let me get a healer."

I was about to say that I did not need one when I felt a little dizzy and all went black.

Chapter 3

When I awoke it was dark and I was somewhere which smelled of incense. I turned and saw that Fótr was asleep in a chair. I quickly realised that I was in a chapel. I sat up and found that my chausses had been removed and my left leg was heavily bandaged. As I tried to swing my legs off the table upon which I was laid pain coursed through my body and I grunted. Fótr awoke.

"You are not to move, lord. The physician was most insistent."

I nodded and held my hand out for the wineskin which was on the chair. Fótr handed it to me and I drank deeply. "Where am I?"

"The chapel in the castle. The rest of the knights are feasting and celebrating our victory."

"Did we lose any men?"

He nodded, "Two of the new ones. Gurth and Jean. They fell ascending the ladder. All else are well. Sir William took charge of our share of the horses and the mail from the knights we slew." He grinned, "Our men at arms and archers profited mightily from being the first over the wall and in the keep. Sir William des Roches is unhappy about the losses we suffered. Twelve knights fell in the battle. He is demanding great ransom for the knights we captured to compensate."

"And my leg?"

"You lost a great deal of blood, my lord. The healer used fire to seal the wound. You have been asleep for six hours." He pointed to the hour candle which flickered in the corner.

"I am ready for some food. If I cannot move then fetch it to me."

When he knew I was awake Sir William returned to me with Fótr and Johann. He was able to tell me in more detail about the battle to take the castle. The enemy had lost over twenty knights. The rest were being ransomed. William was pleased. "We have the warhorses from the five knights our conroi slew. You have seven war horses and I now have one!"

"I will let two of my men at arms have a warhorse too. Ridley the Giant certainly needs one and Edward son of Edgar deserves one. How long do we stay here?"

"A rider came from Angers. The Duke is coming to Le Mans. Lord William wishes to be there when he arrives. We will be heading back on the morrow. The wounded will follow when they are ready."

Return of the Knight

"Then I will leave tomorrow. Fótr, find the chausses from the dead knights; one of them must fit me, find it. "

"Aye lord. Come, Johann, you can help me search and then we will pack the treasure we find in chests. The others are all drinking and feasting. We will find the chests first!"

Our experiences in the Baltic had helped Fótr grow up very quickly. He was an old head on young shoulders. When they had gone I told William what I had discovered. "Templars, lord? That is a worrying development."

"Aye, William, for they always work for themselves. They do not recognise countries. Hospitallers are warrior monks to be respected. Templars are to be feared. The treachery now becomes clearer. If King John is allying with them then he must have promised them something in England. We will keep our eyes and ears open."

We left the next morning. I took my men before the rest of the castle had even risen. I did not wish to ride in the dust of the others and I was anxious to get back to Le Mans. I needed a wagon to take our treasure back to my home and my wife might have heard that I had been wounded. My men, despite losing two of their number, were in an ebullient mood. Their purses were heavier. My new men at arms now had good swords which we had taken from the dead knights and our horses had increased in number. That was a great saving. Warhorses cost more than a hauberk!

Arriving back to Le Mans earlier than the rest of the army allowed me to make enquiries about Sir Ranulf. When he had been at the fortress he had been a shadowy character but by speaking with the steward, sergeants at arms and the servants I began to build up a picture of his activities. It became clear that he was not working alone. Cloaked figures had met with him. Messengers from the east and the west had come and gone. By the time that William des Roches arrived, I had a much better picture. There was a conspiracy. The Templars were at the heart of it as was King John but I worried about the French connection. The messengers from the east had been French. King Philip had, apparently, sworn to support Duke Arthur but the behaviour of Ranulf Avenel suggested other. Until I knew whom I could trust I would keep my own counsel.

My leg was painful and I slept little but the healer had been a good one. He had saved my leg and for that I was grateful. It would heal and I would be able to be a warrior once more. I was happy that we had no plans for the next phase of the campaign. Ballon was the target of our attack but we had lost too many men to attempt to attack it yet. Juhel of Mayenne had arrived too late to help us. We needed knights to replace the ones we had lost. In addition, William des Roches wanted to await the ransoms.

Return of the Knight

Two days after we had returned I met with him, Roger D'Aubrey, Juhel de Mayenne and Sir Guy de Changé. It was the first time I had spoken to him since before we had attacked Sainte-Suzanne. He was in good humour.

"I have to thank all three of you. You all behaved as I would have hoped. Sir Thomas, your capture of the gatehouse saved many lives. I will tell the Duke of your heroic act when he arrives."

I nodded, "Had we had more archers then we might have achieved more and suffered fewer casualties."

Sir Guy de Changé agreed, "Sir Thomas is right. I watched his archers. They cleared the walls and then when they ascended the wall walk, they made sure that we were not attacked when we entered the gates."

William des Roches shook his head, "It is not as easy to get archers here in Normandy and Anjou. This is not England. Ballon is a harder nut to crack and we may well have to build siege engines."

"And that takes time, my lord," I remembered the siege engines we had built in the Holy Land.

William nodded. "We will await the Duke. He will be here soon enough. He can enjoy the victory we achieved in his name. We need to recover our numbers." When the others left William des Roches said, "Remain, if you would, Sir Thomas." I sat again. Just standing had made my leg ache. "You know I was there at Arsuf with the King when you and your father stopped the Seljurks attack. I can still recall you protecting your father's body with the standard. I saw the same reckless courage the other day." I nodded. There was nothing that I could say. He leaned forward, "You do not need to take such risks. Use your household knight and your men at arms. You are too valuable to the Duke of Brittany's cause."

"I cannot change my nature. When I defended my father, it was because I knew it was the right thing to do. It was the same when I ascended the ladder. I have to say that I will continue to do so. If that upsets those with whom I fight then I will still do it. If I think something is right I will fight any!"

He leaned back and his eyes narrowed, "Is there something I should know?"

I shook my head, "Prince Arthur is the rightful King of England but he is young. There are too many people I neither know nor trust. I tell you this, my lord. My avowed aim is to see Prince Arthur, Duke of Brittany, on the throne of England. Until I know more of the people with whom I fight I will be suspicious. I learned of treachery the hard way when I served in the Holy Land."

He spread his arms, "And that is my wish too. We are in accord."

I stood and stared at him, "I hope so. I do not like to be betrayed. If you were at Arsuf then you know that King Richard was not true to his word."

"He was not foresworn!"

27

Return of the Knight

"I lost my birthright. We both know that Cleveland was mine and yet he allowed his brother to take it from me. Perhaps you understand my scepticism. I will watch out for myself until I know more."

"You are a brave man and a good leader. I admire the way your men follow you. Together we can do great things."

I said no more but left.

Prince Arthur arrived two days later. He had with him Raymond, Comte de Senonche. There were also two younger knights. I would not have noticed them save that they were both burned by the sun. Were these Templars too? William des Roches greeted them and his lieutenants hovered in the background.

The young prince was delighted with our news, "We have begun well, my lord! Now we can make inroads into the lands our enemies hold."

"We are still short of knights, your grace."

Raymond, Comte de Senonche smiled. It was a silky smile. It was smooth and meant little save to warn me to be wary. "His majesty has a battle of knights heading in this direction even as we speak. Fighting together we can recover that which was lost."

I became suspicious. As much as I wanted knights to help us I did not want the French to take our territory. I was willing William de Roches to object but he did not. He smiled and said, "That is good news. With our knights, we will capture Ballon and then the whole of Normandy will be ours for the taking!"

I could say nothing for I was a mere knight. Something did not feel right about this. I viewed every knight who had yet to fight alongside me with the greatest of scepticism. I could trust my own knight and my own men but none other. Sir Guy de Changé and Roger D'Aubrey seemed honest enough but who knew where their true loyalties lay. That evening the Lord of Le Mans laid on a great feast. I picked at my food despite the honours which were accorded me. The first of the ransoms had been paid and that added to the good feeling which emanated from the hall. It was boisterous and it was ribald. It was too much for me. I left the hall. I needed to breathe the cool evening air.

When I stepped into the inner ward it was as though I had walked into a church it seemed so peaceful. The sentries walked the wall walks and it was silent save for the drum of their feet on the wood.

"Is there aught the matter, my lord?"

I turned and saw Prince Arthur. "No, your grace. I needed air."

He nodded, "Would you walk with me? I am no drinker and I, too, needed to breathe." We walked towards the stairs leading to the wall walk. Arthur looked young but he had been raised by King Richard. The Lionheart had chosen him as his heir. I reminded myself not to judge him. I had had greatness thrust upon me when I had been young.

Return of the Knight

We reached the fighting platform and the sentries moved aside to afford us some privacy. "I saw your face, my lord when the Comte spoke of the French knights. What worries you?"

"Your uncle, King Richard, never trusted the French. He died trying to take one of their castles. If Philip sends knights to aid you then there must be an ulterior motive. What if he wishes the castles we take for himself?"

"Then we would have to resist him. However, Sir Thomas, do not blacken his name yet. So far, he has shown us nothing but kindness. He could have used his men to take my castles could he not?"

"He would have lost many men in doing so." I sighed, "Your grace, does it not seem strange that he waited until we had taken Sainte-Suzanne and lost knights before committing? You know we had a traitor in the hall?"

He nodded, "Sir Ranulf and you slew him."

"Who was he working for?"

"Why John Lackland of course!"

"I am not so sure. Be aware, your Grace, that I will be vigilant. I promise that, if it is in my power, I will do all that I can to regain your lost lands."

He smiled, "You have an honourable name. My uncle told me of your actions at Arsuf and since. He was impressed by you."

It was in my mind to say '*not enough to return my lands to me*' but I said nothing.

"I know I am young and do not know enough about war yet but I am a quick learner. If I make mistakes I pray that you will tell me so that I may learn from them."

"I am afraid, your Grace, that if you do make mistakes then it may be too late to rectify them. But I will do as you ask."

Over the next few days, the French knights arrived as well as other knights who came to serve Prince Arthur, the Duke of Brittany. I viewed each stranger with suspicion. I confided in William and the two of us made sure that one of us was always close to Prince Arthur. I did not think there would be an attempt on his life but there were other ways to hurt our cause. I needed my sole household knight as I was often involved with William des Roches and the Comte de Senonche on the planning.

The Comte proved to be a useful source of information. "The castle has a good position. It controls the bridge over the Orne. Whoever holds the castle can hold the gate to Normandy."

"And the defences?" William des Roches knew how to get to the heart of the matter.

"A good question, my lord. The castle appears to be one that could be captured easily but that assumption would be erroneous. There is a curtain wall and the castle itself has a great Donjon. It is made of stone. The inner wall is triangular. There is a double ditch and these are seeded with traps. Siege

29

engines would be of little use for the castle is built on the highest piece of ground. It has a large mound with steep sides."

I could see Juhel frowning. I explained, "My lord if you are to use a siege engine or stone-thrower you need to have a higher piece of ground or, at the very least a level one. If they have dug the ditch and used that to increase the height of an existing feature then we will have to attack it the hard way, with ladders and men!"

He nodded, "Or starve them out."

I confess that would have been my preferred option. We had been lucky attacking the first castle with ladders. If this one had a mound and a donjon then we would not have ladders long enough. When I had been in the Holy Land I had spoken at length with the Master of the Hospitallers. He had a great deal of experience of sieges and castle fighting.

As I listened to the debate about how we would take the castle an idea came to me. We reached an impasse and no one could agree on the best way to take this castle. When silence descended I gave my suggestion. "We tunnel."

They looked at me as though I was speaking in tongues. Prince Arthur said, "I am sorry, Sir Thomas, I am not sure I understand."

"It is simple. When you build a castle on a mound, then the foundations do not go all the way to ground level. That only happens when you build a tower and put the mound around it." I looked at the Comte. "That was not how this was built, was it?"

He leaned forward and looked animated, "No, you are right. There was a wooden keep and the wall and the donjon were built in stone and replaced it."

"Then we tunnel close to the junction of the donjon and the wall. We do not need to be close to the donjon. The hard part would be beginning the tunnel. Once it was started then the diggers would be protected by the tunnel itself. You shore up the sides with wood as you go. When you are directly under the wall then you fill the tunnel with kindling and set fire to it. The wooden supports burn and the walls collapse."

They all looked at each other. "Where did you learn that?"

"The Holy Land; there it is harder to tunnel for it is rocky but even so they did. Here we know that we will be tunnelling through the spoil from the ditch. It will be much easier but you need miners."

"Miners?"

"Short men with broad shoulders and powerful arms. If you have any Welshmen they are particularly good."

William des Roches was nothing if not energetic. Once he had an idea to sink his teeth in then he was like a terrier and would not let go. "When this council of war is over I will find such men." He grinned at me. "You are full of surprises."

Perhaps my words had made the Comte warm to me. He added more information without being pressed. "I should warn you that there is another castle not far north at Bourg-le-Roi. They may choose to come and relieve the siege."

Sir Guy de Changé laughed, "Then we do what we do best, we field a force of knights and meet them in the open. Let the moles dig, we warriors will fight."

It was a good plan. William des Roches quickly sought not only the miners but the wood which would be used to shore up the sides of the tunnels. It was still being prepared when we headed for Ballon. I left Skuld and two of my war horses at Le Mans. We did not have far to travel. It was just thirteen miles. I could see why the Lord of Le Mans was so keen to eliminate this threat. As we rode my former squire asked after my wound.

I knew the reason for his question. He had yet to suffer a severe wound. "It is painful, William, and I would not like to stand on it for too long. This attack will not be up ladders and besides, I think we will let others have that glory. My leg is at the stage where it itches almost as much as it hurts. That means that it is healing. Thank you for your concern."

He nodded, "Lord, now that I have coin I would have my own men to lead. What think you?"

"I think it is a good idea so long as you choose well. I would have David of Wales and Edward son of Edgar cast their eye over any warriors you think to choose. We both know that there are some who appear honest but are deceitful."

"Aye lord. The reason I ask is that some of the men at arms who served the knights who died asked if they could follow my banner. I said I would consider when we return from Bourg-le-Roi."

"You are learning. That is the wise thing to do. If they truly seek work they will be waiting when we return."

Juhel of Mayenne was keen to impress all of us and he led his men to surround the castle. He led his knights, men at arms and crossbowmen to capture the bridge north and thereby cut off the defenders from help. By the time we arrived the walls were manned and the gates closed. That was to be expected. I rode, with William des Roches, the Duke and the inevitable Comte to survey their lines and defences. William had been right. It was a formidable fortress. It was not the largest castle I had ever seen but it was much better positioned than the one at Sainte-Suzanne. I saw that the Orne River was just four hundred paces from the castle. Juhel de Mayenne and his men were already camped there as we rode around.

This time we made an armed camp. We did not wish to be surprised and we knew that we would be here for some time. A tunnel cannot be dug overnight although we would be doing most of the digging at night. I made certain that

31

our horses were also well guarded. If they tried to break the siege then they would bring knights from the west. Normandy had sided with John Lackland. If they chose not to relieve the siege then it would tell us that they were not committed. They might be suborned to our side.

I had enough men at arms now to assign two of them to watch the horses. We would not be needed for the mining. They would only be needed for the assault and that would be many days away. Being so close to Le Mans meant that we had plenty of supplies. We had fresh bread. It took half a day to reach us but fresh bread puts heart into a warrior. There was grazing aplenty for our horses and we found a farm which had a good supply of oats. Our horses would eat well. The French knights who joined us kept a screen of scouts and knights to the north and the west. We would be warned of an attack.

Of course, the defenders would have to get a message out. Juhel assured us that none had managed to leave before he surrounded it but I did not believe him. Normans, loyal to King John, would already be preparing to relieve the siege.

My archers were used to keep down the heads of the defenders while the tunnel was begun. We had to place hurdles over the ditch and the defenders sent stones and bolts at the men who hacked away a hole. My archers slew six or seven men on the walls. Even so, four of the men who would be miners perished before it was started. Once it had been begun then we worked at night. It added to the length of the siege but at the cost of just four men, it was worth it.

I had the time to stay in the camp and I used my time wisely. I wandered the camp looking for signs of Templars. The two younger knights who had appeared with the Comte disappeared soon after the siege began. I asked the Comte where they had gone and he smiled his silky smile and said that they were delivering a message to the King. That did not make me any less apprehensive. I found another three knights who appeared as though they might be Templars. Part of it was their routine. The Templars followed a strict discipline and the three knights prayed at the appropriate times and did all that might be expected of a warrior priest. I had no doubt about the fighting abilities of the Templars; it was their motives I questioned.

The days and nights followed a predictable routine. The miners worked in shifts. The changes of shifts were the dangerous times. The one before dawn was the least dangerous but the one after noon required the presence of my archers. In addition, men at arms had to protect them with shields while they entered the mine entrance. The spoil from the tunnel simply tumbled down the slope. Each time it rained more was washed into the ditches. I had a new shield made. My other had almost cost me my life. While the men at arms and foot soldiers watched the walls the knights and squires who were not riding on patrol would see to our horses. A warhorse was the most pampered of animals.

Return of the Knight

Each night one of the miners would report to the Prince. He would detail the progress. They used a piece of knotted cord to measure the distance. We wanted the tunnel to go beyond the wall.

Ten days after they had begun they were almost complete. On that night we would begin to fill the tunnel with kindling. It was that day that they sent a relief force from Bourg-le-Roi. The French knights had done their job. They had kept a watch on the castle and reported the daily arrival of more knights. It was another reason we had kept our horses in a constant state of readiness. As soon as the battle was reported to be on the road we mounted. We would fight in three battles. A battle was the way we fought. It was easier to manoeuvre groups of perhaps eight or ninety knights rather than one enormous mass of two or three hundred. The centre one would be the knights of Anjou and Brittany led by William des Roches. This would be the largest battle. There were over one hundred knights. To the left were the French knights led by the Comte de Senonche. With eighty knights they were almost our equal. Our weakest force was the knights of Maine led by Juhel of Mayenne. There were just fifty of them. The scouts had reported over one hundred and fifty knights supported by a hundred men at arms.

The rest of the knights with whom I rode were armed with a lance. I still preferred the long spear. To me, it was both easier to use and to replace. William emulated me. We still had a gonfanon but I saw that some of the other knights were confused at my choice of weapon. We did not ride far. William des Roches had made his battle plan the day we had arrived. It was a good one. I had learned that William des Roches had learned well from the Lionheart. He had an eye for a battlefield.

Lucé-sous-Ballon lay just two and a half miles from the siege works. It was ten miles from Bourg-le-Roi. William wanted our foes to be more tired than we. The ground was flat and would suit our horses. In addition, there was a slight slope which favoured us. There had been showers, mainly at night, and the ground was not as firm there. In places, it was slick and in others boggy. Horses would labour up the slight slope. Our aim was simple. We would defeat the knights and turn back the relief force. Some of the less experienced knights thought it would be easy. I knew that many things could go awry in a battle. The three knights I suspected of being Templars rode with the French. They were in the van. Their position told me that they were allied to the French. That meant that Sir Ranulf had not been King John's spy but King Philip's.

The slightly elevated piece of land we had chosen allowed us to view their progress. As soon as they saw our banners they deployed into their own battles. I did not recognise the banners. Until recently I had not fought in this part of the Angevin Empire and I had never fought in England. The Baltic and Outremer were my battlefields. They were the standards I recognised. They, however, would know mine. The ransoms for the knights had been paid and I had no doubt that some of them would be with the horsemen who rode towards us. They would have told them about the hired sword who had captured the gatehouse. Men would ride for my banner. I would be worth capturing and ransoming.

Fótr rode behind me with the gryphon banner. He held it in his left hand and his shield protected it. That had been my suggestion. I remembered Arsuf. He was a good rider and would be able to defend himself. He did not ride a warhorse but Flame. Flame was a clever and nimble palfrey. Fótr just needed to stay close to me and avoid the knights.

The enemy host stopped. William de Roches recognised their banners. "They are led by Richard, Viscount of Beaumont-en-Maine. He is a good warrior. Do not underestimate him."

We rode with the banner of Brittany but the Prince was not with us. He had wanted to but William des Roches had been adamant that we did not want to risk the figurehead in the savage fight which would ensue. In our battle, there were sixty knights in the front rank with our squires behind. William's second in command, Richard de Clare, led the rest of the knights as a reserve. William allowed the enemy knights to begin their attack. When they were two hundred paces from us William ordered the charge. We did not gallop. We spurred our horses but kept our line. We were boot to boot and the lances of the knights were raised. It was a foolish knight or a novice who rode with it horizontal for any length of time.

I was to the left of William des Roches and Walther Reedwood to his right. We would be the subject of their attack. Already I could see that their line was no longer straight. It had become an arrowhead with the Viscount of Beaumont-en-Maine eager for glory and to take William des Roches.

Once I knew that I could see the knight with whom I would be fighting. He was to the right of the Viscount. He had a green shield with three yellow fesses. He had his lance lowered. It wavered up and down. He had not yet learned to rest it on his horse's head. I pulled my shield a little tighter to my body. He would aim for my chest. He had seen me and chosen me too for we were now closing rapidly. The slightly slippery slope was causing problems for the enemy line. They were riding too quickly and the hooves of the horses were slipping slightly. We were still boot to boot but there were gaps in their line.

I lowered my spear when we were fifteen paces from the enemy. I was one of the last to do so. It was easier for me to do so as my weapon was lighter. To my left my household knight, William, copied me. I pulled back my arm when I was five paces from the green shield with three yellow fesses. His lance was longer and he would hit me first. I saw his arm pull back. The end of the spear moved up and down so much that I wondered if he would hit me at all. He must have had great strength for he struck my shield. I had it angled so that the head slid off my new shield and it cracked and shattered on the wood at the rear

34

of my saddle. I punched with my spear. It was a shorter and more accurate weapon. I hit him in the thigh. Although my spear shattered it had penetrated not only the knight's chausses and leg but also pricked his horse which reared and threw him.

I drew my sword. Fótr had my banner and I could not afford the time to replace the spear. As our lines had clashed then all momentum had stopped. It was a mêlée. In such a fight a lance was an encumbrance. I spurred my newly acquired warhorse, Dragon, towards the nearest knight to my right. His spear turned slowly towards me. Again, it wavered up and down. He was also trying to turn his horse to meet me square on. As he punched I spurred Dragon and the lance hit fresh air. I brought my sword backhand to strike him in the back. His turn, my blow and the slippery ground made him tumble from the saddle. Fótr was close behind and as the knight lay prostrate my squire placed my banner to the knight's throat. "Yield to Sir Thomas or die."

The knight nodded and I heard a mumbled, "I yield."

I left Fótr with the captured knight and his warhorse. William was still with me and he had his spear. I shouted, "Follow me!"

The men at arms were hurrying up the slope to get to us. I saw our chance. We had broken through the line of knights. The banner of Richard, Viscount of Beaumont-en-Maine still flew. I saw it waving close by the banner of Brittany. The two of us rode from behind the enemy knights. One must have sensed our approach and he turned. His long and heavy lance took an age to swing around and William's spear hit him in the side knocking him from his saddle. I saw the Viscount's standard-bearer. It was a knight. He was guarded by two other knights. William held his spear above his shoulder and threw it. Perhaps God directed his arm or he may have just been lucky but the spear embedded itself in the back of one of the standard's protectors. They both turned. The standard's falling would be the signal for the army to fall back. They could not allow that. William rode for the standard-bearer and I for the more dangerous of the two, the standard's protector.

I was the one riding up the slope and I deliberately slowed down Dragon so that his hooves could gain purchase and grip the slope which was now slick with mud and blood. The knight had a war axe. He rode towards me and swung his axe. I did not meet it with my shield. I turned Dragon so that I was on his right and blocked it with my sword. The knight was strong and my arm shivered with the force of it but I stopped it and only the edge of the axe scored a line down my helmet. I had taken a sliver of wood from the axe's haft. An axe is heavy and as he pulled it back I lunged with my sword at his throat. He jerked his head back but my blade tore across the mail of his ventail. The mail coif was no longer whole. He turned his horse to mirror mine. He swung his axe and my sword was behind me. I just managed to get my shield between us. My left arm shivered. As he swung his arm back I stood in my stirrups and

35

brought my sword down towards his head. His shield was on the wrong side and he used his axe to block it. Already weakened my sword smashed it in two and the head fell to the ground. In an instant, my sword was at his throat. I pricked the skin through his broken mail. "Yield!"

He nodded and took off his helmet. I turned and saw that Johann had managed to give William a spear and the Viscount's banner fell to the ground as William skewered the standard-bearer. Battles do not end instantly but the effect of the falling of the standard was dramatic. All those who were within sight of it stopped fighting. William des Roches took advantage of the dismay to force the Viscount to yield and the advancing men at arms and foot first stopped and then, seeing that their leaders were captured, began to run back to Bourg-le-Roi! We had won.

I turned to William and Fótr, "Today you achieved more in one battle than many knights achieve in a lifetime. I am immensely proud of you both."

Sir William took off his helmet and smiled, "We have learned from you, Sir Thomas!"

Chapter 4

With Richard, Viscount of Beaumont-en-Maine as our prisoner there would be no more attacks from Bourg-le-Roi. I had taken two knights as a prisoner and two war horses. My personal treasure was growing. For me, that meant more men and archers! We headed back to the siege. Knights had been lost but, as we had held the field, none were taken for ransom. Those who had yielded were saved as their captors fled. Such was war. Only a handful of knights had fallen on each side. Had the men at arms and crossbows joined in then it might have been a different story. I saw that the three Templars now had captives of their own. That confirmed, to me, that they were not working for King John. The French knights had done well too.

The Comte de Senonche and William des Roches were in high spirits as we headed back. They were both fulsome in their praise of both me and William. His timely spear-thrust had won the day and both were grateful. With only two miles to travel back, we were soon at our camp. My men at arms and archers looked up as we rode into our camp with the two war horses. Soon we would have the mail from the knights and two more of my men at arms would be attired as knights. Sir Guy and Sir Roger had not understood why I did not have more knights to serve me. The answer was simple. I was well served by my men at arms and until Fótr and Johann were ready to be knighted then I would not change my system.

The Prince was also eager to speak with us. However, I was disturbed that he first went to speak with the Comte before asking either William des Roches or myself what had happened. I think the Lord of Le Mans was surprised and I became even more disturbed when the three Templars also joined them.

"I like not that, Sir Thomas. The Duke is young and he has spent a great deal of time with the French. I fear that he is being used."

"Then, my lord, it is up to us to see that he is not. Let us make a pact to keep him away from the French as much as possible."

He smiled at me, "In that case, I would suggest you stay close to him. He seems somewhat in awe of you, the hero of Arsuf."

I did not like that but if I could use my influence on the impressionable young prince then I would do so.

"Should we see how the tunnel goes?"

"If we can fire it tonight then we can exploit the victory of today. Our knights will be in good humour."

David of Wales and my archers were the closest to the workings. During daylight hours they maintained a close watch on the walls. The defenders had learned how accurate they were. The only way that they could defeat a mine was to countermine beneath it and that would take more time than they had. "How goes it, David of Wales?"

"My lord, they are well under the wall. The mine is empty now and the miners are resting. As soon as it is dark they will pack the kindling and then it will be ready to fire."

William des Roches nodded, "Then we make it a dawn attack I would like to see the walls fall. This will be a long war and I do not want to lose men when we do not need to."

When we returned to our tents Prince Arthur approached us. We both bowed. "Have I offended you, lords? I wished to have conference with you."

William des Roches shook his head, "No offence intended, your Grace. We were inspecting the mine and besides, you had the Comte to speak with." He gave a bow. "And now, if you will excuse me, I will go and arrange for the ransoms."

It was a brusque answer and I could see that he had hurt the young Prince's feelings. "What have I done wrong?"

"Can I speak honestly, your Grace, without offending you?"

"Of course."

"The Lord of Le Mans and myself feel that you are too close to the French. It is good that they help us but Sir William and I believe it is to take parts of your land."

He shook his head, "No, lord, you are wrong. The Comte has assured me that all that King Philip wants is to see me on the throne of England."

I sighed, "And why would he wish that, my lord?"

The Prince was silent, "Perhaps he thinks he can control me." I nodded. "But he cannot. The Lionheart trained me well! Do not worry about me, lord. My mother has also made me strong. I know what the French King intends and I will thwart him and my uncle. My subjects need to have faith in me. My noble sire, Henry the Second, was not much older than I was when he took the throne. He had the help of his mother too. It is an omen!"

I could not help but like the young prince but I was not certain that he was right. He seemed to me to have more enemies than friends.

"Then know this, my lord, my men and I will do all in our power to see that you attain the throne." I meant it and I hoped that he would achieve the throne for if he did then I would regain my lands!

I was up well before dawn. William des Roches and Prince Arthur joined the Norman and Angevin knights as the miners set fire to the tunnel. It was spectacular. The miner who threw in the burning brand barely escaped with his life. The flames, fuelled by oil and straw, took hold immediately. There was a cheer from all of those outside who watched while from inside we heard a wail of despair. All of those inside knew what we intended. Once the initial flames died we just saw the glow from the tunnel and smoke began to pour out of the entrance. The wind fanned the flames and ensured that they would burn a long time. It was late in the morning when we saw the first evidence of the fire. A large crack appeared in the mound. The soil was shifting. It was sliding down to the ditch.

David of Wales had sharp eyes and he pointed, "Look, lord! The tower!"

A tiny crack began to zig-zag up the donjon. Even as I saw it widen there was an audible crack and a large lump of earth suddenly descended. As it did so the wall which adjoined the tower collapsed in a crash of stones and mortar. It tumbled down to the ditch. The wall was so weakened that its collapse continued on the side away from the tower. Then the crack in the donjon became so wide that we could see inside and suddenly the corner collapsed. It, too, fell but it struck the mound where the tunnel had been. As the soil was moved so the flames were fanned and they burned the wood which had fallen with the corner of the donjon.

We were almost mesmerized and then William des Roches shouted, "To arms! We take Ballon!"

I drew my sword and shouted, "Follow me!" I ran to the hurdles which covered the ditch.

I had barely made the mound when I saw the standard which had still been flying when the donjon collapsed lowered and Geoffrey de Brûlon appeared. "We surrender! We yield!"

It was an anti-climax but we had lost no men and for that I was grateful. It became obvious to me, as the knights trooped out of the castle, that they had been relying on the relief force destroying us. They did not have enough to defend the castle.

Prince Arthur was ecstatic. We had begun two sieges and both had ended well. Even as the knights and men at arms were moving from the castle the rest of the donjon suddenly collapsed. Ten men at arms died as the stones tumbled over them. After that, we evacuated the castle. We would not enter until we were certain that it had settled.

The prisoners were guarded and a request for ransom was sent. The day was spent preparing a feast to celebrate. Prince Arthur told us that King Philip would be joining us for the feast. That worried me. Sir William and I left the feast early before King Philip had arrived. I did not relish the thought. We went to the stables to see to our horses. They were behind a stand of trees where there was good grazing. Our horses were separate from the rest and Edward son of Edgar had been watching over them. We relieved him. Although neither had been wounded or injured in the battle we checked them over again. I was lost in my thoughts and William was dutifully silent. Thus it was that we heard what we were not supposed to hear.

Return of the Knight

As we were grooming our mounts we heard the sound of horses and I heard the Comte de Senonche's voice. The French tents were on the other side of the stand of trees. He greeted his king. King Philip had arrived. For some reason, the King and the Comte, along with three others I could not identify, came closer to the trees. It was, I presumed so that they could talk without being overheard.

"You have done well, Valery. And you too, my lord Raymond. Will the young Breton go along with our plans?"

I heard the Comte speak. I recognised his silky tones, "He will, your majesty."

"Good, then there is no problem."

"I am afraid it is not as simple as that, majesty. There are two problems, William des Roches and Sir Thomas of La Flèche. They are both suspicious."

"It matters not. So long as we control the Prince then those who serve him will have to go along with what we say. Are your men ready to move into the castle as soon as the feast is over?"

The voice I did not recognise answered, "Yes, your majesty."

"Then we will have possession of the castle and the two knights can bleat all they like it will not make any difference. And now let us go and greet the would-be Duke."

As soon as they had gone I grabbed William. "Go and fetch all of our men. Do so silently. Have them fetch the tools the miners used."

"What do you intend lord?"

"We cannot afford a war against France but I can deny them this castle. We will destroy it. Meet me by the donjon. Tell the men to be silent."

There was still smoke rising from the tunnel and the ground and stones felt warm. As I slipped across the bridge and into the half-demolished castle I could see that most of the work had been done for us. We had two sides of the donjon to destroy and the gatehouse. There was plenty of material that would burn. I knew what we had to do. Once my men arrived I explained my plan. I was pleased by their attitude. They set about it with gusto. We could make as much noise as we liked for the feast was in full swing. The animals the garrison had kept for a long siege were now being served to the victors. I split my men into two. Half collected wood and flammable material while the other half used mattocks and crowbars to pull out keystones. The plan was for us to prepare it to fire and then they would return to our camp while Sir William, Edward, David and I set it alight. I intended for the cause of the destruction to be a mystery. They might suspect who had done it but there would be no proof for we would be close by the French King when the fire took hold. I was anxious to see King Philip's reaction.

It took longer than I had expected but eventually, we were ready and I sent my men back to the camp. The four of us lit the oil-soaked kindling and then hurled the brands into the corner of the donjon where we had piled all the wood we could find. The tapestries still hung from the walls and they would burn well. We disappeared in the dark. We had reached our own camp when the first shout from the camp was given. There had been plenty of drink and most of the knights were slow to react. William and I went into our tents and removed our smoky surcoats. We put on fresh ones and then joined the other knights who were watching the blaze and listening to the crack and thunder as the walls collapsed. I saw King Philip, Prince Arthur and the Comte de Senonche in close conference. The King turned and saw me. Then he looked back as a sudden flare of flame leapt into the air. The castle would be destroyed. Of that, I had no doubt. It might be rebuilt but that would take time. If King Philip thought he had taken a prize he was mistaken.

William des Roches joined me, "What do you think happened, Sir Thomas?"

I shrugged, "Perhaps we weakened it more than we thought."

"And the fire?"

"Who knows? It may have been just an ember which was fanned by the breeze."

Just then we heard King Philip. He was shouting angrily for his men to put out the fire. William des Roches shook his head, "Why is he so concerned about the castle? It was not his. The only losers are us for we have lost an important fortress. If I thought this was sabotage…" I pointed. The three Templars were close by the King and he was speaking to them. They disappeared. William des Roches turned to me, "What is that you know, Sir Thomas. I pray to tell me."

I had to trust him. Outside of the Prince, there was no one else to trust. "Sir Ranulf was a Templar. I think he was in the employ of France. When he fled us, he was just being clever. We thought he served King John. He did not. Who knows, he might have persuaded King John that he was on his side. I overheard the French King talking to the Templars. He intended to take Ballon as his own castle. That way he could control this border crossing."

"But why would we give away such a fortress?"

"Would you go to war over it?"

"Would the French?"

I shrugged, "We will discover all when daylight comes and men can talk. I for one will be interested to hear what the French have to say. I told you before. I do not trust the French. I am happy that we have defeated King John's allies. It bodes well for the future. We may well be able to take all of the castles. With Normandy and Maine in our possession, we could think about taking England."

"I am not so certain. Is Prince Arthur strong enough to be king?"

"He is stronger than you think."

"But if he sides with the French…"

41

Return of the Knight

"I cannot see that. We will wait until the morrow."

As I turned he grabbed my arm, "You destroyed the castle."

I gave him what I hoped was an innocent smile, "I am just a simple knight. You grant me too much intelligence."

"You are clever but I cannot yet fathom your true purpose. I do believe that you have the interests of this army and Prince Arthur at heart. But be careful my young friend. This is not a game of dice. This is a game of thrones."

The next morning, I awoke refreshed. Whatever plan the French had been hatching had been disrupted by our action. What would happen next? I was summoned, along with Sir Guy, Sir Roger and the other senior knights. Worryingly it was not Prince Arthur who spoke to us but Philip of France.

"My friends, we have won a great victory here and defeated King John and his English knights. The castle may have been destroyed but a new one will rise from the ashes," he laughed, "quite literally! It will have, as its seneschal, Raymond Comte de Senonche!"

I looked at William des Roches. His face was a mask of anger, "Your majesty! The castle is in Maine! It is not French!"

King Philip had a thin smile on his face, "It is now and Prince Arthur here agrees, do you not?"

This was the moment when Arthur should have stood up to King Philip. He did not and, in doing so, signed his own death warrant. He shook his head, "The castle will not be built for some time. Let us not fight over a pile of rubble. King Philip has promised that his army will help wrest Normandy from King John! When that is achieved we will discuss Ballon! An act of God has destroyed the castle. It is a sign that we are to put aside our differences and join together to fight King John."

The announcement left a bad taste in the mouths of the knights of Anjou and Brittany. None of us wanted a war with France. We did not have enough men to fight both France and England but Prince Arthur had now handed over command of the war to King Philip.

William des Roches came over to speak with me. "You knew this might happen. You said as much to me. Prince Arthur is a liability. He will sell us out to the French."

I looked over and saw that Juhel de Mayenne was laughing and joking with the Comte de Senonche and the three Templars. Now that the King of France was here they openly wore the surcoats of the Templars. Their plain apparel had been a disguise. Prince Arthur stood forlornly alone. He did not even have a household knight with him. It was as though they had all distanced themselves from him. He had made a mistake and the visible sign of it was that he was alone.

Return of the Knight

I shook my head as William des Roches and I watched the scene. "I knew that the French and their spies were up to something but I thought that Prince Arthur would stand up to the French King."

The Lord of Le Mans nodded, "I will return to Le Mans. There are ransoms to be collected. I suppose one good thing to come of this is that we have weakened Normandy. When we choose to attack them, they will not have as many knights with which to defend their castles."

"That is cold comfort, lord. I will speak with Prince Arthur and discover his intentions."

Prince Arthur saw me coming and hung his head. He looked like a naughty boy caught out in some mischief. I had been wrong to put my faith in one so young. I said nothing when I was next to him. I waited for him to raise his eyes from the ground. "Sir Thomas, what could I do? King Philip said that he would cease to support me if I did not yield the castle of Ballon. Surely it is better this way? We have an ally and can fight and defeat King John."

"Why did you speak with the King alone? The Lord of Le Mans could have offered support and advice. You are young. You said that you were stronger than men thought. Was this an attempt to impress us by showing that you could negotiate with a king?"

The guilt was written all over his face but he did not reply immediately. "What will you do now, Sir Thomas?"

"Maine is now protected from an attack from Normandy. I came north with you soon after I had arrived in Anjou. My wife is there. I will return home."

He looked almost relieved, "Then I would beg an escort from you. My mother is in Angers with Viscount Aimery. I would seek advice from them."

"And what of William des Roches? He has served you well."

He looked over. William was pointedly sat with Sir Guy and Sir Roger. "I will seek advice from my mother. She has steered my course thus far. I still have enemies in this land. I trust you. I know I have disappointed you and yet you do not berate me and you offer your support. You are a true knight."

I nodded, "Then the sooner we leave the better."

My men were delighted to be leaving. They had bulging purses and there were some, like Ridley the Giant, who had wives. They would be keen to share their bounty. The others wanted to spend their gold and silver. Angers was not riven with war. They would be able to spend it well.

I gained satisfaction from the disappointment on King Philip's face when we said that we were leaving. "We are close to victory, Duke Arthur. We can advance into Normandy."

"I take no men from the army, your majesty. The Lord of Le Mans is still here to command the army of Brittany and Anjou. I will be but a short while. There are things I need to do in Angers."

43

Return of the Knight

For the first time, King Philip switched his reptilian gaze to me. If he thought to mesmerize and cow me he was mistaken. "And you take Sir Thomas with you? Sir Thomas, you need to be careful. Those who play with fire often have their fingers burned."

I smiled, "True, your majesty and those who sleep with the devil always regret that decision."

His face darkened. I knew that the burning of the castle could not remain a secret for long. Men talk and there was gossip that the men of La Flèche had returned to the feast smelling of fire. His eyes flickered to the three Templars who stood close by and then he smiled, "I am pleased that the Duke of Brittany will have such an escort. If King John's men should capture him then it would be the end of the war. We still have much to do." He turned to William des Roches. "When the ransoms are in we will discuss our strategy to take the border castles of Normandy." It was a deliberate snub to Prince Arthur. It was as though he did not exist.

William nodded, "Yes your majesty."

Leaving the Duke's servants to see to him I returned to my camp to give my men the good news. As we were packing up William des Roches came to me. "I am sorry that we must part like this. You are a true knight and a great warrior. I hope that Prince Arthur realises what he owes you."

"He is my liege lord and I cannot support King John." I looked over to King Philip, "If I were you, my friend, I would keep a close eye on the King. He is up to something. I cannot see him risking his best knights just to regain Normandy for Prince Arthur. I fear he means to take it for himself."

"Then he will have me to contend with. Our task is not easy, my lord, we must save the young prince from himself. With time and a good mentor, he may become a leader who can face up to King John but, until then, we must save the Dukedom!" he clasped my arm. You can be assured that I will send your share of the ransom to La Flèche. Will you return to the army?"

"When I have safely delivered Prince Arthur to Angers and set my affairs at La Flèche in order then I will bring my men back here." I smiled, "By then my young knight will have hired more men at arms and we will be even stronger."

He looked relieved, "Good, then go with God!"

We left on a bright June morning. With over seventy miles to travel we could not make the journey in one day; not with servants and baggage. I decided to break the journey at my home. It would be a long forty miles but the thought of my wife would spur me on.

Chapter 5

I was not a fool. I had a great responsibility. The Duke of Brittany had just six household knights and squires with him. All were young. None had taken part in the two sieges nor the battle north of Ballon. They were untried. They had the best of helmets and they had fine armour and war horses but I knew not how they would deal with danger. I would be relying on the common man and not the nobles. I had the six knights and their squires riding with Prince Arthur. If nothing else they could slow down an enemy who might try to do him harm. I had ten of my men at arms at the rear with the baggage and the horses. The rest rode in two lines flanking the household knights. My archers were spread in a scouting screen ahead of us and Sir William, Fótr and Johann rode ahead of Prince Arthur. I know that he thought he was being snubbed for, as we neared the cathedral of St. Julien Le Mans, he asked me so.

"Why do you keep apart, my lord? We are travelling through my lord des Roches' town. Surely we are safe here and you can speak with me and make this journey more pleasant."

I had stopped and turned to speak to him, "Prince Arthur, your safety is all. If I am distracted then, in that moment, you could be harmed. If anything happened to you then King John has won for there is no other of your family to fight him. You have neither wife nor child. Your sister cannot rule but she could be married off by your uncle. When we reach La Flèche I will chatter like a magpie. Until then we will be vigilant, even when passing a cathedral!"

South of Le Mans the land was devoid of castles. Mine at La Flèche was the only one of any substance. There were fortified halls but no walls and that was another reason for hurrying. I would not risk a camp in the open. King Philip's words still rang in my ears, *'If King John's men should capture him then it would be the end of the war. We still have much to do.'* I feared John but I feared King Philip even more.

The household knights complained and moaned about the speed with which we travelled. I ignored them. When we stopped, it was for the horses. My men did not complain. They were alert and spoke little. The household knights sounded like ladies sewing a tapestry as they chattered on about trivialities like who had hunted the largest pig or speared the greatest stag. I noticed that Prince Arthur said little. He had more serious matters to engage him.

We were not moving as swiftly as I wished. A combination of the wagons and the need for the household knights and squires to stop and make water meant that I did not think we would reach our home until dusk. I was eager to see my bride and the changes she would have wrought in the old castle. It was late afternoon and we had just emerged from the forest at La Fontaine-Saint-Martin when Griff Jameson rode in. "Lord there are riders ahead of us."

I did not stop to worry about who they might be. I immediately began to plan how to defeat them. I held up my hand, "Ambush ahead. Prince Arthur, you and your household knights stay here." I turned to William, "Ride back to the rear guard. I fear there will be more men who are approaching from that direction."

"Yes, lord and you?"

"I will clear the road."

"But you know not whom you face."

"It matters not. They stand between me and my home. Change your horse for your warhorse. Fótr, fetch Dragon."

Prince Arthur rode up to me, "Ambush? Who dares to do this?"

"Who would not dare, my lord?" He looked shocked by my effrontery. I dismounted, "Until you surround yourself with warriors rather than these preening popinjays then you will always be in danger."

One of his knights, Sir Hugo bridled, "My lord that is too much!"

"Silence! Until your sword is notched and bloodied then hold your tongue! I have man's work to do. Prince Arthur, continue up the road but be ready to fight. My men at arms will no longer flank you. Sir William will guard your rear but draw your weapons and be prepared to defend yourselves." Fótr returned with Dragon and I changed horses. He handed me a spear. "You stay with Sir William and the horses. He may need you."

"But I am your squire!"

I waved my hand at Edward and the others who were heading to me. They had changed horses and taken a spear. They knew we had to fight. "And I have these. Whoever these ambushers are they are in for a shock."

I had thirteen archers and twelve men at arms. It would have to do. I rode to the slight rise where David and my archers waited. They had dismounted and their bows were strung. He pointed to the riders five hundred paces from us. "There are thirty-four of them, lord; I counted them. Almost all look to be mailed."

That was not enough to take us. There would be even more at the rear. "Gruffyd son of Tomas, take your brother and two others. Go support Sir William with the baggage. You will be attacked."

"Aye lord."

The fact that the enemy had not attacked us told me that they were waiting for the attack at the rear to distract us which gave me time to assess the situation. I peered south. "David, you have better eyes than me, who are they?"

"They wear the liveries of the men we slew and captured at Ballon lord but they are led by the knight you said was a Templar."

"How can you tell? They wear full-face helmets."

Return of the Knight

"The palfreys they ride. All three have a white star blaze on their heads. I saw them at Ballon. They have just taken shields and surcoats from those we defeated."

That told me all that I needed to know. It was King Philip. I do not think he wished harm to Prince Arthur but he needed him at his side so that he could control him. I turned to the men at arms, "We have the advantage of fresh horses. These have ridden hard to be ahead of us. Thanks to the knights of the Prince we are fresher than they are." They laughed. "They outnumber us. David, take your archers and flank them. Use your arrows to thin them out for us. We ride in a wedge. The ones with the white blaze are Templars. Do not underestimate them. They may be treacherous but they are all good warriors."

The men formed up behind me. David divided his archers into four archers and five. They rode south. I could see that our action had spurred the ambushers. They formed two lines. They intended to charge us. I had no banner above me but Fótr had brought me a spear with a gonfanon. That would have to do as the rallying point. We began to move down the road. The Templars were as experienced as I was. They kept together and did not gallop. I guessed that half of their men were knights. They would be French knights. They knew that I had just Sir William. Like me, they would have dismissed the household knights. They had fought in tourneys and jousts. For this, you needed men who could kill. They would underestimate my men at arms. That was my secret weapon.

I was aiming at the three Templars. They had lances. They would have practised every day since they had been young men. They would hit us and hit us hard. I would have three lances aimed at me. I would not be able to stop them all. I would be hit. I spurred Dragon a little. I was riding a warhorse. They had to be riding palfreys for David had identified three of them. My horse was bigger. They would be striking upwards. I would have one chance to hit the knight in the centre. I knew that he would be the knight called Valery. I had learned that his name was Sir Valery of Lyon. He was Burgundian. The three Templars showed their experience by resting their lances on the cantles of their saddles. When they hit, they would strike where they aimed.

We were now closing rapidly. I heard a couple of cries and shouts from the flanks. I smiled without looking. David and the archers were thinning the numbers and weakening the resolve of the men we attacked. I saw that we were just twenty paces from them. I lowered my spear and pulled it back slightly. I pulled my shield up and leaned forward in the saddle. I had the top of my helmet towards the enemy. I was flanked by Harry Longsword and Edward son of Edgar. Both knew how to use a spear. They would both have a free strike as three lances would try to unhorse or kill me.

Sir Valery's lance struck my shield. He punched hard. Had I not been riding a warhorse I might have been unhorsed but Dragon did not miss a step. The second lance hit my helmet and made my head ring. Even as I rammed my spear at the cantle of Sir Valery's horse I felt the lance tear through the mail covering my arm. It drew blood. Dragon did what every good warhorse did. He lunged and bit at one of the horses. As luck would have it that was the horse to my right; the one whose rider had lanced me. As my spear struck flesh I twisted and then felt the ash shaft shatter. Sir Valery tried to keep his saddle but he had a metal head and an arm's length of spear in his guts. He fell.

Edward took advantage of Dragon's bite and his spear hit the second Templar in the chest. He tumbled backwards over the back of his horse. As I drew my sword I could not see how Harry fared but I knew that two of my most dangerous enemies were down. I felt the blood pouring down my arm. I prayed that it was a clean wound and that there were no wooden splinters embedded there.

I was the first to reach their second line. I saw that the riders had no mail. They were protected by metal-studded leather. They were armed with spears. I brought my shield over to protect my chest and held my sword out horizontally. Edward was just behind me. As the spear shattered on my shield the rider rode into my outstretched arm. The blade tore through the surcoat and into the leather. He fell backwards over his horse's rump. I heard the crack and the scream as Edward's horse crushed his chest.

There were none before us and I whipped Dragon around. I saw that Harry Longsword lay dead. The Templar who had killed him was galloping towards the Prince. He had eight riders left with him. Some of my men were still engaged with the survivors of the ambush.

"Edward! With me!"

I saw that the protectors of the Prince were showing their inexperience. They did not form a line. They charged, recklessly and without order towards the Templar and his eight men. I glanced to my right and saw that David and his archers were turning to send their arrows after the Templar and his men. They had to check for they were thwarted; the Prince's retinue had met the enemy and my archers had no clear target. Four of the Prince's knights and two men at arms fell as the nine riders galloped through. Their deaths allowed David and his men to send their arrows at the enemy and four fell from their horses.

The deaths of the knights had not been in vain. It takes time to kill a man and they had had to stop their horses to despatch them. Edward and I were gaining. The Prince was just sitting on his horse. He was not moving. To the north, I saw Sir William, Johann and Ridley the Giant galloping to the Prince's aid. They would not make it in time. I spurred Dragon and, in leaping forward, he brought me close to the rearmost warrior. Blood was seeping from my wound but I still had enough strength to swing my blade hard into the spine of the knight I chased. The blade came away bloody and he slipped from the saddle. His death grip pulled his horse with him. The Templar had just three men with him and as Edward brought his sword down to split the spine of another one then he was down to two. It was then that the Prince reacted. He ran. Luckily, he ran back down the road towards Sir William. It was the best thing he could have done.

As Edward and I brought our swords into the backs of the two men at arms following the Templar. Ridley and Sir William hit the Templar from two sides. Ridley the Giant had a long broad sword. While Sir William's sword hacked through the Templar's arm, Ridley's sliced through his body, cutting him in two.

"Johann, fetch back the Prince, by force if needs be!" I reined in Dragon and dismounted. I trusted the judgement of David of Wales but I needed confirmation. I took off the helmet of the dead knight. It was one of the Templars. I took off my own helmet and looked up at William. "How was it at the rear?"

"The archers saw them off. When they realised we were ready they fled north but Alf Smiths'son fell."

I nodded, "Well done Ridley. The horse and this knight's bounty is yours."

"Thank you, lord but I would change it for Alf alive and laughing once more."

"I know. Have the rest of the enemy horses and war gear collected. Leave their corpses where they lie. They fought under false colours."

As I mounted Johann rode back with the Prince. Prince Arthur looked at me, "You were right, my lord. My men were naïve. I will listen to you in the future."

"These men were sent by Philip of France. Do you still put your faith in him?"

"They may have acted alone. You cannot know."

I shook my head, "If you will not listen to my advice my lord then I have done with you. I will take you to Angers and let your mother act as an adviser. I hope she has more luck than I have had."

Fótr shouted, "Lord. You are wounded!"

I had forgotten. The blood flowed freely. Ridley looked up and tore a long piece of cloth from the dead Templar he had been stripping. He tied it above the wound and tightened it. The blood stopped and he nodded his satisfaction. "That should hold until we reach our castle, lord."

Sir William said, "You and Fótr ride. We will clear the field!"

I shook my head, "I will wait."

Sir William shook his head and said, forcefully, "Lord, do you not trust me and your men? Take the archers and the remains of the household knights. We will fetch the wagons and the horses. If you ride hard then you can be there before the blood needs letting."

Return of the Knight

Edward son of Edgar put his hands together to help me to mount, "Come along my lord, there's a good fellow, do as young Sir William says! If you lose your arm we will have to face the wrath of Lady Margaret!" He said it with a smile and I nodded.

"Come, Prince Arthur, we will ride!"

David of Wales and my archers were clearing up the bodies at the ambush site. Fótr said, "My lord is wounded, David of Wales, you will escort us. Godwin of Battle, have the men at arms help, Sir William?"

Both men ginned and knuckled their forehead, "Aye my lord!"

I knew Ridley had been right as we headed south. I felt slightly dizzy. It was the same feeling I had had when I had been wounded in my leg. As we closed to within a mile or two of my castle Fótr put his heels in his horse's flanks. "I will have all prepared, my lord!"

David was on one side of me and he laughed, "That one is growing, lord. Soon you will be able to knight him!"

I nodded, "He has become a man overnight, it seems."

Prince Arthur was on my other side. He had been silent since the ambush but now he spoke, "Better than some knights, it seems."

One of the knights who had survived heard him, "We will strive to do better, Your Grace."

The Prince shook his head, "But for a young knight and a man at arms I would now be dead! It is a little late to say you will do better."

He relapsed into silence. The attack had unnerved him. Hitherto he had seen death and violence from a distance. His sword had remained sheathed. The last Templar had been within two blade strokes from ending his life.

As we rode through the gates I saw that Margaret had her women ready along with the steward, Geoffrey, and Father Michel. The Prince and his men were some way behind my archers. While the other women, Marguerite apart, looked tearful, my wife looked stoic. She saw me riding and therein lay hope. I smiled at her, "Did Fótr, tell you that Prince Arthur comes to stay the night?"

"He did and the rooms are being readied. Now let us look to you, my husband. I understand that you have two wounds."

"One is almost healed."

"Then you remain at home until both are. You cannot save the Dukedom with one arm!" There was the hint of a smile in her eye. She was mocking me!

I dismounted, grateful that my right leg was whole and I would not wince when I placed my foot on the ground. Father Michel supported me, "Come lord, I have all that we need to sew you back together although I fear I can do nothing about your mail." I saw the torn links. It would be an expensive repair. I hoped they had a good smith here. My wife came in with me. I saw Lady Marguerite throw her arms around William and then whisper in his ear. He shouted loudly. That was unlike him.

Return of the Knight

When we reached the door to the chapel my wife kissed me, "I shall be a good hostess. Tell me, what ails the Prince? He looks out of sorts."

"He has been duped and betrayed and he is finding it hard to handle. He thought he was ready to rule and he is not. I feel sorry for him but he has many people depending upon him."

Father Michel was a good healer and he was thorough. He had Fótr strip me completely. As soon as the improvised bandage came off the blood began to flow again. Although the flow was not as quick as before Father Michel had to be quick with the cloth to staunch the bleeding. It took some time to stop the blood from pouring. He used honey and lemon to smear into the wound. It stung but I knew that it would prevent my arm from putrefying. Then he stitched it. I noticed he had hands like a woman. His fingers were long and delicate. He did a good job. Then he looked at the wound on my leg.

"Not a bad job although I would have stitched. Who used the fire?"

"A priest."

"A lazy priest then but the wound is healing well, but the scar..." he shook his head. "I will speak with the cook and have a special diet for you. It will make you stronger and replace the blood you have lost."

"Replace the blood?"

He laughed, "You knights know how to spill the blood but not how it is made. The body makes blood. However, it is possible to help the body to make it quicker. We will do that. Fótr, you can help him to dress. I would suggest you take it easy but I have spoken with Lady Margaret and know that is not in your nature. You must wear a sling!"

I felt foolish but I knew that he was right. Fótr helped me into my gambeson and surcoat. Father Michel adjusted the sling and helped me to the hall.

"Fótr, take the mail to the blacksmith. Ask him to repair it or, if he cannot, then he can make me a new one."

Father Michel left me at the door to the hall and went back to the chapel to clean up the blood. He was a fastidious man. The hall was empty for my wife was showing our guests to their rooms. This was one of the first times I had been alone in the Great Hall. It was large but not as large as the one at Stockton. This would do but I still had the dream of a home in England. This was an exile only.

I went to my chambers. I barely knew the servants but they were in the room already. My chests were being unpacked. Both wounds were aching and I waved them away. I slumped onto the bed. Margaret came in and, sitting next to me, began to comb my hair. I found it soothing.

"I am sorry I was so long, my husband, but I was speaking with the Prince. He is like a little boy. He told me you had abandoned him." I nodded. "You cannot do that. He never knew his father. When he was born his father was already dead. He has been brought up by his mother. She is a troubled woman.

Her husbands were chosen for her. They were forced marriages. None were happy. His sister will be like a prize cow to be married off. You owe it to them both to try to help them." She laid down the comb and took out a clean kyrtle. "The Earl of Cleveland spent his life looking after Empress Matilda and her son Henry. You can do no less."

I knew why my wife felt this way. She had almost been forced into marriage for her fortune. She had lost that fortune. On the voyage south, she said that I was more valuable than the fortune she had lost. She was, however, correct, I was honour bound to help the three of them. I knew it was a lost cause but I was a knight and a knight of England. I had been dubbed by a king.

"You are right. What did I do to deserve you?"

"Come, stand and I will bathe and then dress you. Your arm will take some time to heal. At least that means you will not be involved in this war for a while."

As she washed me she told me the news of the manor. She detailed all the improvements she had made and whom she had seen. She was impressed with Geoffrey the Steward and could find no fault with the servants. Sir Philip and his predecessors had chosen well. Suddenly she stopped, "I am a featherbrain! I have forgotten to tell you the most important news. Sir William and Marguerite are to be parents. She is with child!"

Now I understood the shouts and the excitement. I was pleased for them.

That evening the Prince and his knights were subdued which was in direct contrast to Sir William, Fótr and Johann who were full of high spirits. My wife said as the cheese and ham were brought in with some fresh bread, "Husband, sit with the Prince. Build bridges."

"Yes, my love."

I swapped seats with my wife. It went against all protocol but this was my castle and I would make the rules. "What is amiss, Prince Arthur?"

"Today I saw the enormity of my task. I have lost knights and I fear I will lose my Dukedom. My mother told me that I just had to assert myself and all would be well."

"This is a game, my lord, and you do not yet know the rules. I tried to warn you that King Philip had his own motives. All is not lost. William des Roches is a fine leader. He fought with your uncle at Arsuf. So long as he commands then you will not lose your Dukedom."

He looked at me and then nodded, "But you do not think that I can retake Normandy!"

I could not lie to him. Too many people had done that already. "No, you cannot. There will come a time when you will be able to. But that is in the future. You need to learn how to use the men you can trust and how to deceive those you cannot."

Return of the Knight

"You have only one knight and yet you are able to defeat all your enemies. How is that?"

"I learned in the harsh sun of the Crusades. There you either learned to fight or you died. I went to war when I had seen but ten summers. I did not fight for three more but I learned by watching. I did as Fótr and Johann do. I brought horses and spears to my father while avoiding the swords and the arrows of our foes." I lowered my voice. "And I learned to choose good men. When I came from the Holy Land I had but five and young William. Now you see that I lead over thirty men. By the time my arm is healed, I will have another fifteen."

Sir Richard of Nantes leaned forward, "I felt ashamed today, lord, when you and your men did what we could not. They are common men and have had none of the advantages we have enjoyed yet they killed Templars!"

"How many men have you killed?"

He shook his head, "None."

"The first is always the hardest. My men fought to save their lives. They fought without armour and with poor swords. Now they have the best of both and they are better for it. When you go into a battle you have to believe that you are better than those you face. You must try to kill."

Prince Arthur said, "But what about ransom?"

"You cannot have ransom if you are dead. Worry about surviving first and ransom second. The ransom will come when you defeat your enemies."

By the end of the evening, they all seemed happier for they had something to do. I knew that it would be at least two months before I could even think about going to war again. In the event I did not have two months and my world was turned upside down once more.

The next day my wife insisted that I stay in the castle and Sir William and my men at arms escorted Prince Arthur back to Angers. Before he left we spoke.

"I have learned my lesson, Sir Thomas. Perhaps you are right. My knights and I should learn to walk before we run. Tell me this; can I count on your support when I try to wrest Normandy from King John?"

I smiled, "Of course, you need not ask. I am your man."

He visibly brightened and looked like a young boy. Was the game he was playing the right one?

La Flèche

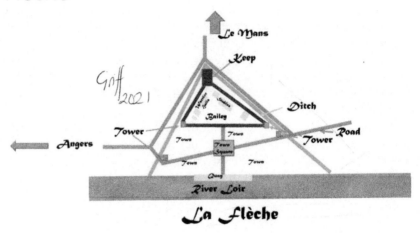

Chapter 6

Thirty days after he had left us I was allowed to begin to train with my men once more. It had been frustrating not to do so. However, I knew that both my wife and the healer were right. I needed my sword arm. David of Wales and Edward son of Edgar managed to hire two more archers and four more men at arms. I had not been idle when recuperating. I had been allowed to walk my walls and I had examined my castle. It had been well built. Like many such castles, it was triangular with the keep at the narrow end. The longest wall was the one closest to the town. The gatehouse was not the biggest but Sir Leofric had cleverly built three easily defended gates for the town. One was on the river and the other two at the east and the west of the road which ran alongside the river. It meant an attacker, if he wanted to reach the gates, had to move along two walls where archers could make life difficult for them. Or they could try attacking the keep and that was a substantial building for it was built on a mound and had the moat before it.

However, as I walked the walls with Fótr and Sir William, I noticed improvements we could introduce. The ditches which ran around the two walls were deep enough but it suddenly occurred to me that we could flood them from the river. All that we would need to do would be to build two bridges. I knew that they would need to be substantial ones. I set my men at arms and archers on building the bridges. When they were in place then we would break through the earth and flood them. I also had the boggy land to the west of my town flooded. If the French came from that direction they would get a shock. I made it competitive by having each group of men work on one of the bridges. My wound prevented me from helping but Fótr and Johann joined in. While they were being constructed I spoke with the merchants in the town. My wife had got to know them while I had been on the campaign. That made it easier when I went around to speak with them.

Sir Philip had told me that Sir Leofric had created a town council that still operated and I met with them.

The head of the council was the leading winemaker, Roger of Meaux, "My lord, we are honoured that you have chosen to live here as lord of the manor. For many years we have served the castellan. Under our hand, the town has grown and we enjoy a prosperity that other towns envy. We know that this is due, in no small part, to the power your family wields."

I nodded, "As you know there is a war going on. At the moment we are safe here. The Duke of Brittany is in Angers and has promised that he will do all in his power to keep it so. However, I am a realist. King John may well choose to make war on us. And I have no doubt that King Philip might cast a greedy eye in our direction." I saw some of them shifting uncomfortably. They did not want to hear this. I smiled, "I am a man of war. You are men of commerce. I will keep you safe so that you may continue to make coin. We all benefit." They smiled. I had said the right thing. "If war comes then I wish all of you to continue to go about your business. The river is the lifeline of the town. I propose that we defend that lifeline."

"Defend it, lord? How? We already have walls."

"The walls defend the town. I am talking about the river. If we are attacked then we will put chains across the river at the two ends of the walls. I would have any attack come from the land." They looked relieved.

"And how can we help?"

"I am making the ditches into moats. My men will do that and I will bear the expense. We will make two bridges which we can remove in times of danger. I would have the town make the two chains to bar progress along the river. Does that seem reasonable?"

They smiled. Roger of Meaux nodded, "Perfectly."

"And if we are attacked then I would expect the men of the town to defend its walls."

Although less acceptable, they understood the reality of the situation. They all nodded.

"Of course, my lord, but it will not come to that, surely?"

I gave what I hoped was a reassuring smile and said, "I pray to God that it will not but we all know that the Lord helps those who help themselves!"

With the two bridges in place and the ditches deepened I watched as my men began to break through the narrow piece of earth which lay beneath them. The piles which had been driven into what would become the banks had been secured by rocks. My men had large stones which would also be placed next to the piles once the dams were broken. I nodded and both sets of men toiled to make the break through. It was not as spectacular as I might have hoped but the effect was all that I had wished. The dampness at the bottom of the ditch became a puddle and gradually it rose to become a moat. When the water flowed faster it washed away the soil back to the stones. We had good defences.

I summoned Geoffrey, my steward, and asked him about the supplies we had in our cellars. He misunderstood me, "Do you have a feast in the next few days lord? We have plenty of supplies I can assure you."

"No, Geoffrey. Do we have enough to last us for a month? Is there enough grain for the horses? How many wells do we have?"

"A month?"

"If war comes we may be besieged. If we are then we need to feed ourselves and our horses. Have we enough?"

56

Return of the Knight

He shook his head, "No, lord." He looked fearful as though I might berate him for an oversight.

I smiled, "Then start today. I want grain, salted meat, salted fish. I want a good water supply."

"But the cost, lord!"

"How many chests of treasure did I bring back with me?"

He smiled, "Sorry, lord. Sir Philip rarely brought treasure. Of course, we have enough coin but I am not certain where we would store it."

"Find somewhere; if there is nowhere then build a granary. If my men can defend this town then you can feed it! See to it!" I did not doubt that he would manage it. He had just not thought of the problem was all.

My plans were seen to be prescient when a messenger arrived to tell us that King John had landed in Normandy and invaded Maine from the direction of Argentan. It seemed our victories had spurred him to go on the offensive. Had I been fit then I might have contemplated riding north to fight him. Sometimes fate intervenes in our lives in ways we do not understand. Had I not been wounded I might have ridden north that September and then I would have been close to Le Mans and present at the battle of Lavardin. There King Philip was soundly defeated by King John and the Duke of Brittany suddenly found himself without an ally. I followed the rider who brought the news, along with Sir William and some of my men at arms to speak with the Duke in Angers.

I watched Arthur's face as he heard the news. He looked crushed. As we had ridden into the city I had seen evidence of the build-up of his forces. He had not been idle but in the three months since he had ridden south he had had little time to gather a large army. His mother was with him. I could tell that she did not like me. She glowered and glared at me. There were other counts, earls and barons in the court and all of them had suggestions. This was not a place in which I was comfortable.

The Prince still looked up to me, "Sir Thomas, we value your advice. What do you suggest that we do?"

All eyes turned to look at me. "William des Roches still commands Le Mans. That cannot be taken easily. You have already begun to prepare an army to fight King John. All this battle means is that King Philip is no longer there for you. As you know, your Grace, I never liked the alliance. This may be a good thing."

Constance, his mother, snapped, "A good thing? This is a disaster! If this is the quality of your advice then keep it to yourself! You are nothing better than a mercenary! You are a sword for hire!"

She had a savage tongue but her barbs did not penetrate. She was right. I had been a mercenary. However, my advice was still good. Arthur reprimanded his mother, "Sir Thomas has been my most stalwart friend. What else should we do?"

Return of the Knight

"Winter is coming. Armies find it hard to campaign in winter. Prepare for sieges. If John tries to live off the land then he will starve. By spring we should be in a position to meet him sword to sword."

"That is your advice? Sit and do nothing?" Constance sounded like a harpy.

"Preparing for a siege is not nothing, your ladyship."

"I have heard enough. You are dismissed from my son's court! We will send for William des Roches. He will offer better advice."

Summarily sent north I rode in silence. I was not angry. If anything, I was saddened by the events. I now understood why Arthur was the way he was. His mother lived in the past. It was a past that did not exist. She thought she could pick and choose from the advice she was given. That was wrong. She was right in one respect; William des Roches was Arthur's only hope.

Rather than wait for disaster to strike us I had men put the chains in place in the river. I instructed the council to initiate the town watch and within the castle, I doubled the sentries. My men did not mind. We all had coin we wished to keep and families to protect. Six of my men now had wives and children. That was an incentive. In addition, I rode each day, with Sir William, on the road north. The initial flood of refugees fleeing fighting fell to a trickle after a couple of days and I grew hopeful.

Then, six days after we had heard the news of the battle a pair of riders was seen coming down the road. I recognised one as Viscount Aimery from the standard his companion carried. He was one of the lords who served Prince Arthur and he had been with William des Roches. At last, we would discover something approaching the truth rather the rumour and gossip which had followed the refugees.

We reined in and waited. Viscount Aimery's face was dark when he spoke to me, "Sir Thomas, I bring dire news. William des Roches has been persuaded to join with King John. He is the new seneschal of Angers."

I was not often stuck for words but I was then. What could have made William des Roches become a traitor to Prince Arthur? Had I been such a poor judge of character?

"I go to warn the Prince. He, his mother and his sister must flee. Sir William is coming down the road with his army even as we speak."

I had recovered enough to regain my voice. "The Seneschal will need to get past my castle. He will not find that easy. Where will the Prince go?"

The Viscount shrugged, "Perhaps to Aquitaine. Eleanor is still the matriarch. If any can save the boy it is she."

I nodded and whipped my horse's head around. "We will escort you to my castle."

We had not sought it but war was coming to my little valley and as we headed south I wondered just how many of the people we passed would suffer? The lords, the high and the mighty, even the church would not care what

58

happened to them. They each fought for themselves and no one fought for the people. I turned and said to Robert of La Flèche. "Take two men and warn the farmers and those who till the land north of La Flèche that war may be coming. Tell them that they are more than welcome to take refuge with me."

I saw the relief on my man at arms' face. This was his land and these were his people, "I will do so, lord."

The Viscount was impressed with my defences as we rode along my walls. "You have not been idle, Sir Thomas."

"No, Viscount, my travels have taught me that nothing remains at peace forever. A wise man hopes for peace and prepares for war."

My wife was like a rock. While some of the other women became almost hysterical she was calmness personified. "Ladies, Lady Marguerite is about to go into labour. Let us deal with her while our men do what they do best and protect us."

I nodded my thanks to her and sought the council. They too were fearful. A rampaging army was unheard of in my sleepy little town. I had to calm things down. They were all agitated and already speaking as though we were defeated. "Firstly, they may not be rampaging. I may have misjudged William des Roches but I know that he is a gentleman. From what I have seen of him he might try to reduce our walls but he will not hurt those within. We must be strong. From this moment we ration our food. I know not how long we will have to hold out. If you wish to send your ships away then do so but this evening I have the chains deployed. We will be in a state of siege."

Grateful for something to do those who had ships filled them with their valuables and the goods they had to trade and sent them downriver. Brittany was still held by the Duke's men and their goods could be traded safely there. By the time the evening came, I was exhausted but our exhaustion was relieved somewhat when Sir William became a father. It was a son. "I would name him after your father, Sir Thomas. He will be Samuel of La Flèche."

It seemed a good omen and everyone's spirits were lifted. That night as I crept wearily into my bed my wife snuggled next to me. "I did not wish to say anything before Marguerite's baby was born but I believe that I am with child."

I could not see her face in the dark but I squeezed her hard, "When is the baby due?"

"March or so the ladies who deliver babies tell me. They have been watching me when they came to speak with Marguerite and I have felt the bairn move. It is a lively baby."

"I will make sure that you are both safe, my love."

As we settled down to sleep I had something else to worry me. I not only had a Dukedom and a town to save, but I also had a family who now needed me.

Return of the Knight

As much as I wanted to be with my wife I was needed by my town and my castle. My archers already had many arrows but now they began preparing more. One legacy of Sir Leofric was that my town had more archers than any other castle this side of the English Channel. The smithies rang to the sound of swords and spearheads being beaten. Men were cutting and bringing in as much hay and grass as they could. Our horses would be needed once the siege was lifted. We began slaughtering some of the animals we would not be able to feed. The pig fat would be reserved in case we needed to deter attackers. The meat would be salted. I did not think it would be a long siege. We were not big enough to warrant it but King John might wish to make an example of us.

The first scouts came down from the north two days later. I recognised them. They belonged to Sir Richard de Trevers. He was a good knight and his men were the equal of any I had seen in the battle of William des Roches. They did not approach the castle directly. They halted four hundred paces from the fork in the road. Sir Leofric had placed his keep where it could be the most effective. Any army heading south would have to leave the road or risk the arrows, stones and bolts from the keep and the walls.

We watched as the army grew behind the scouts. I saw the banners of William des Roches. Would this day be the day I fought an old comrade? I watched him and three other knights take off their helmets and ride to the edge of the moat. There was no bridge. Sometimes I had thought that a curse but now I saw that it had been a wise decision of Sir Leofric. They stopped and waited for me to appear. I only had one knight, Sir William. We stood on the wall walk at the northern edge of the keep. Our squires flanked us.

"My lord I am disappointed. I hear that you have sided with John Lackland."

He nodded, "King John was most persuasive. We both know that Prince Arthur cannot stand up to King Philip. You were there at Ballon. We could not endure that. King Philip would have Anjou, Maine and Normandy!"

"We could have fought both of them. You know that."

He did not answer directly. "I am the Seneschal of Angers and Tours. Will you bar our passage?"

"Perhaps." I knew that Viscount Aimery had been in Angers for three days. I was certain that they would have fled for Poitou and the dowager Queen, Eleanor. If I could avoid fighting then I would. "What do you intend?"

"I will go to the Duke and explain why I have, apparently, betrayed him. King John has assured me that he wishes no harm to his nephew."

I laughed, "And you believe him? The man does not know how to speak the truth."

"He is King of England."

"Aye but not the rightful one. An ancestor of mine spent his whole life fighting for the rightful King of England. I can do no less. However, we have been brothers in arms and if, as you say, the Duke is safe then I will allow you to pass unhindered but know this, if anything happens to Prince Arthur while he is in your care then you will pay with your life. I do not speak lightly."

"I know and I realise that you are honourable. Fear not. I swear that while he is in my custody he will be safe."

And so, we watched the army march past our walls. We scrutinised them for we knew that we might well have to fight them at some point. We saw many crossbows but few bows. That gave us hope. When they had disappeared, I summoned my most experienced men at arms. "I would have you build two stone-throwers. I want one on the northwest tower and one on the northeast tower. If an army comes to do us harm then we will make life difficult for them. Build the machines in situ. It will save time."

"Aye lord. And we will have men collecting stones."

I turned to Sir William, "You take charge here. Have the men fix forks to the end of long poles. We will use them to send the ladders back to earth should they try that attack. I will take my archers and ride east. You may tell the people that we are not under siege. They can go about their business. Have them continue to work in the fields and send the horses out to graze."

"You trust William des Roches?"

"It matters not what he does. I have two worries now and they are both kings. If King John is abroad then he might well remember me and come to do me harm and King Philip is also someone who may well be casting avaricious glances in our direction. I will see if any are close."

I used Skuld and I did not wear mail. Instead, I donned a leather jerkin beneath my surcoat. I needed speed. We headed north and west first. We were just twenty odd miles from Le Mans. If that was now in King John's hands then I had to discover if he had men out seeking us. We would then head east to see if King Philip had advanced. There were just fifteen of us. If danger came then we would be more than capable of bloodying our attackers' noses and still escaping.

We rode swiftly but I had my best archers at the fore. They had shown me, over the years, that they could sniff out danger. We rode fifteen miles northwest and saw no sign of danger. We spoke with farmers who confirmed that there had been no scouts heading from Le Mans. King John would be waiting for William des Roches to apprehend Prince Arthur. I hoped that the young Breton was safe with Eleanor of Aquitaine. There he would be safe. We turned and headed due east. The French might well have scouts out. That might not spell danger for us, they could be seeking King John's forces, but I wanted to know where they were.

We were nearing Chateau-sur-le-Loir when we found the French. That surprised me for it was William des Roches' castle. He had not lived there since he had become lord of Le Mans but I had assumed that he had men garrisoned there. It was a knight, squire and twenty men at arms that we spied. They were not riding warhorses but they were mailed with helmets and shields. We saw them first and I had my archers dismount and ready their bows. Beyond them, I could see the towers of Chateau-sur-le-Loir. I turned to Fótr, "You have better eyes than I do, tell me if that is the standard of des Roches which flies from the tower."

He peered into the distance. My archers had strung their bows. "No lord, but I have seen it before. It belonged to one of the knights who was in the retinue of the Comte de Senonche. It is a white bird on a red background."

I nodded, "Then William des Roches has lost his castle."

David of Wales said, "Lord they are moving towards us."

"Are you worried?"

He laughed, "Of course not lord but I thought you should know."

"If they get too close discourage them." I turned to Fótr, "And unless I am mistaken that is a red shield with something white upon it too; on the shields of the men at arms."

"It is, lord, but the knight has a black shield with the same bird."

I heard arrows as they were sent towards the advancing riders. They were less than two hundred paces away. The movement of the horsemen meant it had been difficult for me to see the devices clearly. The squire flew backwards over his saddle clutching his shoulder. A man at arms was hit in the head. Another had his leg pinned to his horse. The rest managed to get shields up but the arrows which had struck had, effectively, ended their interest. Gathering their wounded, they turned and ran. The squire's horse galloped towards us.

"Fótr, go and fetch the horse."

"Aye, lord!"

"Well done archers. We have seen enough. We will return to the castle. We know that the French are now twenty miles from our castle and I think they will be a threat before King John. This has been a useful exercise eh?"

"Aye my lord. Can we go and search the dead man at arms?"

"Of course. Fótr is still chasing the horse. We have time."

It was almost dark when we reached our castle. The day had gone better than I had hoped and I had knowledge of my enemies. That was always important. I told Sir William of my scouting expedition that evening.

"You see, William, we have enemies to the north and east of us, the north and west and the south. As far as I can see we have no friends at all. Perhaps my decision to leave the Baltic was a bad one."

He laughed, "Bishop Albert would not have allowed you to stay lord. No, this is better. We have more men now than we had. All of us are better armed and this castle is better than any that we saw in Sweden. I would not like to take it."

"Nor would I but I think we can make it even more unpalatable. I plan on damming the river just downstream of the chains. I want the level to rise above the other chain. When the ground is boggy and soggy enough we will release the water."

He nodded, "You would have them struggle to place ladders and to use the ground to the east of us?"

"Aye. We can do little about the ground to the north but the east is where the first danger will come."

The next day I checked on the progress of the war machines and I was pleased. They were not as large as the ones we might use to batter a wall but they did not need to be. Their purpose would be to destroy any war machines that were sent against us. We used a crane to lower roped piles of stones into the river. It would not completely block it but, with autumn rains it would raise the river's level and make it burst its banks. I wanted an inundation for a few days. It would destroy the grazing close to the castle and deny that to our enemies. It would also make the ground treacherous. The castle of La Flèche and most of the town was built on higher ground. The warehouses by the river might be under water, albeit briefly, but they were empty anyway. It was a small price to pay.

Four days later an emissary came from William des Roches. He sent a man I could trust. It was Sir Guy de Changé. He came to the west gate. He was not alone. He had twenty men with him. I was summoned to the gate, "Yes sir Guy?"

"I am sorry that we meet under these circumstances, my lord but the seneschal of Angers and Tours sent me. We have captured Prince Arthur and his mother. They are now prisoners in Le Mans. My lord thought you should know."

It was a blow but I did not show my disappointment on my face. "He did not flee to Eleanor of Aquitaine then?"

"No, lord. His mother persuaded him to stay and to order William des Roches to changes sides."

I could not believe the woman. She had cost her son his only chance of regaining power. "And all this happened some days ago."

He smiled, "My lord you have something of a reputation. The Seneschal sent the Prince and his mother away from Angers as soon as he could. He did not want you to try to rescue him."

"And how do you know that I will not?"

"I pray you do not, lord. There is a huge army at Le Mans. King John is busy securing the northern parts of Maine. If you were to attempt a rescue it would end in failure and, I think, your death. I would not like that. You are a brave lord and a true knight. I admire what you are doing but it is like spitting into the wind. You cannot change that which is."

"But a true knight does not worry about that. When my father led his household knights to defend King Richard he knew it was like, what did you

63

say? *'Spitting in the wind'*? Yet he did and the King was saved. It cost them their lives but they died true knights."

He nodded, "Then go with God."

We were now utterly alone. I was not a fool. King John would not allow me to change sides, even if I wanted to. I had bloodied his nose too often and he hated my family. I was fated to fight him. I was undaunted by the odds. If he brought his whole army to bear on my little castle it would send a message to others that it was possible to defy this Lackland King! We would not go quietly if we were to perish.

In the end, it was not King John who came to test our defences, it was the forces of the French King. I had kept patrols out and they told me that French scouts had been seen. Those French scouts had also been killed. However, it meant that we knew they were coming. We could make them blind but, eventually, they would reach us. The swampy, boggy ground to the east would be a surprise. The weather had become wetter. It was almost as though God was on our side for it rained for seven days non-stop.

We pulled all of our people within our walls. With most of the crops already harvested, we had every farmer and his family, as well as their animals, from within five miles inside the castle and the town. They were the French who were coming and my men were ready to defend the land with their lives. I hoped it would be French blood that would be spilt. The hiatus of the advance by William des Roches had actually helped us. There was neither panic nor pessimism. All thought we could beat them. I prayed that we could.

Chapter 7

The French arrived a few days later and camped well to the east of us. Our boggy ground made the approach they hoped, impossible. Instead, they headed further north which meant they would be within range of my two war machines when they attacked. Their crews were eager to try them out. My walls were manned but I knew that it would take some time for them to get close enough to attack. They had no high ground upon which they could place their own stone-throwers and tunnelling, because of the moat, was impossible. Had I had more men then I would have considered a quick raid on their camp but my defences made that harder for us. There was no easy way to slip in and out. If we had to escape then that would be by the river.

Our only action was to destroy the houses which lay beyond our walls. They were poor dwellings. The ones who lived there did not pay taxes and they eked out a living working in the port or by gathering in the woods. They were empty now. Their occupants were sheltered inside my walls. We would help them to rebuild when this was over but we could not allow them to be used by the French. As they burned we contented ourselves on counting the banners and identifying our foes. King Philip had sent the Comte de Senonche. Perhaps King Philip had a higher opinion of the knight than I. During our time together, I had seen little evidence of great military skill. All the decisions which had won us castles had been the result of William des Roches or myself.

Sir William was with me. I had allowed him as much time with his new son as I could but he knew that his son's life chances would be increased if we were successful. The two of us, along with Edward and David of Wales, peered north.

"Where will they attack, lord?"

"They cannot use a tower because of the moat and the boggy land. They can make a bridge for the moat." In answering the question, I was clarifying my own thoughts. "They cannot mine for we have made the ground too wet and we are close to the river, a mine would flood. They will use ladders and a ram." I looked south, to the river. "They either use the two roads and attack at the town gates or, if they wish to reduce the castle, then they attack the walls; probably either by the stables or the warrior halls."

Sir William nodded, "Then we will not be fighting here at the keep. Our families will be safe within."

"Only a fool would try to attack here. De Senonche is not a great strategist but he is not a fool. If we fight from these walls then the rest of the town and the castle have fallen and we will have lost. We will have the oldest retainers and the two crews here. I will be on the east wall and you, William, will command the west wall. Edward, you will divide the men into two groups. David, the archers will be on the wall they are attacking."

"And if they attack two walls at once, lord?"

"Then that means they have men to spare and we will be in danger. If that happens then divide the men up. Now arrange all and I will go to the town."

Taking Fótr with me I left through the main gate. It was open and unguarded. When the attack began it would be closed and I would have two men watching it. The people looked at me with a mixture of fear and relief. The fear was of the unknown, the French attack, and the relief was that my presence in their town meant I had not abandoned them. The council were the richest men in the town and all had bought themselves good helmets, hauberks and swords. I was not sure that they would acquit themselves well if it came to battle but they would give the French the illusion that we had more warriors than we did have. Some were even pretentious enough to have had banners made with their device upon them. Now that might work in our favour.

They waited for me to speak. We stood in the central square "It is the French who are here. I have no fear for our defences are well made. There will, however, be no relief. We have to defeat this attack." I pointed to the two gates at the east and the west. "If they attack there then I want you to take all of your people within the castle. There is room for them and they will be safer. My men will defend these walls. If they do not, and they attack the castle walls then you need do nothing except to send your archers into the castle to fight on our walls."

The relief on their faces was palpable. Their helmets and mail might not be needed. "You are certain, my lord, that they cannot breach our walls?"

I smiled, "Jean the Merchant, you have never fought in a battle. The outcome is rarely certain. I am confident that our defences are strong. We are well supplied. They may damage our walls and I have no doubt that I will lose men but I think that when they have gone we will still be here and the food we have laid in store will be used to celebrate Christmas." I sounded more confident than I was. I remembered the castle in the Baltic where we had thought the enemy would not be able to breach our defences and they had. They had been barbarians. The French valued and prized their own lives much more highly than the Estonians. "Keep the three gates manned with your other men. The French may try tricks. With the bridges raised and the water level high they will find it hard to break through. My squire, Fótr, will keep you all informed. God be with you."

We turned and headed back into the castle. As we walked through the gates I said, "Have Robert and Michael stand here. They are both local men and the townsfolk will be reassured. They are also sound warriors. They will not panic. Come we will walk the walls."

Return of the Knight

We walked beyond the east gate tower and climbed the wooden steps. Sir Leofric had built the gate towers so that they were self-contained. They could not be reached from the wall walks. The fighting platform was wide enough for two men. I saw that there were men at arms and archers along the wall. Each one had ten paces of the wall to guard.

Fótr noticed that, "Lord is that not too large a gap between warriors?"

"It is but remember this, they cannot attack along the whole length of the wall. We will concentrate wherever they congregate." I stopped and turned to my squire, "This will not be like a battle with horses. You will not have the luxury of waiting with horses. You will be armed and fighting here on this wall of death. Are you ready?"

"I am, lord."

It was as we walked that I realised we still had improvements to make. We could put wooden shelters, embrasures, to protect our men from missiles. We could not do that yet but we would when time allowed.

By the time we reached the keep and began to descend, Edward shouted from the keep, "Sir Thomas, they are making a move."

"I come. Fótr, find Robert and Michael. It is time to close the gate. The siege has begun."

I entered the keep and climbed the stairs to the fighting platform. Sir William greeted me, "It looks like they plan on dividing our forces. They are coming to the east and the west."

I looked to the east. The road was within bow range and they were aware of our skill. They were moving down the road using large shields to protect the men who were moving. They had a ram. They must have brought the parts with them and assembled them in their camp. "Do they have a ram to the west too?"

"Aye, lord."

I looked at the crew of the stone-thrower. "When you practised with this, how far could you send a stone?"

Godwin of Battle grinned, "Beyond the road, lord."

"And how accurate were you?"

"If I am to be truthful, lord, not very but if you are asking me if we can hit that snake of shields moving south then I would confidently say aye!"

"Then let us see if you make the French fill their breeks. David of Wales, have the archers ready to support the stone-thrower. Sir William have the other one begin to send stones at those in the west."

Godwin lifted the stone onto the thrower. They had had the time to select similar-sized stones which would make accuracy better. They were the size of a man's head. I could still see the marks by the road where they had practised. He had four men with him. Once it was loaded he shouted, "Pull!" The five of them launched the stone. It sailed over the line of shields. There were riders to the east of the road and we saw the stone hit a horse.

Return of the Knight

I gave Godwin a wry smile, "A little less power perhaps."

"Sorry, my lord. We were a little eager."

He loaded another one and I saw that the French had reacted. Orders were being shouted. Crossbowmen left the shelter of the shields ready to send bolts at the men at arms. It was a mistake for David of Wales and his archers hated crossbows and those who operated them. Not one bolt reached my walls. They had no protection and they died.

"Pull!"

This time the men at arms used less power and the stone smashed into a shield. As the man fell he pulled another two men with him and my archers managed to send a dozen arrows into the exposed men. The shields closed as another stone struck. This one must have hit the soldier's shoulder. It took his head and spun off taking a mounted man from his horse. My men's accuracy was rewarded for the archers slew two exposed men at arms and knocked a knight from his saddle. The French decided to choose that spot as their place of attack. They risked losing more men as their column progressed down the road south. That too was a mistake. They did not know that we only had two stone-throwers. Had they kept moving down the road, then they would have been out of range.

Their movement did throw off my men at arms briefly while they adjusted their thrower but the movement also allowed my archers to slay some of their men as they hurried forward with the hurdle they were using as a bridge. They were hampered by the muddy ground and by the time they had reached the edge of the moat twelve men lay dead or wounded.

"Concentrate on the ram. My archers will deal with the bridge."

Until the hurdle bridge was in place the ram was a sitting target. It would not move. The first stone was short but managed to hit two men who were trying to move a hurdle. The second third and fourth stones were more effective. By the tenth rock, the ram was broken. Its front wheels had been shattered and the roof had gone. A knight sounded a horn and the men withdrew out of range of the stone thrower and our arrows. I saw a hurried council of war.

"Well done, Godwin of Battle. Fótr, fetch ale. These men deserve it."

As my squire ran off my men at arms began to repair the stone-thrower. Wear and tear caused a deterioration in performance. They used the delay to make sure they would be as effective when they began again. I took the opportunity to go to the west tower. I saw that they had been as effective. The ground around the road was filled with bodies but the ram had not been damaged. It lay too far away. "The ram to the east has been destroyed. It seems whoever commands this assault has more sense."

Sir William nodded, "He is cautious but he lost many men to the thrower and our arrows. What will they do?"

68

Return of the Knight

"If I was in command I would wait until night. Our archers would have to release blindly and they could bring up crossbows. We will see."

By the time I returned to the west tower the men had had their ale and were watching the French. "What are they doing, David of Wales?"

"I think they are licking their wounds and making another camp further east." He pointed. "It seems to me they are trying to make some sort of pathway through the fields. They may try to attack further south."

I nodded. I now regretted not having two more stone-throwers built. Although the town gates were lower they would still have been effective deterrents to an attack there. The men on my walls could support them. The afternoon was an anti-climax. We just watched each other. The bodies of their dead lay before them and I knew that their leaders would be regretting that. We had lost none and yet the French attack had cost them a ram and over fifty dead men. The French would have poor morale. I knew that David of Wales was right. I sent orders to have two men out of every three sent for food and rest. I also commanded pots of fire to be prepared. When night came and they renewed their attack I would make night into day.

I also sent William and our squires for rest. I walked the walls to speak with those who remained on guard. They were confident. Godfrey of Lancaster pointed to some of the bodies. One appeared to be moving, "Look Sir Thomas, rats are already feasting on the corpses. No matter what the outcome of this battle it is the rats who will win."

"It is always the way. You will be in command here this night. They will attack. I intend to have pots of fire so that our archers can send fire arrows across the moat. You have the ladder poles?"

He pointed to them. They were close to the wall. "Do not worry Sir Thomas they will find this a hard nut to crack. The ground at the base of the wall is slippery and wet. If they do manage to get a ladder against the wall it will sink in the mud and this is a high wall."

He was right. There was an optimum height to use ladders. They had to be high enough to reach the top of the wall and strong enough to bear the weight of men climbing them. I had seen ladders break beneath the weight of mailed men. Fótr came to relieve me. "We have eaten, lord, and her ladyship has food ready for you."

Godfrey was also relieved and we both headed for our food. His would be in the warrior hall. I passed the kitchen as I entered the keep. The cooks had fresh bread being prepared. We had enough wheat to last a three-month siege. We also had rye, barley and oats when that ran out. The French, in contrast, would have to get their bread from further afield. The longer the siege went on the harder it would be for them. Already the weather was becoming colder. It never froze in this part of the world but with the cold would come more rain and conditions for the besiegers could only worsen.

69

Return of the Knight

Margaret joined me to eat. She knew better than to talk of the siege. "Samuel is a delight. Marguerite is lucky. She is not using a wet nurse. She feeds him herself and he is a hungry bairn. I hope I am as lucky with our child."

"You are well?"

She laughed, "I can see that you are unfamiliar with the world of women, husband."

I nodded. "My world is the world of warriors and war. I left the world of women when I had seen ten summers. I am learning wife but you shall teach me."

"Good. Then I am well. I feel the baby within and that is good. Sometimes I have minor problems but they should not concern you. They are normal. I make water more than I used to and I eat differently but if there is aught amiss then know that I will tell you, I promise."

"Good, then I am satisfied." I pushed away the empty platter and emptied my goblet of wine. "I should warn you that the French will probably attack this night. It may be noisy. I am not worried about you for you have endured worse but Lady Marguerite may be disturbed."

"She is stronger than you think. Ridley the Giant's wife, Anya, is with her and she is a strong woman." She put her hand on mine. "If you are to stand on the wall all night then get some rest. I promise to call you when you are needed."

I did as I was bid. It was good to take off my mail. I now enjoyed the services of a manservant when in the castle and Henry helped me to disrobe. He promised to awaken me although in truth I barely slept. When I woke it was still light but the sun was already dipping in the west and the east was gloomy. The walls were fully manned. My men had all had some rest and they had had food. I was greeted by smiles and I heard the banter of confident men.

Godwin of Battle nodded east, "They are getting ready my lord. They have been moving around since it began to darken. We have fireballs that we can light but I fear they may weaken the machine."

"I know. It cannot be helped. Just do your best. It may be that you and your men may serve us better on the fighting platform. Discourage them from crossing the moat, if you can. If they can put a bridge across at more than one place then we might be in trouble."

David of Wales was equally worried. "We have fire arrows, lord but they only work if they strike something which burns. Bodies do not."

I pointed to the wrecked ram. It was made of wood. "Light that and we will have our own beacon behind them."

"We can do that, lord. I will take my archers to the walls. This will be too far away from the attack point."

Return of the Knight

"I will come with you. Godwin, take charge here. I want the bridges destroying as they build them. If David can light the ram then you will not need your fireballs."

"We could send a couple over to help him lord and then use stones."

"Have shields ready. When it is dark then expect the bolts from their crossbows."

The ditch was over a hundred paces from the moat. The ram was invitingly close to the moat. If Godwin and David could fire it we would drive the French further away from the stone-thrower. The men in the town would be able to bring their bows to bear. I was not wearing my helmet. None of my men was. We needed good visibility. If our enemies made our walls they would be below us and we should not need them. I would rely on my arming cap, coif and ventail.

"They come, lord!"

I nodded, "Are you ready David of Wales?"

"We are. If they think the light is not good enough for archery they are wrong."

As if to prove the point he pulled and sent an arrow into the head of the sergeant at arms who was exhorting his men to keep a straighter line. His shield had protected his body but not his head. The result was that the line of advancing men slowed and the shields came higher. As they did so they began to slip and slide on the muddy ground which led to the moat. The men behind were easier targets and Godwin sent a stone to crash amongst them. The hurdle bridge they were carrying was shattered. I knew that they had more but each one damaged meant one less bridge across the moat. The light had almost gone when they finally reached the edge of the moat.

"Godwin, send a fireball at the ram! David of Wales, light the sky!"

His men had been waiting for the order. The flaming fireball was like a meteor. Godwin had judged the range perfectly and the ram ignited. David of Wales' arrows accelerated the burn and it became a beacon. They then switched to ordinary arrows as they sent them at the men carrying the hurdles. Godwin's stone thrower added to the destruction. We heard men dying. There were splashes as bodies fell into the moat. More hurdles were destroyed but the sheer weight of numbers meant that eventually, they succeeded in putting a bridge across. Men ran with ladders. Godwin had to adjust the angle of his stone-thrower and then find the range. David of Wales and his men did their best but men still managed to get across.

"Godfrey, are you ready with the ladder poles?"

"Aye lord."

I drew my sword. I did not have my shield. Instead, I would use my mailed left hand as a weapon. I had a dagger and that would be as effective as a shield fighting a man who was below me. Godwin and his men could easily see the

71

bridges and, once they had adjusted their aim, they began to target them. The light of the burning ram helped them and, one by one, they demolished them until just one remained. As it happened that was the closest one to us. The French had got some ladders across.

I heard cries of, "St. Denis!" and "King Philip!" as knights exhorted men to brave our arrows and to cross.

Godfrey and his men at arms used their ladder poles to push the ladders from the walls. The first two were not a problem as there were just two men on them and they were pushed away easily. As more French men poured across the diminishing bridges and our archers tried to kill as many as they could, so they began to ascend in greater numbers.

Godfrey shouted, "Come to me! This one is laden!"

I saw that the French had managed to get five men on a ladder. The first was just two paces from the wall. Dick One Arrow sent an arrow into the shoulder of the man at arms who led them but he was not killed and he still ascended. I saw that there was just one bridge left. If Godwin could destroy that one we had a chance. I joined with Godfrey and pushed the pole. It creaked and it groaned but, as more men joined so the top of the ladder moved away. Once we had momentum on our side it flew. The wounded man at arms fell on top of the ram. The smell of burning flesh filled the air.

Godwin and his crew ran to us. "I am sorry, my lord, the machine is broken. We can repair it but we thought you might need us!"

He was right. "Spread out! We have one bridge. David of Wales, have your men concentrate on those bringing fresh ladders." Every ladder which fell was shattered. They had a finite number of them. They had a foothold on our walls but we needed them to be discouraged. Johann ran to me, "Lord, Sir William has destroyed the ram on the other wall but there are men across the moat."

"Tell him that the command is still to hold them!"

"Aye lord."

This would be a battle of wills. Who would break first? With the added numbers of the stone-throwing crew, my men at arms were able to throw off more of the ladders. When they fell more than half were shattered. As they were brought back across David of Wales and his archers slew the carriers. We were winning.

Johann, bloody and breathless ran to me, "Lord they have made the walls!"

"Fótr, come with me. The rest stay here and send them hence."

I ran and followed Johann. The quickest way was down the stairs and across the ward. I saw that men were on the fighting platform. The enemy had a foothold. Edward son of Edgar was leading men at arms from one side and Sir William from the other. They were slaying Frenchmen but more were climbing the ladders to join them. I saw a chance. The stairs came up in the middle of the French men.

Return of the Knight

"You two, stay behind me. When I make the top one goes to the right and the other to the left." Even as I spoke a French body was pitched over to crash on the ground. I took the stairs two at a time. I drew my dagger. The French were so concerned with the battle on the wall walk that they did not see me. The first that they knew was when I swept my sword across the legs of the knight who stood at the top. He was wearing chausses but it mattered not. He screamed his way to the ward and I leapt up. I lunged with my dagger into the back of a man at arms as I did so and brought my sword down on the skull of the one fighting Sir William. I was in the middle of the French. I had to get to the wall and stop them from pouring over. I had to rely on Fótr and Johann. They would need to watch my back. Using my dagger and sword in a scissor action I took the head from the warrior before me and I found myself at the wall. I felt a sword hack at my left shoulder. Then there was a scream.

A face rose from the ladder. I rammed my dagger into his mouth. Pain shot up my arm. I had been cut. I dared not look around. They had but one ladder. If we could destroy this ladder then the breach would be ended. I was aware of the clash of steel all around me but I had to concentrate on the ladder. I took in the fact that the ram had been destroyed but a hurdle bridge remained. Ridley the Giant and his crew had joined Sir William and were now making inroads into the French who stood on my wall walk. Until they could kill the intruders I would have to hold off those who tried to ascend. I could not use the ladder pole alone.

I spied the pot of burning coals which the archers had used. I sheathed my sword and my dagger. Using my mail mittens, I lifted the pot. It was hot. I reached the parapet and the heat was almost unbearable. I just pushed and the coals slipped over. I let the pot fall too. The coals struck the knight who was climbing and he threw himself from the ladder in his efforts to stop the burning coals searing his eyes. The pot hit the man at arms who followed him. Their falling bodies cleared the ladder of those ascending and I took my chance. I leaned over and pushed the ladder. Freed from any weight it began to tumble to the side. A crossbow bolt cracked into the wall by my head but I was not deflected from my task. The ladder fell to lie next to my wall. It was not broken and could be reused but they would have to do so while my men used ladder poles to discourage them. Unsheathing my sword, I turned but the last of the French were being slain.

"I am sorry, Sir Thomas. We did not manage to push the ladders away."

"Do not worry, we beat them back. Now I must return to my wall. We are winning! Be strong and we will prevail!" I saw that both Fótr and Johann were besmirched with blood. They were warriors now. "Come, Fótr, back to our wall."

The cut to my left arm was not serious but it was bleeding. My hands were still feeling the effects of the burning pot but we had still to yield any part of

73

our wall. For me, that meant we were winning. Godwin and Godfrey had kept the walls clear. I joined them at the fighting platform.

"Godwin, see if you can repair the stone thrower. If we can destroy that bridge then we have a chance."

"Aye lord. Come on lads."

I saw that two of my men at arms lay dead. I had seen three wounded or dying on the other wall. We had fewer men than the French. Despite the number we had slain, they could afford the losses. They were now concentrating on this one ladder. They had men with shields protecting those who crossed it. My archers were not enjoying the success they had before.

Godfrey picked up an axe that had fallen in the attack. "David of Wales, cover me. Peter, son of Richard, hold my legs." Almost without waiting he went to the parapet and leaned over. Peter son of Richard was almost as broad as Ridley the Giant and he threw his body at Godfrey's legs. I saw the axe rise and then heard it as it smashed through the wood of the ladder and into the wall. "Pull me back!"

I leaned over as my man at arms was retrieved. Although Godfrey had only managed to break four of the rungs, they were close to the top. They would not be able to use it. Someone on the French side saw that and a horn sounded. The French withdrew. The attack was over. A short while later we heard the same call from the west wall. The French had, briefly, abandoned their attack. "Well done!" Cupping my hands, I shouted, "Geoffrey, have the stewards fetch food and ale for the men on the walls. This is not over yet!"

When dawn broke they had still not returned to the attack and, as the sun rose in the east we saw that they had withdrawn to their camp. In the dark, they had moved most of their dead but those who lay next to our walls had not been touched.

"Godfrey, take ten men at arms. Leave by the east town gate. Strip the bodies of anything which is of value. Throw the bodies to the other side of the moat. Let the French endure the stench and destroy the bridge and any ladders which remain."

"Aye lord."

"Fótr, go and tell Edward son of Edgar to do the same on the other side of the castle."

David of Wales said, "They will build more siege machines. Next time they will find a different point to attack."

"I know and they will make just one attack next time. However, David, we fight one battle at a time. We are alone and we must depend upon ourselves."

They did not come that day, nor did they return at night. We heard them hammering in the woods to the north of us. It was tempting to ride and raid but that would have been a mistake. We rested. We kept a watch at night but all of us, men at arms, archers and townsfolk had sleep. We had hot food and we had

74

our wounds tended. Father Michel stitched my arm. It would be stiff but I would be able to use it. The French had to endure the open air and cold fare. Morale would help us to win through.

They had learned their lesson. They would not come at night. Nor, it appeared, would they try a dual attack. Instead, they moved down the road to the east of us. They kept men at arms with pavise and shields to shield them from view as they headed towards the river. Godwin and the stone-thrower slew ten of them. David of Wales and his archers killed another eight but they managed to join the road where it was beyond the range of both archers and stone-thrower. They were heading for the east town gate. As soon as it became apparent I sent for every man at arms and archer to head for the town. I sent Fótr to order the townsfolk into the castle. We had planned for this and I would implement that plan.

"Godfrey, you stay here until the walls and the keep are manned by the townsfolk. Fótr and Johann will take charge. When you have done that put some pig fat onto heat. Leave one of your men to watch it."

During the last day, we had discussed this and I had decided to trust the two squires. The townsfolk might baulk at taking commands from a man at arms but a squire was a different matter. When I reached the gatehouse, I mused again that I should have had another two throwers built. It was too late now. This time they would be able to push the ram down the road. We had no stone thrower to destroy it. Our only hope was that they would not be able to bridge the moat. Another advantage we had was that we could line the walls with our archers and fill the gatehouse with our men at arms. If they managed to breach our defences they would pay a heavy price. I had worked out that they had lost twelve knights already. They would be losing heart. William des Roches might not be willing to come to our aid but he might seize the opportunity to raid France. Similarly, King John, at Le Mans, might see the chance to gain French land.

I could hope.

Sir William and his men were the last to join us. "I sent four men to watch the west town gate. I did not wish us to be surprised and I thought it prudent to have it guarded. I pulled the guards from the castle gate. That is now manned by the ones who worked the quay!"

I occupied the tower closest to the river. Here the moat was much wider than where they had made their first attempt to subdue us. They would not be able to use a hurdle. They would have to build a bridge. I saw that they had done just that. They must have had scouts out in the darkness to measure the gap. The town watch had not been as vigilant as my men. I could see the forces arrayed against us. They had built another ram. Without a stone thrower, we would have to destroy it the hard way; with men. They were not as numerous as they had been. I saw fewer banners. Their knights had suffered. The woods to the north must have been severely thinned for the men advancing did so behind large, man-sized wooden shields they had made. Useless in combat they would be very effective in protecting the men hauling the bridge.

David of Wales had his men looking for an opportunity to send arrows at them. He shouted to me, "Sir Thomas we cannot get through the shields but we can get over them."

"Then do so!"

The bridge required twenty men to carry it. It was made of logs split in two and bound with ropes. It was crude but it would breach the gap. They could not carry it and a shield. When the arrows rained down men were hit. As soon as two were struck the movement of the bridge stopped and more men died. I saw a knight wave his banner and shout something. Crossbowmen ran forward to try to engage my archers. That brought them within range of the town's archers who now occupied my south-eastern tower. David and his archers continued to send their deadly missiles at the bridge men while the crossbowmen fell to the flanking arrows of my townsfolk. The French sent more men to help with the bridge. They moved their wooden shields to protect the carriers from the arrows but, the closer they came the easier it was for David and his men to send arrows plunging from on high. It cost them twenty-seven men but the bridge finally reached the moat.

They no longer needed to carry it and, with shields held by others, strong men lifted it vertically. Here was where their measuring skills would come into play. If it was too short then it would simply float and end up in the river. They had one end a couple of paces from the moat. I saw the top sway and then suddenly it fell. As it did so the men pushing it were revealed and David and his archers slew many of them before they had the wit to grab their shields. There was a resounding crash and crack as the massive wooden structure struck the bank. It was long enough. Only by a pace but that would be enough. The French gave a cheer. With men protected by the ram and no stone thrower, they would break through the gate.

As I donned my helmet I said, "Edward son of Edgar, fetch fire and pig fat. Sir William, fetch half of your men. Godwin, bring half of yours. When the ram is on the bridge we will attack it and fire both the ram and the bridge."

I had twenty men with me as we waited for the pig fat. Jack son of Harold brought the fat. I could see the heat rising from it. "You and Robert stay behind us. We will clear the ram and then you soak the ram with the hot fat. We will fire it when we return."

"Aye lord."

Peter shouted from the tower, "Lord, the ram is almost on the bridge."

"Open the gates." The gates had double bars and it took some time to remove them and swing open the metal-studded gates. I stepped out. The ram had rolled onto the bridge. The crudely made bridge creaked but held. I had

Return of the Knight

Edward on one side of me and Sir William and Ridley on the other. "When we reach the ram split into two and slay those within. They will have no shields. Clear those who are following and then get back to the gatehouse."

"Aye lord."

As we moved out into the open bolts thudded into my shield. Those crossbowmen would be slain by my archers but they were a threat. The ram was already on the bridge. The crude wheels did not move as well on the split wooden logs and the men inside were straining. As we reached the front I saw the fear on the faces of those within. They stopped. It is in a man's nature to defend himself. Their hands went to their swords and daggers. It was to no avail. Edward and I slashed, stabbed and stuck the first five men. The rest on our side fled.

"After them!"

There were mailed men coming behind but the ten survivors from the ram broke up their lines. David of Wales and his archers sent flights of arrows over our heads to further disrupt them. Even so, one knight and four of his men remained ready to fight us. The knight's shield had a white bird and a star on a red background. He was one of de Senonche's knights. He had a mace in his hand. One of the men at arms next to him lunged at me with his sword. I deflected the blow with my shield and swung my sword overhand. I found the gap between shoulder and head. As my blade severed links and tore into flesh the knight swung his mace at my head. I could not bring my shield up in time and I received the full force of the blow. Had I not had such a good helmet then that might have been the end of me. As it was I saw stars and tasted blood. I reeled and staggered back. This was now a mêlée. There were no men at arms behind me and I landed on the wooden bridge. The knight was on me in two strides. I did the only thing I could. I swung my sword at his chausses. I managed to hit him behind his knee. My sword ripped through the mail and into the tendons behind the knee. My blade bit through to the bone and he dropped to one knee. I stood and, swinging my shield into his face knocked his mailed body into the moat.

Already the Comte de Senonche was sending more men to man the ram. My nose was broken and I had lost teeth but I shouted, "Back to the gatehouse!"

Edward was close by and he shouted more loudly, "Sir William, we have done enough, back! His lordship is hurt!"

As we passed the ram I felt the heat from the brands held by Robert and Jack son of Harold. We had just made the gate when there was a mighty whoosh as the brands were thrown onto the ram. The hot pig fat had ignited immediately. As the bars were put in place on the gates I hurried up the steps. My helmet was so badly damaged that I found it hard to see.

"Edward, take my helmet from my head."

Return of the Knight

He had to have Ridley help him for it had been buckled by the blow. When it was removed the air felt cooler but Sir William gasped, "My lord, your nose is spread across your face. You must get to Father Michel."

I shook my head. That was a mistake for it made my head hurt worse. "Let us wait until we see the effects of the fire." The ram burned well and spread to the logs. It was not a swift fire, it was a slow one. The French used buckets to try to quench the flames but David and his archers slew more of them. A further fifteen men were slain before they realised the futility of such action.

Sir William pointed to the far end of the bridge, where the knight had struck me. "They lost mailed men there, lord. I think we have broken their hearts with this fire."

"Let us hope so."

When the bridge collapsed, hissing into the moat then we knew that the attack had ended. Even better, when we saw the French head not north to their camp but on the road east to France, we knew we had won. My men cheered.

We had succeeded in fighting off a French army. There was hope for my people.

Chapter 8

Even my wife was shocked by my injuries. While the rest of the garrison and the town celebrated I had to eat gruel. My face was so swollen that I could barely see. The pain I endured was the worst of any wound I had yet suffered yet I knew that I was fortunate to be alive. I took the helmet to my smith and he agreed to make an even better one. "Lord we know how lucky we are to have you and your men defending us. We lost nothing and that is all thanks to you. I swear that this helmet I make will be surpassed by none."

Edward and my men at arms also expressed their disappointment at not having protected me better. "Lord, you need more men at arms and archers. We are too few to protect you from the army of enemies who gather."

I nodded, "I agree but we both know that they are not easy to get. We will try to get more but for the while, we make our defences better. Are all the bodies of the dead collected and stripped of mail and weapons?"

"Aye lord. David and his archers found great quantities of material they had left at their northern camp. We slew more than a hundred and fifty of their men. We think that fourteen knights perished. We hurt the French and that is why they withdrew."

"Good."

Three days after the siege had been lifted and the chains removed, the first of the ships arrived from the west. They brought news. It was Roger of Meaux who came to my hall to speak with me. My wife had insisted that, until the swelling had completely gone, I did not leave my hall. "Husband you would terrify the townsfolk if they saw you. You are just lucky that the teeth you lost were not at the front. Father Michel says that in a few days you will begin to look like yourself but for now stay in the hall."

I obeyed her. Roger's face showed that he was shocked by my appearance. I tried to smile but I knew that it appeared lopsided. "You have news?"

"Yes lord. Our ships say that there is an uneasy peace. With the Prince in Le Mans, there is no fighting south of Ballon. William des Roches has let it be known that he does not regard you as an enemy. King John is busy in the north battling with the forces of King Philip. You have saved us."

"Temporarily. We will not rest easy though. I want every man in the town available on a Sunday after church. We need to improve the skills of our townsfolk."

"Is this not over, lord? Will more enemies come?"

Return of the Knight

I gave him a grim smile, "Let us say, Roger of Meaux, that there will be those who wish to take our livelihoods from us but, until Prince Arthur rules this land again, we pay no taxes!"

The merchant in him smiled, "Then we will train, lord."

The success of the stone-throwers encouraged me to build two more. By positioning them at the town gates and towers we could protect all of our walls and the river. When they were finished we had some of the townsfolk train with them. As Godwin of Battle reminded me, they would not have the range that the ones operated by the men at arms had but they would deter an enemy. They would use slightly smaller stones than my men at arms used. The boys of the town were paid to collect the right sized stones. It became almost a game for them and we soon had a healthy pile next to each war machine.

Once my wife gave me permission I rode abroad with my men at arms and Sir William. We rode mainly towards the French. I was no friend of King John but so long as he did not bother me I would allow my enmity to lie dormant. I was in no position to do other.

Christmas was approaching. The land, it seemed, was covered not by snow but by an uneasy peace. Just before we celebrated the feast my sentries spied a column of men trudging down the road. They were warriors and so Edward called out the guard. They were spotted from well down the road and so I joined Sir William and my men at arms as they watched them approach.

"Are they a threat Edward? I see spears and helmets."

"Aye lord along with swords, axes and bows but there are no war horses and their trudging gait suggests weariness."

"Then what are they?"

He shrugged, "I could hazard a guess lord but if I was wrong then I would look foolish. They will be upon us within the hour. I will shout down and ask them eh, Sir Thomas?"

My man at arms was chastising me. He was probably right. The closer they came the less of a threat they were. Four of them had no boots but marched with a cloth about their feet. They had but three cloaks between them. What they all had and marked them as soldiers were weapons and, more than that, weapons that looked cared for. They halted at the crossroads. It was less than thirty paces from the keep.

Their leader was a grey-haired man. He had a leather jerkin studded with metal and a basinet helmet. His sword was the type that required two hands to wield effectively. I spoke to him, "You and your men look weary. Have you travelled far?"

"Aye my lord. We left Le Mans before dawn."

I became wary. Le Mans was controlled by Prince John. "And why leave there in winter. You are warriors. I am certain that John Lackland would offer you employment."

Return of the Knight

"No, lord, for we served Gilbert de Vesci. He was the nephew of Eustace de Vesci who served with King Richard in the Holy Land. His family own Alnwick Castle. He brought us to Normandy to fight for Prince Arthur. When we lost the battle of Mortain, two months since, our lord, his squire, Geoffrey, and twenty of our number were killed. We were captured. We have been kept prisoner until yesterday. William des Roches was visiting and he persuaded the Seneschal of Le Mans to let us go with our weapons. He said it was the Christian thing to do as we had only been obeying our lord's lawful commands."

"And what would you do now?"

"If I am to be truthful, Sir Thomas, we would serve you. Sir Gilbert spoke well of you but I can see that we do not present an attractive prospect at the moment. We have little to offer, save our weapons and our loyalty."

"We cannot turn away fellow Englishmen. Come into the castle. We will feed you and we will talk. You have walked far enough this day. Follow the road to the town gate and Edward will meet you there."

As we went back inside Sir William said, "This could be a trap, lord. It is just the sort of device that King John would use. He has men feigning friendship and when we are asleep they open the gates to their confederates."

I looked at Edward, "You may be right. Edward, you have a nose for such things. Is Sir William right?"

"He could be but, with due respect Sir William, I think not. Either these men are travelling mummers who act out the holy plays or they are what they say they are. Besides they will be in the warrior hall. If they are trying to deceive us then it will soon become clear."

I went to my hall and spoke with my wife. I told her Sir William's worries, "But I think that is because he is worried about his son and his wife."

My wife nodded, "It is almost Christmas. We cannot turn any away. Our Lord was turned away as a bairn. We will welcome them into our home. It is the Christian thing to do."

"And you, my love, are a saint!"

She clasped her cross, "Do not blaspheme, now go and greet them. I have orders to give to the kitchen."

We reached the gate to the town before they did. The townspeople were peering at them with fear and apprehension as well as a great deal of curiosity. Edward was keeping them from asking too many questions and I saw the gratitude on the old warrior's face as they stepped through my main gate.

He nodded appreciatively, "A well-made castle lord. We heard that the French had tried to take it and lost more men than they could afford." He bowed, "I am James Broadsword of Amble, my lord. You have saved lives this day."

Return of the Knight

"It is almost Christmas. How could we have done other? Edward, take them to one of the warrior halls. My wife is arranging food." I turned to James Broadsword. "We captured a great deal of war gear from the French. I am sure it would fit and would be better than the rags your men wear. There are boots too. It would be an improvement on going barefoot. I will speak with you after you have eaten."

I saw my wife, well wrapped against the cold, watching from the door to the keep. I headed towards her and she watched the line of weary warriors enter the warrior hall. When I reached her, she threw her arms around me and began to weep.

"What is amiss my love? Is it the baby?"

She shook her head. "It is a mixture of things. Those men and what they have endured and your face. Our son will never see the handsome man I married. He will see you with teeth missing and a broken nose. He will see your misshapen face."

I laughed and put my arm around her. "He will see a warrior. He will see a man. My face and my body are the result of what I have done. They are part of me. It could be worse. Think of the knights we have known who have lost limbs. This baby... I suddenly stopped. "You said 'he'. You know it is a boy?"

She smiled, "I dreamed for the last three nights. Each dream was different save in one regard. The baby I bore was a boy and this," she touched the unborn child, "feels like a boy." She stepped away from me, "But do not be angry if it is not."

"You goose! I will not be unhappy whatever it is. Come, this cold can do neither of you any good at all."

Sir William still voiced his concern as we ate. My wife put him in his place. "When you came upon Johann and me up in the cold northlands we could have been spies. We could have been a danger."

He laughed, "Of course you couldn't. How could you have hurt us?"

She smiled, "Because we are women we cannot kill? We do not wear mail but we can fight. We could have been sent by your enemies to poison you or to deliver a blade in the dark. We did not. My husband is a good judge of character and he will judge these poor men. I watched as they came in, Sir William, they have been ill-treated. It is Christmas let us see what the lord has sent us."

Chastened William nodded. He came with me after we had eaten and I visited the warrior hall. "I am not sure I understood what Lady Margaret meant lord. I knew that Lady Margaret and Johann needed our help. These soldiers are different."

"Because they are not noble? Because of the way that they look? You must learn to look beyond that and see the man beneath. William des Roches betrayed us but, at heart, he is still a good man. He has done what he has

Return of the Knight

because he believes it is right for Normandy and Anjou. He is wrong but I can understand his motives."

We entered the hall and everyone stood. This was the smaller of the halls. It was the one which had the most room as eight of my men were married and had homes close to the wall we had spare space.

"Sit, we came merely to see if there was anything else you needed. The food was satisfactory?"

James Broadsword grinned, "The last food I ate that was as good as that was when we feasted at Bamburgh. I shall sleep well tonight, lord. And the wine was better than any I have ever tasted. We are grateful." He looked at his men. They were willing him to say more. I could sense it. "Sir Thomas, what say you to our offer to be your men?"

"I say that I would have you think about it. Stay here for the twelve days of Christmas feasting. There will be no war for any of us. Enjoy the time and see if we are warriors you would like to join." He was about to speak and I held up my hand, "We are now alone. We sent the French packing but they will return. I have ships and I can offer you passage back to Amble or anywhere in England. Do not feel that you have to stay here and to serve me. When you have spoken with my men and my people and when we have feasted then you can come again to me and ask me. Until then enjoy yourselves. Here you are safe. This, for the next fortnight, is your home and after that, if you still wish it then you shall be given my livery and become warriors of the gryphon."

James Broadsword stood, "My lads, his lordship could not say fairer and that's no error. We will take up your offer, lord, but I can tell you now that our minds will not be changed."

For all of us in that castle, this was our first Christmas where we all felt safe. That was almost a contradiction for we were surrounded by a sea of those who wished us gone but we had prevailed against odds which should have seen us drown. It was a happy time and reminded me of those Christmases in Stockton. My face had settled down. Father Michel had managed to straighten my nose. The missing teeth were an inconvenience. I had to think about how I ate. I was alive when but for my helmet I would be dead! My only sadness was that I had not received a letter from my aunt. I had sent a message as soon as I had reached my home. I prayed that all was well. The fact that Eustace de Vesci appeared to be opposed to King John gave me hope for Alnwick was just a two-day ride from my former home.

During the twelve days of feasting, I discovered more about the new men who wished to join us. There were thirteen archers and sixteen men at arms. They would be an invaluable boost to my numbers. Eight of them, five men at arms and three archers were men who were past their prime. What they did possess was experience and it was that experience that had enabled them to stay together and to stay alive. The younger ones were looked after by the ones like

Return of the Knight

James Broadsword. Edward son of Edgar and David of Wales confirmed what I had thought. They were honest men. Their lord had been killed and they needed a banner to follow. My men felt sympathy for many of them had been in a similar position. What was interesting was that Edward discovered that there were more men such as these. Not every lord supported King John. They were not opposing the King openly but I had hope that I might have allies.

All of the men remained true to their word. They all confirmed that they wished to join me. I gave them the opportunity to join me or to become Sir William's men. My former squire had realised that he was wrong and he was happy to be the leader of such men. Twenty of them, all the younger ones, chose to follow Sir William. I did not mind. I had to hide my smile as Sir William realised that he would have to have surcoats made. I had more than enough for my men. He also needed more horses. That was when we came up with the idea of a chevauchée. The French had shown us that we were enemies. I would not risk the ire of William des Roches or King John but the French were a different matter. If we raided them we could take horses and weapons. Both would be needed. My child would be born in March. I decided to raid in February. It would be cold but the new grass would be growing and new horses would have been foaled.

Before that happened, I received a letter from my aunt.

You know who you are and I hope you know that I think of you every day! Each night you are in my prayers.

I was overjoyed to read your letter. And that you had returned to La Flèche. And we are both delighted that you have taken a wife. The family name will live on.

As for England, I have to tell you that it is not a happy place. The taxes are too high and people starve. The King does not care. His Sheriffs are a law unto themselves. There is much unrest amongst the barons. I fear the war which is in Normandy may well spread to England soon.

Are you safe in La Flèche? There are rumours that the Duke of Brittany has been captured and King John is winning. We both pray that you are safe. I am afraid that we are both too old to travel to visit with you. God willing the tyranny that is John will end soon enough

We pray for you each night as do all those who live in the manor. Our family is still well thought of. Our home is your home and always will be.

Xxx

I showed the letter to my wife. She had read the others. "Your Aunt Ruth sounds like a strong woman. If there are more like her in England then perhaps King John might be defeated."

Return of the Knight

I did not argue with my wife but she was wrong. It would take a force of arms to defeat John Lackland!

I did not take the new men on the chevauchée. We were going to get horses for them and I wanted my castle defended. As chevauchée went ours was a small one. I intended to attack the Chateau-sur-le-Loir. There were a number of reasons. It was close. It had been captured by de Senonche and it had belonged to William des Roches. Like my betters, I could play these games. I still believed that William des Roches would see through the falsehood of John Lackland and we would fight together once again. By trying to hurt those who had taken his castle from him I was putting him in my debt.

We left before dawn and headed north and then east along the small roads which criss-crossed the valley of the Loir. It was cold and there was dampness in the air. I was riding Skuld and I carried my new helmet. My face had healed as had my arm and my leg but the cold and the damp made them ache. In England, it would be a living hell! I carried the helmet deliberately. I needed to see and hear well. A chevauchée relied on surprise and speed. I hoped that we would have the former but our horses were the best and I knew that we would have speed. My local men acted as scouts. We would not be foolish enough to risk attacking the actual castle but there were many smaller halls. William des Roches' knights had lost their land. Their animals and workers still lived there.

The first farm we found had a tower in the hall. However, the fields with the horses were unguarded. As I led my men at arms into the fields to collect the horses my archers formed a protective screen. When the French knight sent his men to stop us they soon discovered how effective my archers were. It cost him four dead men to gain that knowledge. Amongst the eight horses was a warhorse. We headed south and east and saw smoke from a hall. It was on the other side of a hill and a wood. Leaving two men with the new horses in the woods we filtered through them and found a field filled with horses. There were fourteen of them. None were warhorses but they were palfreys and that was just as good for an archer or a man at arms. This time we had complete surprise for we descended from the woods like wolves. Our archers did not have to draw bows. We almost had enough horses and we had too many to risk another raid. We turned and headed west.

Sir William was ebullient. "That was easy!"

"But when we return tomorrow for more horses it will not be as easy. They will be ready for us and we will have to fight. The difference is that we will have more men. We can bring your men at arms and my new ones too. If they were counting our spears today then they are in for a shock tomorrow!"

We left Sir William's archers and the old guards to watch the castle. William was surprised when James Broadsword and the older warriors who had joined me came with us. "Why not leave those to guard the castle and bring my archers, my lord?"

Return of the Knight

"For what we do we do not need archers as much as experienced men at arms and I would see them in action."

"You think that we will have to fight to take horses today?"

"I know it. Yesterday we rang a bell of alarm for the French. They will heed it. Whoever is now master of the castle and the lands thereabouts will wonder if it is us or if it is King John. Chateau sur le Loir is now the border. You and I know that knights who guard a border cannot afford raiders."

We headed further south towards the Tours road. We rode through land which was tilled and showed signs of new growth. We passed vineyards and terraces. Then we turned north. The vineyards became fewer. We saw more cattle in the fields. The fields were smaller as were the farms and let them be. We were after horses. If we found a larger herd of cattle or sheep then we would take them. Our scouts found just such a farm. It lay tucked away in a shallow valley. There was a fortified hall but there were horses, ten of them, and a small herd of cattle. There was also a banner flying. It had a green background and two white birds. It belonged to a knight who was a relative of de Senonche.

Will son of Robin had found a place where the archers could dismount and, using the cover of a small copse, cover us with their bows. It overlooked both the hall and the fields with the animals. I led the largest number of men at arms since the Baltic. More than half, however, were new to me. I would be wary. I rode at the fore with my squires, Sir William and my most experienced men at arms. James Broadsword and the new men rode at the rear.

There were horse guards. The six of them fled at the sound of our galloping hooves. I heard a horn from the direction of the hall and I drew my sword. I was not wearing my helmet. That hung from my cantle. "James Broadsword, have the men begin to drive the cattle and horses south."

"Aye lord."

Even as they did so I saw that the knight with the two birds had been ready for us. Armed men galloped towards us. There were the gonfanons of three knights and there were more than thirty riders. There were another thirty on foot. I did not think they had seen our approach. That became obvious when David of Wales and his archers rained arrows on their right flank. They had just been prepared was all.

I spurred Skuld and hefted my shield to my side. We had to ensure that James Broadsword and his men had time to begin to drive the animals south. We could not drive animals and fight off the French. Fótr and I were flanked by Ridley the Giant and Edward son of Edgar. Now that Ridley rode one of the captured warhorses he did not look so ridiculous on the back of a horse. In fact, he looked intimidating. He carried a war axe with a long handle. He was one of the few warriors with the size to be able to do so. For the first time, William was protected by four of his new men at arms. Eight of us hit the approaching

Return of the Knight

French. Our archers made the French to our left wary. Their right sides were exposed and I saw a knot of them turn to ride up the slope towards the copse. It diminished the effect of the attack.

Perhaps the French knights thought to capture us and take ransom or that their superior numbers would guarantee them victory. Either way, they were wrong. Ridley's axe almost hacked in two the horseman with the banner who rode next to one of the knights. I took a blow from my left with my shield and, without a helmet I had a better view and I was able to duck beneath the backhand sweep from the other knight. I lunged with my sword and the speed of the knight's horse brought him across my sword. I rasped the blade across his mail and, as he fell from his saddle I saw that my blade was bloody.

Skuld kept going. The ones behind their front rank were looser in formation. I did not have two men to deal with. I stood in my saddle and brought my sword down hard across the shield of the man at arms who rode at me. He had on a bascinet helmet and I saw his face fill with fear. He was already jerking around his horse's head as my blade smashed into his shield and arm. Horse and rider fell in a jumble.

Seeing those before me were on foot and slowing I turned, "Back! We have done enough!"

One of the knights still maintained his saddle and he galloped at me. Skuld was stationary. Skuld had wonderful reflexes. Once I determined the knight's approach I waited until the last moment and then spurred Skuld while pulling the reins to the left. The knight's speed took him past me and I swung my sword across his back. His arms went into the air and his back arced. He was hurt.

As I rejoined my men I saw that we had not escaped unscathed. Roger of Lymm lay dead. Two of my men at arms were putting his body over the saddle of one of the French horses. Others sported wounds. The clash had yielded us another six horses including a warhorse. I could ill afford a dead man at arms but casualties were to be expected. We also had a prisoner. One of the squires had yielded to Johann. We took him back with us. I was not concerned about ransom but I wanted the information which the young squire might yield. Johann guarded him closely.

Despite our losses, there was an ebullient mood as we crossed the bridge and entered the eastern gate of my town. People looked up as we drove the horses and the small herd of cattle through the town square and then into the castle. Since the siege, we had cleared the land between the road and the moat. Now we would use it for the cattle. First, we would examine them. Any that were sickly would be slaughtered.

As we dismounted I said, "Fótr find the man who lost his home in the siege, Jean of Durtal."

"Aye lord."

87

Return of the Knight

"Johann, take your prisoner into the hall." Once his helmet had been removed we had seen that the squire had seen barely fourteen summers. I wondered if Johann would be disappointed at the ransom we could expect. As the horses were led away I realised we would need a third stable. As a temporary measure, we would let the horses graze in the ward. There was plenty of grass.

"Good horses, lord."

"Aye James Broadsword. The French were waiting for us."

"You handled them well, lord. You use archers like a general. I heard that your family used them well. Growing up in Amble I heard the stories of the Warlord and his archers. You have inherited that skill."

I nodded, "It seems to me, James, that when an English knight uses men at arms and archers then he is invincible."

Fótr hurried up with Jean of Durtal. He was not a young man. He had with him his two sons. His farm had been the most serious loss in the siege. He had farmed north of the woods and although he and his family had been safe within my walls his farm had been razed to the ground. All that he had possessed was lost. I had been seeking a way to repay him.

I pointed to the cattle. The three sickly ones had been taken towards the kitchens. There remained sixteen cows. "Jean of Durtal I give these cattle to you." We had already discussed the site of the farm. Jean had come up with the idea of extending the moat with ditches to keep the cattle from straying and to provide protection for a new farmhouse. We had yet to begin building it.

"My lord, you are too generous."

"Your rent for the farm and the cattle will be four gallons of milk a week for the castle. What say you?"

He dropped to one knee, "That I am your man lord and I accept your offer."

As I walked back to the hall James Broadsword said, "You remind me of Sir Gilbert. He was like you. He worried and fretted about his folk. Many barons do not. We were right to come here. Perhaps our footsteps were guided eh lord?"

"Perhaps."

We set the men to building the new stables and some went to help our new tenant farmer to dig the ditch and his home. He knew how parlous his existence was but if war came again he and his family would not have as far to flee. Sir William and I questioned Johann's captive.

We learned that he was Jocelyn of La Chartres sur Loir. His father was a knight and had been one I had unhorsed. He told us all. He wanted us to think we had been outwitted. We let him talk. "We knew that you were coming. Sir Raymond de Senonche predicted that you would attack the manors to the south."

"He was right."

88

Return of the Knight

"And that was why we had men waiting and so few horses in the field. They were to tempt you." It was on the tip of my tongue to say that it did not seem to make a difference. We had defeated them and taken their horses and cattle. However, it was a lesson. I should have been a little less arrogant about my opponents. "My father will pay a ransom." He gave a sly look. "La Chartres sur Loir is a rich manor. As is this one and the Comte will soon have it."

I saw Sir William colour. I gave a slight shake of the head. "He has tried once."

"Next time he will succeed. As soon as the peace talks are concluded then you will be even more alone."

I rose and gestured for Johann and Sir William to follow me. "You had better go to the nearest French village and send a message that we have Jocelyn of La Chartres sur Loir. Set your price." I smiled. "He is an arrogant pup. Ask what you will. Sir William, take command here. I will ride with some men to Angers. I would speak with William des Roches."

"Is that wise, lord?"

"We are blind without more knowledge. We knew nothing about this peace meeting. If William is not in Angers then it means they are meeting now and if he is there I can discover when and where it is. In one respect the boy is right. If the French, Normans and the English combine against us then we cannot hold out. We would have to find somewhere else to live."

"And we are running out of such places."

I left the next morning with six archers and six men at arms. I took my most experienced men including James Broadsword. He would know those who had fought for Prince Arthur. I needed those men identifying. The weather was improving day by day but we still rode with thick, grey cloaks about us. They also helped to disguise our livery. The land was at peace. Farmers were in the fields and there was no appetite for war. Our numbers would not intimidate but would offer protection from bandits and brigands. Since the war had ended there were such bands wandering the countryside. Like those we had taken on they had lost their lords but they had chosen the route of banditry. None had come close to my land. Perhaps my name had frightened them.

We knew the road well but it had been some time since we had travelled it. I now saw standards flying from castles which reflected the new owners. King John and his seneschal, William des Riches, had wasted no time in evicting the supporters of Duke Arthur and replacing them with men loyal to King John. We had been lucky.

When we neared the gate, I spoke quietly to my men. "We go in peace but we are prepared for flight. While we are in Angers keep your eyes and ears open. Fótr and I will go alone to the keep. The rest of you," I smiled, "wander the streets but keep your eyes and ears open."

"Aye lord."

Return of the Knight

Both Edward and David had been given coin by the men they led. Angers was much bigger than La Flèche. The markets were better and there was a larger range of goods. When I had finished my business, I would have to order more bolts of cloth for both mine and Sir William's surcoats.

The sentry recognised me by my horse. He was a grizzled old sergeant at arms. Skuld was always prominent on the battlefield and William des Roches had used his own men as guards. They had seen me fight. "My lord, can I ask your business here in Angers?"

"I am here to speak with the seneschal. Is he at home?"

"He is lord but you have barely caught him. He leaves on the morrow for…he will tell you if you need to know. Before I can allow you to enter do I have your word that you wish none within this castle harm?"

I adopted a serious expression, "Does John Lackland reside in this castle?"

He looked puzzled, "No, Sir Thomas."

I smiled, "Then all within are safe from both my ire and my blade."

He stood aside and we passed through. Edward chuckled, "Not the sharpest of blades was he lord? He looked to have taken too many blows to the head."

I nodded, "Meet us at the gate to the keep. Makes sure the lads stay out of trouble."

"They will lord."

We were admitted to the inner ward where we left our horses. I hung my cloak and helmet from the cantle. I no longer needed a disguise. I turned to Fótr, "Stay around the inner ward. Someone may say something we find useful."

I could not help smiling as I was taken into the Great Hall by four guards. I must have worried them. William des Roches had his head down and was poring over a map with four of his lieutenants. He looked up, in irritation at first, at the interruption then smiled when he saw it was me. "I can see you now at Arsuf! Does nothing make you afraid? You come into the heart of this castle which is ruled by your greatest enemy and yet you come alone."

"Not alone, Seneschal, I have my squire and twelve of my men with me besides when last we spoke you said we were not enemies."

"Nor are we." He turned to his lieutenants, "We will continue this later. I must speak with Sir Thomas." He turned to his squire, Guy of Chateau-sur-le-Loir. "Guy, have the maps made ready for me."

"Yes, my lord."

He put his arm around my shoulders and led me outside. "Come we will walk the inner wall. I almost did not recognise you. Were it not for your beard and your voice I would have wondered who you were."

"A mace in the siege. I was lucky."

As we walked he said, "You managed to defeat de Senonche I hear?"

"Perhaps the defeat of the French by King John weakened them."

90

"Perhaps but it was remarkable with so few men. I would that you were on our side."

"When you are on the side of Prince Arthur then I will be. I can only follow one master at a time."

"He is weak and worse, he is led by his mother." We had reached the wall walk and the Seneschal waved a hand so that we had privacy. "There are few barons who support him. Even the dowager Queen does not support him."

"I will admit he is not ready yet but even as he is he is a better ruler than John Lackland."

"King John is stronger than you know. He will stand up to the French. He appointed me as Seneschal of Anjou to make sure that the French did not take it. I will be moving to Tours after the treaty is signed. There I can make sure that the French keep their side of the treaty."

"How did you lose your castle?"

He gave me a sharp look. I could see him wondering how I came by that information, "I took too many men with me to Le Mans."

"I raided the French barons there. I think they will not be happy. I expect retribution." He nodded. I had made him think of his former home. "One of the prisoners told me that there is a meeting between the two kings."

"Aye, in May at Le Goulet on the Seine, not far from the Vexin."

"And will Prince Arthur be there?"

"He will be as will I. I can promise you that all will be done well. They may not be done to your satisfaction but Prince Arthur will be treated fairly. I swear that I will do all in my power to watch over the youth."

"Good. I would come but I suspect that I would be the subject of the ire of the two monarchs."

"That you would." He laughed then stopped and turned to face me, "Seriously, Sir Thomas, as soon as the treaty is signed your position will become almost impossible. King Philip cannot allow you to flaunt your independence before the rest of France and King John has endured much at your hands. I will not fight you but there are many others, like the de Ferrers family, who would be more than happy to ravage your lands and take your castle. None of them are as good as you but they would weaken you with every attack."

I nodded and then said, "I have taken into my retinue the men of Gilbert de Vesci."

He looked genuinely pleased, "I thought they might come to you. I liked Gilbert. Like you he was obstinate but he had honour."

"I intend to take on as many others who have fought John and lost. You say I will become weaker. I intend the opposite. I will become a refuge for any who wishes to fight against King John. You know there is treason talked in England?"

Return of the Knight

"I heard. That is your country and not mine. I know that the King will not return hence until the situation in Normandy and Anjou is settled." He paused, "And Brittany."

"So not content with preventing Arthur ruling Anjou and Normandy he is taking from him his Dukedom. I do not call that seeing things well done, William des Roches. What you mean is that you will see that Arthur has a decent burial." I turned, "Farewell. You are not the knight I thought you were. Farewell."

"Sir Thomas…"

I stormed down the steps. The two guards who waited close by the door to the great Hall stepped towards me. I glared at them and then saw them look beyond me. They stepped back and away from me. Turning I saw William des Roches. He had ordered them to stand down. I forced myself to calm down. I had been let down, again. However, if I raged and ranted it would do no good. I had to use my time in Angers well.

When I reached Fótr and the horses I was calm. "Did you learn anything, Fótr?"

"Yes lord. The Seneschal leaves tomorrow. All the greatest counts, earls and barons in the Dukedom accompany him. His own retinue leave tomorrow for Tours."

"Good. We need to find our men. Do you know where they are?"

"Yes lord, Edward said that he heard the '*Angel's Kiss*' by the river was a good alehouse and popular with English sailors. He was going there."

We led our horses and wound our way through the busy town. We heard many accents and dialects. There was Angevin, Norman, Breton, French and English spoken. A plan was forming in my mind. We passed some of our men buying wares but the bulk of them were at the inn. I could see why it was popular. It was as close to the quay as one could get. A ship docking would find it before any other alehouse. Sailors rarely wanted to walk far for their drink. Edward, David and James Broadsword were closeted together.

Edward rose, "Are we leaving, lord?"

Not yet." A servant appeared, "More beer for this table."

He looked at me as though I had two heads, "Beer, lord?"

"I am English, humour me. Beer." I leaned forward and spoke more quietly, "I believe that Prince Arthur will be betrayed by everyone. Bad as that will be for Prince Arthur it could be worse for us. It could well mean even more enemies. Thanks to James here we have more men but we need to recruit even more. James, I want you and David to spend another three or four days here. Take rooms." I took out a purse of coins. "Use this to hire, as quietly as you can, as many men at arms and archers as you can. We do not want the dregs of the river. We want men we are happy to have as shield brothers. Have them

92

make their way to La Flèche as soon as they are hired. That way it will appear like a trickle."

The beer arrived. I held my beaker aloft, "England and a decent King!"

They echoed the toast. Interestingly I saw only smiles and no scowls. Edward had chosen the right place. We talked a while about how we would be able to pay for such men and then, after finishing my ale I said, "Fótr, stay here. I will soon return."

I was gambling that *'Swan of Stockton'* was still in port. I knew that the captain, Henry the son of William of Kingston, would be ensuring that he had a full manifest. If he was not still in port then I would find another English captain. I could trust Henry the son of William of Kingston and more importantly so could my aunt. I needed her help once more.

The ship was in port but I could see by the activity that she was getting ready to sail. The crew knew me and I was admitted on board, "You are just in time my lord, if you wish to sail. We leave before the middle of the afternoon."

"No, Henry. Have you parchment and pen?"

Most sea captains kept such items to make charts and to keep records. "Aye my lord." He took me to his cabin. "I must get ready to sail."

"I will not keep you." I sat and wrote three sentences. I neither addressed nor signed the letter. I did not seal it nor did I use the sign of the gryphon. I trusted Henry and my aunt would know from whence it came. I went up on deck. "I would have you deliver this for me."

He looked at me, "There is no address, my lord."

"You need not one." I took a gold coin and pressed it into his hand.

"You need not, my lord."

"I know. God speed."

I stepped ashore and waited until the ship had cast off and set sail. I felt much happier.

Chapter 9

James and David were both more than capable of blending in. I had chosen James rather than Edward because he was unknown in Angers and would arouse little suspicion. Similarly, David of Wales was so quiet that he was easily overlooked. With loaded sumpters, the rest of us headed north. We would have daylight for most of the journey and it would only be the last three miles we would travel in the dark.

Before I had left James had said, "Sir Thomas, what if there are knights who wish to join us?"

I had not considered that possibility. "Then tell them to ride to my home. They will not need coin as an inducement."

"Most men will not need coin. If they ask for coin then I will not take them. They fight for the right!"

I knew that I had made the correct decision.

The next day I met with Sir William and my wife to tell them the news that I had discovered. I confess that Margaret showed less interest than she might normally. Half way through my opening statement about the conference she winced and said, "The baby!"

Her ladies whisked her away. I made to follow them but Sir William restrained me, "They do not need us, lord. In this respect you are the novice and I am the veteran. Come, tell me the news you were about to impart."

It proved to be good advice and it took my mind off the birth. When I had finished he asked, "Could we not go to Le Goulet? Perhaps we could help the Prince directly."

The thought had crossed my mind but it was a risk. "William des Roches was quite right. We would antagonise both monarchs and make it worse for the Prince. However, we could go north and be close to Le Goulet. We could stay hidden. I want to be close at hand and learn quickly what the terms of the treaty are to be."

"We have forty days then, lord?"

"Aye and by then I hope that we will have more men to lead."

"We need more horses, warrior halls and stables and, unless they bring it with them, coin."

"We have forty days before we ride north. I want us to begin raiding our French neighbours in the next five. We shall use them as our treasury and stables! Their lords will be at Le Goulet. Angers had been emptied of barons. The two kings will want as many barons present as possible. By the time we leave for Le Goulet we will have more men, more horses, more coin and more grain. Our walls will be higher and we will have more war machines. My conversation with the Seneschal showed me the size of this problem. We have two choices. We run away or we fight to make this enclave a county!"

The birth took a whole day. It was dark of night and Sir William and I were still seated with a flagon of wine when Lady Marguerite came in, "Lord, you have a son. Mother and child are doing well but Lady Margaret is tired. Do not stay too long. She needs her rest."

My wife looked pale but she was smiling. "I told you, lord, a boy and a healthy one too. I am surprised you were not alarmed by his cry when he came into this world. He will make his mark."

I kissed her and she thrust the swaddled babe into my arms. I held the little reddened bundle. One eye opened and stared at me, "Son, I am your father. You come from a long line of great knights and you, I have no doubt will gain as much honour as any of them. I swear that I will teach you to become the best that you can be."

His other eye opened and his mouth seemed to smile. I know it was my imagination for every father believes this to be true but in that moment, we were bonded.

"And his name, husband? What will this young knight be called?"

"That is easy. I will name him Alfred after the Warlord who sired this clan. He will be Alfred of La Flèche but one day he will be Alfred of Stockton!"

The birth delayed the start of our chevauchée and that proved a blessing in disguise for the first of the men sent by James arrived. Like James and his men, they were underfed and ragged but their weapons were sharp. Their arrival meant that I could take more of the garrison. When we left, a day late, Sir William and I headed south east with over forty men. The French were going to experience rampant English warriors.

We headed for Dessay. It was ten miles south east of Chateau-sur-le-Loir. They had a castle and it was made of stone but I had no intention of bleeding upon its walls. We now had twenty archers with us and I used them to ride far ahead of us and get between us and the castle. I intended to be the beaters driving the game towards the archers.

As luck would have it we came upon ten French men at arms. They were heading along the road in our direction. Perhaps I was still distracted by the birth of my new son but whatever the reason it was Sir William who reacted quickest. He spurred his horse and led his column of men towards the men at arms. I drew my sword and led mine a heartbeat later. The men at arms tried to turn but our horses were well fed and fast. Sir William and the men clattered into them. Three at the rear escaped but the rest were killed or wounded so swift was our attack. The four wounded were tended to while the horses and arms were collected. We discovered that the Comte de Senonche had ordered his lords to send out patrols while the barons were absent from their homes.

Return of the Knight

I pointed south, "Head south and you may be safe. If we find you again you will pay with your lives. Without horses, the four men gratefully limped south and we continued east. As we galloped down the road people fled, leaving homes empty. We would search them on our way back. We found our archers and the last three men at arms just a mile from the castle.

Cedric Warbow was laughing, "What is so funny, Cedric Warbow?"

"They were so scared that when they saw us they left their animals and fled for the castle." He pointed to the animals which were flocking nearby.

We headed back. Every field was cleared of animals, which we drove before us. We knew there would be no pursuit. We had slain the best of their warriors. Each house and hall was searched. We took back thirty head of horse, twenty cattle and fifty sheep not to mention twelve pigs and countless fowl. With the mail and weapons from the six dead men at arms we had made a good start.

Over the next few days we repeated our raids. This time I was not foolish enough to be predictable. There were more than enough French manors within half a day of riding from us. When James and David finally returned from Angers we had another thirty men. Twenty were men at arms but ten were archers. All were either English or Welsh. They were the golden treasure we had not found in the manors. They were not valued in this land and they were eager to serve an English lord who knew how to reward them. Between us Sir William and I had thirty-six archers. That was a formidable force. With his own retinue now as powerful as mine Sir William raided on his own.

By the time April came and we had done that which I had intended, scorching the borderlands, we had horses enough. We had mail and weapons to spare and our coffers were full. Geoffrey, my steward, would be able to buy for the town that which we could not produce. The first thing we bought was stone. I had local masons begin to make two barbicans so that the moats and gatehouses were protected. It would take a year to complete but I now had a vision of what my manor could become, a fortress against all enemies. The siege had shown me the weaknesses and I would eradicate them.

I took James Broadsword with me and walked my walls. Sir William was with me. "I wish you to be castellan here. When I travel north to Le Goulet I want our families protecting. I wish you, while I am gone to have wooden towers built on the two long walls. Begin with one tower on each wall in the middle. Then divide that with others. I want towers that can be used by archers." I pointed north. The wood in which the French had camped was too close to my walls for my liking. "Use the trees from the southern end of that wood."

He nodded. He was an old soldier and knew the value of strong defences. "You have the keep which is the strongpoint and with two barbicans then the gates will be safer. The weakness is the two walls. Aye we can do that and we can make the walls harder to attack by building embrasures. With wooden shutters in place we can protect the archers too." He rubbed his hands. "I have often sought a home. Now I can help make one."

With just twenty or so days before I rode north I spent as much time with my new son as I could. He had changed dramatically since he had emerged red and misshapen. Now he looked like a baby. He had the bluest and most piercing eyes I have ever seen. I was still fearful of holding him badly and also of terrifying him with my visage. I became so concerned that I had Fótr shave my beard and moustache so that I looked less frightening to my son. At the same time, I had my hair close cropped. My wife did not like it but I felt more comfortable. Even then a plan was forming in my mind.

I would be leaving Sir William and his men to guard my home along with James Broadsword. Until our defences were improved we were still vulnerable. When Sir William walked with James and myself to examine the defences he said, "If we were to extend the moat around the barbicans they would make a small lake. It would help Jean of Durtal and make the barbicans almost impossible to take without great loss of life. The new towers James will be building will allow more archers to bring their arrows to bear." It was a good idea. William, like me, now had a family to consider and he was making our home as strong as it could be.

I chose just ten archers and ten men at arms to accompany me. I chose the ones who had been in the Holy Land and the Baltic. They were the oldest but they had the most experience. I had fought alongside some of them for nine years. In that time, we had learned how each fought. We would be hiding from plain view and seeking an opportunity to come to the aid of Prince Arthur. For that I needed a stiletto and not a cudgel.

It was hard to leave my wife. Her soft eyes smiled at me, "You are a true knight. You go to do that which is right. Yours is the kind of tale sung by troubadours. We will be safe and God will watch over you for what you do is noble."

We left and headed north. We had spare horses but I did not take war horses save one for Ridley the Giant! I had scouts out and we rode beneath anonymous grey cloaks and with no banners to mark us. The danger would come when we neared the Seine. That would be where all the barons were gathered and it was the northern border of Normandy. By then we would be deep within land which was hostile to us. We had a hundred and fifty miles to travel. That would only take us five days but I intended to make a camp twenty or so miles from the Seine. There was a huge forest north east of Le Mans and there we could hide. I had a plan in my head. I would not speak of it until we were camped for it was audacious.

We travelled north east along the quiet roads. There was just civilian traffic. They were wary of mailed horsemen but unworried. There had been peace for almost a year and the ones we spoke with assumed that we were Normans heading for the Seine and the meeting. My archers found us a dell in the woods with grazing, water and shelter in the form of charcoal burner's huts.

We knew that the meeting was due to take place in May but as men had been travelling north for some time I assumed it would be imminent. As we had travelled north Edward son of Edgar had asked me about that. "Lord, if they are to have a meeting then why not pick a day, have the meeting and be done with it. Gathering so many men for so long merely asks for trouble. Men at arms gathered in one place with little to do is a recipe for trouble."

"You do not understand kings and princes. These are nobles. I know this place. There are forests close by where they can hunt. They will feast. They will joust. All the while they will be seeking support from the counts and dukes who are present. King John and King Philip are masters of this game but Prince Arthur is not. When each side has their supporters arranged they will then each make their demands. It is like the game of chess. There are pawns which will be discarded because they are unimportant. Prince Arthur will be such a pawn."

"And what can we do, lord?"

"We can offer sanctuary. We can offer the Prince the chance to build his army from within our walls. There are others, like me and Sir William who support the Prince. He will be the magnet which draws them to us."

When the camp was set up I chose the men I had decided I would take with me. "Ridley and David, you will stay here and guard the camp. I will take Fótr, Edward son of Edgar, Philippe of Poitou and Griff Jameson north to the Seine. I am going to pretend to be a knight of the Livonian order. Three of us can speak Swedish. I doubt that there will be many at the meeting who can do so. It will allow us to speak in front of others and not be understood. We will say that we are seeking a new lord."

"But you will be recognised!"

"No David of Wales. The blow from the mace changed my face. I have no beard and my hair is cropped. I even have a brand-new helmet. We will wear plain surcoats and leave our shields here. If we can we will buy new ones at Vernon. It is close to Le Goulet but if not then no matter."

"They will know Skuld."

"And I will not take her. I will ride Ridley's war horse. I will use Philippe and Griff to keep you informed of any changes to my plan. If you do not hear from me then keep a watch on the road from the Seine and, if there is pursuit when we come you will ambush them."

"And how long do we wait?"

"If we have not returned in a fortnight then we are dead or captured. If we are captured there will be a demand for ransom. Do not pay it. I will escape for I will not yield for ransom."

"Be careful, lord. I would not wish to be the bearer of such news."

"Nor will you be. Enjoy the hunting around here! It looks like the land teems with game!"

I sensed nervousness amongst my men. "We will stay in the background. I intend to avoid both King John and King Philip but I will try to speak with Prince Arthur."

"And William des Roches, lord?"

"We definitely avoid him but he is not the one I worry about. It is the Comte de Senonches. Some of his men may know of my wound. We keep to ourselves. Philippe and Griff, you do not speak Swedish. Pretend you are mute when we do so. Bring a spare palfrey. If we can we will rescue Prince Arthur."

"Aye lord."

We reached Vernon. I could see why it was important. There was a stone bridge across the Seine and they were building a castle. King Philip had only gained the site four years earlier. We found an inn and arranged rooms. None were surprised at our visit. I discovered that they had had a steady flow of knights heading to Le Goulet. The only surprise was that we were so late. Philippe managed to buy four plain shields and I felt better when we left, the next morning, with shields hung from our cantles. What we had discovered was that we would not have accommodation. We would have to camp. It was summer and so we would risk the open air.

We spied the camp from afar. The lesser barons and knights were camped well away from the hall and castle of Le Goulet. We had passed perhaps five tents when a Norman voice shouted, "I would not waste your time friend. The best spots have been taken."

I nodded and said, in Swedish, "We will camp here. Find a spot."

Edgar smiled and replied in Swedish, "Yes, Lord Petr." We had decided on that name in memory of Birger's brother.

I dismounted, "Thank you."

"You are not Norman? Your mail and helmet look Norman."

I pointed vaguely north, "We served in the Baltic Crusade. We heard there might be coin to be made here for swords without masters."

"Aye as did we all but I fear that we will get crumbs. There will be no war. The best that we can hope is that one of the knights who gains a castle close to the border needs knights and men at arms. You may be better off than most. There is just you, a squire and three men. You will be cheap." He waved a hand around his fire, "There are five knights here and five squires. With England at peace and now Normandy… perhaps we will try Sicily. I am Sir Richard D'Arcy."

"Petr Bergeson. Perhaps I will see you around."

"Perhaps. We have heard that the two kings will sign the charter in two days' time. Then those who came for war will leave and it will just be those like my comrades who will serve any so long as we are paid."

Return of the Knight

As I walked towards a waving Fótr I passed similar camps with knights whose armour needed attention and whose conversation showed their lack of hope. Although well away from the road Edward had managed to find a spot close to the stream and two small crab apple trees. We would be able to make a shelter with our cloaks. Leaving my helmet and shield I said, "Edward get a fire going and something cooking. I will take Fótr and see if I can locate Prince Arthur."

I put the hood of my cloak over my head. The sun was shining brightly and others had adopted this method of staying cool in the hot sun. It allowed me to look for faces I might know. The closer we came to the castle the more defined became the camps. There were Angevin, Breton, Norman, French, English. I was surprised to see the camps of the men of Flanders and Boulogne. Every representative of the old Plantagenet Empire was here. I stopped short of the small wooden castle and its gate. English and French sentries stood there. I saw the standards of England and France fluttering from the keep and I also saw the banner of Brittany. Prince Arthur was in the castle. I had little chance of getting in there. Every face would be scrutinised.

The small town began just paces from the castle. I saw the river beyond and there, in the middle of the river was a long island, on which there was a tent. I was intrigued and I led Fótr to the inn which stood by the bridge which led to the river. There were no sentries on the bridge but there were men working on the tent. It looked to me as though they were building some sort of dais.

It was a pleasant day and there were crudely made tables outside the inn. Two knights stood and left. We grabbed their seats before any others could. We ordered some wine, bread and cheese. I spoke in Swedish to Fótr. It added to the illusion and made it unlikely that we would be overheard. "I am guessing that the island will be where the document is signed. That way many can watch but only a few will actually be present."

The servant with the food and drink arrived. He presented the bill. It was ridiculously exorbitant. My face reflected my shock. The man said, "With so many people the owner charges what he likes. When all of you have gone then the prices will return to normal. You can take it, my lord, or leave it."

"We will take it!"

I decided to make both the food and the wine last as long as possible. We continued to talk in Swedish. The more we did so the easier it became. "Prince Arthur will have to come across this bridge to get to the tent. We need to get a message to him."

"That will not be easy, lord. I am guessing that both kings will have him guarded and William des Roches will be close at hand not to mention the Comte de Senonche."

"We have two days." I gave a wry smile. "I just hope that our money lasts."

Return of the Knight

Just then Sir Richard D'Arcy and another knight walked down the road towards the bridge. He laughed when he saw us drinking, "Perhaps I should try the Baltic. If you can afford this brigand's prices then they must pay well."

The owner, who was standing close by, just sniffed and turned away. "They do pay well but it is a cold land and they have little wine." I pointed to the island. "That is where the high and mighty will congregate?"

"It is. We are going to wander across. It might be as close as we ever get but hopefully someone will see our livery from the castle and seek us out." He shrugged. "It is worth the effort. I am surprised you have no livery."

"We served with the Birger Brosa and his livery was the gryphon. We were attacked at Le Mans whilst wearing it."

He laughed, "How unfortunate. That is the livery of the renegade Thomas of La Flèche."

His friend said, "Or Stockton?"

"And even Aqua Bella. He is the most interesting knight in this land and the most unfortunate."

"How so?"

"Every man's hand is turned against him. None will serve except for those with a death wish. I have never met him but his name is spoken throughout the land. Get yourself a livery my friend and then you will be noticed."

"Thank you for the advice friend although if I wait get gain a position with a lord I can save myself more coin!"

The two knights left. It was then that I noticed that they wore no cloaks and their liveries were bright and colourful. They would be seen. That was their plan. They were desperate. We had almost eaten all of the bread and the sun was setting when I decided that we would leave. As we rose I saw two priests heading for the river. Behind them were two men at arms and behind them another two. Betwixt them, hidden, was another figure. As we headed back up the road I saw that it was Prince Arthur.

I had to think quickly and trust that the Prince could think as quickly. I stopped before the priests and dropped to one knee. I spoke in accented Norman. "Father I need your blessing. I have been on Crusade in the Baltic and I seek employment here. Your blessing will help me to serve God once more."

The priests had to stop. I could tell from the look of distaste on his face that the priest disapproved of my action but I had mentioned Holy Crusade and he had to do something. The guards and Prince Arthur had also stopped. I lifted my head slightly and, catching Prince Arthur's eye, winked.

The priest said, "So long as you do God's work you will have God's blessing." He made a dismissive sign of the cross and I stood.

I saw that the Prince had recognised me. I stood. "Then this time tomorrow I will visit the island and pray to God there." I saw Prince Arthur nod.

Return of the Knight

We headed back to the camp. I saw my men peering anxiously for our return. Their relief was obvious. Edward spoke in Swedish, "When you were away so long we became concerned."

"We have found the Prince. This time tomorrow I will get to see him again. We may be able to leave tomorrow night."

We ate and drank the wine we had brought from home with us. We spoke quietly but, whenever any came close, the three of us who could, spoke Swedish. Mainly we listened to the conversation. From what we could gather the two kings had come to an agreement. Alarmingly there was no mention of Brittany. We heard a heated debate from some knights about Flanders. The rumour was that King John was giving up his suzerainty of the county. The men of Flanders were unhappy about being beneath the French yoke. Sir Richard D'Arcy had thought that the land was ripe for peace. I was not so sure.

When I awoke I wandered the camp seeking Bretons. Breton warriors wore distinctive armour. They still used an open helmet too. I took my borrowed warhorse. That way I would appear to have a reason to be wandering abroad. There were remarkably few Bretons to be found. I had seen a few in Angers when I had met with Prince Arthur. If they were here then they would be in the castle. The few who were camped were barons who had come to discover what would happen to their Dukedom. I chanced upon one Breton baron who was walking his horse along the road too. He appeared to have a genuine reason for walking it. He kept stopping to examine its withers.

I paused, "Is there a problem?"

He nodded, "It is an infernally long way from Mont Saint Michel to here and he has not been stepping out as he should." He looked up and saw my horse. "That is a fine warhorse. You must have coin to afford such a horse."

"When I had coin I spent it wisely but now it is running out. I seek a lord. Is that your quest?"

He shook his head, "Ours is a simpler mission. We need to know who rules in our land. Is it the French, Lackland or that whey faced boy Arthur?" He was obviously not a supporter of the young prince. I now understood a little more why William des Roches had done as he had done. "As soon as I find out then I can pledge my allegiance and may hold onto my manor. I have a wife and family to support." He seemed to notice my lack of livery, "And you, where do you hail from?"

"I have just returned from the Baltic Crusade. I had heard that lords here might need a knight, squire and three warriors for the working day."

He laughed, "Aye you and a hundred and more knights feel the same. When this carnival is over there will be many hundreds of you tramping this land. If you have been on Crusade you may be a good man but most of the knights here would slit a throat to get a manor."

"Would you?"

"Honestly spoken. I can see that you are a crusader. If I am to be truthful, aye. I like none of the leaders here but I will swear to serve one of them. God will forgive any sins."

"Amen to that. Are there others who feel as you do?"

"The majority do not wish Arthur to be our Duke. He is no leader. Even William des Roches abandoned him. He is our hope. He is one of John Lackland's favourites. If he made him the Duke then I would have hope for he would defend us from our greedy neighbours."

I returned to the camp more disturbed than when I had left. I had hoped that there would be support for the young Prince. Now it seemed he had none at home, not even from his own barons. If I was to save the Dukedom for him then I would need a coalition against John. Arthur would have to be a figurehead.

Fótr and I prepared to head for the island in the middle of the afternoon. With the upcoming ceremony planned for the next day there were many knights and barons wandering both the camp and the town. The bridge and the island were busy with people. That suited me. There were trees on the island. It was a pleasant place to be. I suspected that come September it would be filled with mosquitoes and other biting insects but on that May evening it was a good place to watch the sun set in the west.

We chose a place beneath a tree. We would be seen as soon as any stepped on the bridge. I spied Richard of Nantes one of the Prince's household knights. I recognised him. He recognised Fótr and came over. He seemed surprised when I spoke, "Sir Thomas, I did not know it was you."

"Does the Prince come? I have a horse to take him away."

"I do not think he will leave, lord. He has hopes that the treaty will be in his favour. He has been treated well by King John."

"And that is when I would be the most suspicious. Does he come here?"

"He comes, lord. It will be after dark. The other three knights will be with him and he will be cloaked. I will await them at the bridge."

As he left I said, "Fótr, go and tell the others that we do not leave this night. I will try to persuade the Prince to leave tomorrow." Each moment we spent in this vast camp spelled more danger for all of us. I remained hooded. I was still fearful of discovery. My beard had begun to grow and soon I would be recognisable once more.

I heard footfall and looked up. Sir Richard of Nantes was with a hooded figure. The Prince clasped my arm, "Sir Thomas, it is good to see you. At least you have not abandoned me."

"Prince Arthur you must come with me. Here you are in danger."

"Not so. My mother assures me that King Philip has my best interests at heart and King John has told me that I will remain as Duke of Brittany no matter what happens. It is mine so long as I live."

That sent shudders down my spine. "You say your mother spoke to you? Were you not involved in the discussions?"

"I was at first but they were so tedious. Besides there is more unrest over Boulogne and Flanders than my Dukedom. I was disappointed when William des Roches abandoned me but now I spy a kind of hope."

"What does William say?"

The Prince frowned, "It is strange, he has been kept from me. I suspect they think I am still angry with him." He lowered his voice, "But you, Sir Thomas, are in grave danger. The Comte de Senonche wishes all of us to come and crush your manor! If you are seen here then you will be taken. Go to Nantes. There you will be safe."

"I came here to save you. I am camped with the other knights. I will leave when they do. If you need me then send Sir Richard to find me. I will find a way to rescue you."

One of the other knights, Geoffrey of Carentan put his arm to help the Prince to his feet. "Come, Your Grace, we have tarried here long enough. There may be an attempt on your life."

"Prince Arthur I promised to support you. Get word to me if you need me. I will come, no matter where you are."

"Thank you, you are a true knight."

The five of them disappeared into the crowds. I stood and made my way back to the camp. He was naïve and he was inexperienced. He was being played with and his mother was complicit in the charade. When the announcement was made I would ride back to my men and we would return to La Flèche. We would be an island in a sea of enemies but that did not stop my resolve. A knight did what was right, not that which was easy.

Chapter 10

We packed our horses and made our way to the riverbank early so that we could hear all that was said. Edward, David and Philippe waited for us at the road with the horses. They were ready to leave as soon as we arrived back. Fótr and I found a good place to listen. The tent was closed. Suddenly the flap was opened as a panoply of horns sounded. There were bishops and priests in great number and they stepped out first. Then the two kings and Prince Arthur appeared. Behind them came the leading counts and earls. I recognised William de Roches and the Comte de Senonche. They stood as far away from each other as it was possible to get.

Two priests held the document. As soon as King Philip stepped forward to read it then I feared the worst. "I Philip of France recognise John son of King Henry as King of England, heir of his brother Richard. I formally abandon my misguided support for Arthur I, Duke of Brittany, the son of King John's late brother, Geoffrey of Brittany."

I saw Arthur's face. He was crestfallen. King John smiled and stepped forward, "I John, King of England and Ireland, Count of Anjou, Duke of Normandy and Maine, formally recognise the new status of the lost Norman territories. I acknowledge the Counts of Boulogne and Flanders as vassals of the kings of France. They no longer owe a duty to England. Furthermore, I recognise King Philip as the suzerain of the continental lands in the Angevin Empire. I also promise not to support any rebellions on the part of the counts of Boulogne and Flanders. I concede the Vexin to France with the exception of Chateau Galliard. Prince Arthur, my nephew, will remain as Duke of Brittany and he has my full support."

If the two kings thought that their announcement would be greeted with cheers they were mistaken. It was obvious they had carved up the Empire of Henry II and both had abandoned Flanders, Boulogne and Brittany. They all returned back into the tent. I felt as though all hope had been sucked from me. Would Prince Arthur need me? We made our way back to the horses. I could see that Edward was agitated and that David had strung his bow. There was danger.

I trusted my archer and I turned to Fótr, "We get to the horses and we ride! We may have to fight our way out of this place."

At that moment my three men mounted and I saw Geoffrey of Carentan point towards us and shout, "There is the traitor! There is Thomas of La Flèche." We had been betrayed. Geoffrey of Carentan was leading twenty men at arms in the livery of the King of France. They were led by a knight. As the knight raised his sword David's arrow struck him in the chest. Even as we ran and mounted our horses two more men at arms fell to his deadly missiles. Everyone took shelter behind shields and we mounted and put spur to horse. My war horse ensured that no knights were foolish enough to get in his way. No other knights were mounted. We had time but there would be pursuit.

The first six miles would take us along a road which twisted and turned through a wood. It had been a hunting forest of King Henry I of England. They would not see us. The road was not straight. I hoped they might think that we had turned off. We would keep riding hard until we reached my men. The journey back to Ridley and the others would be shorter as we would not be heading to Vernon. We would ride directly to the forest where Ridley the Giant and my men waited for us. The spare horse would enable us to ride just that little bit further and faster. We had a head start. It took time to saddle a horse and mount a pursuit. It would actually suit us for them to come at us piecemeal. We kept our heads down and rode. We did not speak for there was no need. One of the Prince's men had betrayed us. Could the others be trusted? It was a moot point in any case. The Prince had tacitly agreed to King John being his overlord. Now any action he took would be seen as rebellion. He had been outwitted. King Richard had died far too soon. He had not been the best King of England but he was better than his brother and, under his guidance, Arthur might have become a decent king. Now we would never know.

I began to rein back. It was not that I wished to be caught but I did not want to thrash our horses to death. They had had a couple of days rest and we had chosen the best of them. The odds were in our favour. There was a gap of, perhaps, six miles between the road through which we rode and the one where my men waited. I felt almost naked as we burst out of the shady gloom into the bright open countryside. Annoyingly the road was also straight. There was no hiding place. When we were a mile down the open road, I risked a glance behind for the hairs on the back of my neck were prickling. I saw knights and men at arms. They were French. The same bird on the white background was on their shields. There was a temptation to gallop harder. I resisted. We still had five miles to go and I was aware that they were catching us. It was impossible for me to count how many there were and would have been pointless anyway. It was just a number.

By the time we were three miles from the relative safety of my archers and men at arms, the pursuers were less than half a mile behind us. Their horses were lathered. They cared not about conserving their mounts. They wanted me. I was a prize worth a horse or two. My manor would be a rich reward for my capture and death.

David of Wales shouted, "Should I send an arrow or two back towards them, lord, to discourage them?"

Return of the Knight

"Stick with the plan. So long as our horses are game we ride on. They are hurting theirs."

Edward son of Edgar shouted, "That is the French for you! Horse eaters!"

For some reason that made me laugh. We ate horse. We ate anything but our men had this prejudice that the French ate things out of choice which we did out of necessity.

The next time I looked around we were two miles from the forest and the leading riders were just two hundred paces behind. Now, however, they were strung out in a line. It was a long line. I slid my sword in and out of my scabbard. If the leading rider caught us I would turn and engage them. I would have to be quicker than he was. I could now hear the hooves of the horses pursuing us. They could see my face for I was not wearing my helmet. As I turned and saw the leading four horsemen just a hundred paces behind me, I realised they had taken the time to don their helmets. They would not have a good view. That gave us an advantage.

I looked ahead, at the woods just a mile away. I could not see anyone. I was trusting that my men were there. If not then once in the forest we would perish. The French were just thirty paces behind me and the leading horse was in a bad way.

"When we enter the woods ride twenty paces, turn and face our foes. I will not kill these fine beasts!"

It was as I turned Ridley's horse that I glimpsed some of my men. They were ten paces inside the wood and spread out on both sides. As I whipped the war horse around I drew my sword and pulled up my shield. I would have no time to don my helmet. The knight with the lathered horse laboured up towards me. My men were too experienced to attack prematurely. They would wait until more of our pursuers were within the range of our swords and bows. The knight also drew his sword and lifted his shield as he saw me turn. If I had not seen my men waiting at the ambush then he would have no idea he was about to spring the trap. He was a dead man riding.

I shouted and gave him a chance to live. "Yield or die!"

"You killed my cousin. It is you that will die!"

His weary horse lumbered towards me. I deftly stepped my horse to the side so that his sword faced my shield. I stood in my stirrups as he swung his sword at the shield. In order to avoid his horse's head his swing was higher than it should have been. It hit my shield at the broadest part. In standing I was above his shield and I brought my blade down on his helmet. He did not see the blow coming. I stunned him. Pulling my left arm back I punched him in the shoulder with my shield. His weary horse lurched and both mount and rider crashed into a tree. The rider lay still. The second knight had had the misfortune of trying to fight Fótr and Edward. Edward knew how to kill and his sword bit into the neck of the knight who fell to the ground.

Return of the Knight

The others who were pursuing had closed up a little and I saw that there were twenty of them. There were four more knights at the fore. The four of us were abreast of each other and David of Wales had dismounted so that he could use his bow. One of the knights flew over the rump of his horse as David's arrow struck him in the chest.

I heard the roar from Cedric Warbow, "Release!" The men at arms who were at the rear were all struck. A second flight emptied the saddles of the men at arms. My men stepped from the woods with weapons pointed at the four remaining knights.

"Yield or we will butcher you where you stand."

Their leader said, "We yield." He took off his helmet. Staring at me he said, "You cannot win. Soon a French army will come to La Flèche and this time we will not leave until it is a pile of rubble!"

"What is your name?"

I saw that he was a young knight. He looked little older than Sir William and the other three were equally young. "I am Valery de Montparnasse."

I nodded, "You are young and so I will excuse your impertinence. There are certain protocols to be observed when a knight surrenders. You yield your sword, your horse, and your armour to your captor. In return you are treated as a guest until the ransom is paid. However, if the knight who yields does not behave as a knight should then he may be imprisoned and treated as a common criminal. Speak to me like that again Valery de Montparnasse and you and your friends will languish in a cell."

Ridley the Giant was standing next to the young knight and his head was level with the young knight's shoulders. I saw Ridley smile, "I would do what his lordship says, little man! Boo!" He roared at the young knight who reeled back so far that he fell from his saddle.

We had no time to waste, "Dick One Arrow, take one of these horses and ride back down the road. See if this is the only pursuit."

"Aye lord."

"Michael of Anjou examine the men at arms and see if one is still alive. Have the mail and weapons collected and put on the horses. Give the horses some water. These French knights know not how to care for them but as they are ours now we will endeavour to save them." I dismounted and handed the reins of his war horse to Ridley. "You have a good horse there, Ridley. Game as any!"

"Thank you, lord."

I walked over to the knight I had knocked from his saddle. His helmet had fallen and I could see that his neck was broken. He was older than the four we had captured. As Fótr gave his horse water I said, "What is the name of this knight?"

108

Return of the Knight

Valery de Montparnasse had recovered his feet and stood next to me. "He was my uncle; Charles of Blois. You have killed a most powerful knight and the nephew of the Comte de Senonche."

I turned and cast a cold eye at the young man, "I have killed many powerful knights. Think on that!"

Michael of Anjou brought along a man at arms. He had been hit by two arrows: one in the upper arm and one in the ankle. Michael had to support him. I saw that his wounds had been bandaged. "Give him the best of the horses that are left." I looked at him. "You will live." Relief flooded his face. "These four knights will be taken to my home. I wish the ransom for them to be brought there."

He nodded, "Yes, Sir Thomas. Thank you for my life, lord."

"I have not finished. The ransom includes a surety that my castle will not be attacked for one year from this date. Whoever brings the ransom must so swear!"

Valery de Montparnasse shouted, "You cannot ask that!"

Ridley the Giant smacked him hard on the back of the head, "Young pup, bark again and I will give you more than a love tap! You are a prisoner! Behave like one!"

A horse had been brought and Dick One Arrow galloped up. "Take the horse and ride." The man at arms needed no urging and he was helped into the saddle and galloped north. "Well, Dick, any pursuit?"

"Not that I could see."

"We will walk the horses back to the camp. They have ridden hard. Then we head home."

The four knights were less than happy about being forced to walk but they endured it in silence for Ridley and Edward walked behind them. The camp was just two miles into the woods. The French must have been confident that a column of twenty-two men would easily catch and capture just five men. Once the man at arms arrived back they would realise their mistake. I thought it would take him a couple of hours to get back. He would not be able to push his horse. We had that time to put as much distance between us as we could. If we could survive until dark then we had a good chance of reaching our home. The worst thing to do would be to panic.

I turned to Fótr and Edward. "If you were riding down this road, through these woods and you found a couple of logs across the road what would you think?"

"That there was an ambush ahead."

"And you would dismount and send men into the woods to check. Edward have two trees felled. David of Wales, make traps in the woods so that they think there will be men waiting. This will give the horses a short rest. It is the best that we can do."

Return of the Knight

We ate and drank along with our horses. We discarded all that we would no longer need. I had the horses packed more efficiently and we left just as the sun was dipping past its zenith. With archers ahead and behind my men at arms led the horses. I rode in silence for I had much on my mind. King John had conceded the Vexin. That had been a contentious piece of land since the time of the first King Henry. It was a plateau on the right north bank of the Seine running roughly east to west between Pontoise and Romilly-sur-Andelle and north to south between Auteuil and the Seine near Vernon. I saw now why Le Goulet had been chosen for the meeting but what had made him do that? He had kept the mighty fortress of Chateau Galliard but he had given King Philip a route into Normandy. Why had King Philip given up his claims to the Angevin Empire? King John had to accept that, in those territories he had to acknowledge Philip as his lord but that meant little. It merely prevented open war. There was much I needed to discover. I was also interested in Prince Arthur's motives in all of this. Had he initiated the betrayal or was he also as surprised by his faithless knight.

We rode until dark. By my reckoning we still had forty miles to go to reach my castle. I intended to do so the next day. After a night's rest the horses would be fresher and we had remounts now. Once we reached La Flèche then I would make sure that all of the horses fully recovered. It looked likely that we would have great need of them in the future. I had used a stick to smash a wasps' nest. I knew what the consequences were. The four knights were also less than happy about the cold fare we ate in our improvised camp. My men at arms brooding presence ensured that they behaved.

The four young knights became even more agitated, the next day, as we left the forests to join the road which would take us the last eight miles to my home. They began to chatter away to each other. Robert of La Flèche rode behind them, silent and taciturn. They forgot he was there and my man at arms learned much about them and their families. We stopped to water the horses at a trough just six miles from my home. Robert walked up to me, "Lord they are thinking of fleeing and heading east to Chateau-sur-le-Loir." They were waiting until we stopped and then remounted." He laughed, "They think I am a fool. They think I am like Ridley and an Englishman."

"Thank you." I walked back to the four of them. "You are planning on running." I said it plainly and the truth could be seen on their faces. "You are welcome to try. Cedric Warbow. There is an ash tree two hundred paces away. Show these arrogant young warriors just how good you are."

"With pleasure, lord." He strung his bow, casually nocked an arrow and, in the twinkling of an eye had struck the tree dead centre.

"Feel free to run. The arrow which hits you will not kill you. It will lame you. I am certain that a knight who limps on one leg will be able to find something to do other than being a knight! You gave your word. You could have fought on but you did not. You yielded and you have learned a harsh lesson."

Valery de Montparnasse said, "We will not run but you will rue this day. My mother is the cousin of the King. He will not suffer this dishonour."

"The dishonour is yours not mine."

As we neared the castle I was pleased to see that, in the few days we had been away, progress had been made. There were now two wooden towers one in the centre of each of my long walls. The ditch around Jean of Durtal's farm was almost complete and I saw men working on another two towers. With the extra manpower I had brought back from the Seine we would make even more progress. My wife was pleased to see me. She and Sir William greeted me when I dismounted. She glanced at the four sulky looking knights, "I see that you have made new friends, husband."

There was a twinkle in her eye. I kissed her and laughed, "Of course. We are now completely alone. King John and King Philip have made peace. I expect to have visitors before midsummer day."

Sir William said, "And Prince Arthur?"

"Confirmed as Duke of Brittany but I fear that is a parlous position."

He pointed to the walls. "The men have worked hard and the masons have laid the foundations for the two barbicans." He smiled, "We may be a pariah amongst the rest of this land but there are still those who choose to come and live close to us. Two farmers came yesterday and asked if they could farm to the west of the town between the moat and the road. I pointed out that those buildings had been destroyed when the French last attacked. They seemed happy enough." He pointed to the east. "They are bringing their families in the next day or so."

"We had better put these four knights somewhere safe."

When Sir Leofric had built the castle he had built the keep first and then piled the earth and spoil from the moat around it. The result was that the gate to the keep was actually a good fifteen paces above the ground. There were large storage rooms. When we had been besieged they had all been packed with barrels and supplies. Now one was empty. It was dry and, with summer coming it would be cool. More importantly it had a door which could be locked. They would be secure. I did not trust the four of them.

When all was done I went to play with my son. As Margaret said he was not yet at the playing stage but I enjoyed making ridiculous noises and pulling faces. I swore that he smiled but my wife said it was wind.

Seven days after our return and with two more wooden towers completed, James Broadsword, in the tower of the keep, spied banners. "Sir Thomas, we have company!"

I had been expecting this. "Sir William, fetch the captives. Have the men stand to."

111

Return of the Knight

"Should we have the gates barred?"

I looked to the north. Now that we had cleared some of the trees for timber we had a much better view. The column was more than a mile away and I could not see siege engines. It looked to be made up of horsemen. "I think not. That would make them think that we were afraid of them. If they show belligerence we have time enough to close the gates." I saw that there were four sumpters with what looked like chests. When I had discovered the identity of the captives I knew that they would pay a healthy ransom.

As they closed with us I saw that they were going to take the eastern road. Jean of Durtal had wisely removed the bridge over the ditch to his farm but he continued to work on the fences he was building. I saw that the banner of the King of France was amongst the French standards. I recognised that of the Comte de Senonche and others that I had seen at Le Goulet. My beard had grown and I was more recognisable. I headed, with Sir William, to the east town gate. I left the captives to be watched by Ridley the Giant, Father Michel and our two squires. My archers lined the wall.

Roger of Meaux looked worried as we crossed the town square, "Does this mean trouble, lord?"

"I think not. They come to pay ransom. There will be more gold spent in my town. It is all good."

The men at work on the barbican had stopped. At the moment it looked a mess. I smiled to myself. It was not a dignified entrance to my castle and town. I did not think the Comte de Senonche would be happy. Sir William and I stood in the gateway. The riders approached. I held up my hand, "I do not intend to allow such a large group in my town. Comte choose six men and bring in the sumpters and the horses for your knights. You will have to dismount to enter my castle. The gate does not accommodate riders."

When I had first come I had found the gate into my castle an annoyance. Now I could see why Sir Leofric had built it as he had. It could accommodate a led wagon and a horse but not a rider on a horse. When we rode to war we used the town square to mount. It was a minor inconvenience.

The Comte dismounted and handed his reins to one of the men he had selected to accompany him. He smiled at me although it was not a friendly smile. It was the smile of a reptile. "Having work done on your walls I see, Sir Thomas."

"Some of the neighbours were a little exuberant. We are just putting it to rights. When next you visit you will find it much cosier."

The smile left his face, "You cannot win you know. I admire your courage but it is misplaced. You can do nothing for Prince Arthur. King Philip will attend to you once Boulogne and Flanders are brought to heel."

I stopped, "In which case this meeting is ended."

"What?"

112

Return of the Knight

"I made it quite clear that part of the ransom price was peace for one year. If King Philip is planning to attack me then I will keep the knights here and hang them, one by one when the attack begins."

"But Sir Valery is a relative of the King!"

It was my turn to smile. "I know." I shouted, "Take the prisoners back to their cell there will be no exchange this day."

"Wait!" he glared at me, "Very well. We will agree to peace for a year."

I pointed at Father Michel. He held a Bible. "You will swear on the Bible."

I saw his face fall. He nodded.

As we turned I noticed that, amongst the men with him was Guy of Chateau-sur-le-Loir, William des Roches' squire. "I am surprised to see you in such company Guy of Chateau-sur-le-Loir."

He nodded, "The Seneschal of Anjou sent me to make certain that all was done well."

"Good." There was more to it than that but I would bide my time.

The swearing was done first. Then I had Father Michel count out the coin. While that was going on Guy of Chateau-sur-le-Loir sidled over to me and spoke quietly to me in English. "My lord also sent me with a message and with news. Prince Arthur has had enough and he has fled to the court of King John in Rouen."

I could not keep the dismay from my face.

He nodded. "The Seneschal said that he has people watching the Duke and he is safe. He also said to tell you that King John bribed King Philip with twenty thousand gold marks. The King of France now has coin to make war where he will. He warned you to watch your back."

I pointed to the Bible, "The Comte has sworn for France!"

"You were at Le Goulet. Do you remember all those knights seeking a master? Now King Philip has the coin and they all have a master. They did not swear. King Philip plays these games well. My master is your friend but…"

"But I have placed myself in this hole and I need to get myself out."

He nodded, "Just so, my lord."

Chapter 11

I had been warned and so I took precautions. I divided my men at arms and archers into patrols of six men; four men at arms and two archers. Each day one patrol would ride east and one west. They would meet up at the road to Le Mans and ride in together. To vary it and confuse any who might be watching, one random day in three they would reverse the route. The result as that we would be warned of any threat to us. They also scouted out the French manors which lay close to us. I had not given up on the idea of taking them as a buffer and to enlarge the number of men who would fight for me.

At the end of August men arrived from Angers. They had come from England. They came in response to the letter I had sent to my aunt. A knight led them. He was young. There were twenty-four of them and they had walked. They looked weary. My sentries spotted them in the west when they were half a mile away and their weariness showed for I reached the gate well before they did. They stopped at the gate and the knight gave a slight bow. I saw that his boots had seen better days and his armour was the old-fashioned scale armour.

"I am Henry fitz Percy, lord. I have here a letter from," he gave a tired smile, "you know the lady and I will not use her name. We have all been sent here for we have a mutual hate for King John, his taxes and his tyranny. We wish to fight against him. The choice is obvious: become an outlaw and live in the forests or join Sir Thomas of La Flèche. When the lady… offered to send us here on the *'Swan of Stockton'* we leapt at the chance. There are more waiting to join us but the ship had a full cargo. We had to sleep on the deck."

"Then you are welcome. "Godwin of Battle, take the men to the warrior hall. Come Sir Henry, bring your squire."

He shook his head, "Do not accord me false title, my lord. I have trained as a knight but King John refused to knight me for I am the bastard son of William Percy who died last year. He denied me knighthood so that he could take the family manor of Topcliffe. That is why I come to you as an impoverished knight. In England there was nothing for me. I will go to the warrior hall if my presence offends you or your good lady."

"The greatest knights I knew were impoverished knights. They were the Hospitallers in Outremer. I am more than happy to dub you as a knight but I cannot promise that you will make your fortune. I have been a sword for hire and know the pitfalls."

"We care not for a fortune do we, Richard?"

The squire was younger than Johann. He grinned, "No lord. But a roof and a bed which did not roll and was dry would be good."

114

Return of the Knight

I liked them both immediately. I was learning how to judge people and these two, without even reading my aunt's letter, felt right. Edward and James would get to the bottom of the motives of the archers and men at arms who had come. We needed them, of that there was no doubt. As I headed up to my keep I wondered how I would fund them. If I raided again then I would be breaking the peace I had brokered. The alternative was to tax my people and, so far, I had avoided that. The only tax my people paid was the tithe to the church. Soon the harvest would be collected in. Even if they wished war the peace would still hold for another month or two. If we could get to October without war then we could begin to sell our surplus and bring in coin to our beleaguered manor.

I called Fótr over. "Find Geoffrey and have this knight and his squire given rooms."

He grinned, "Yes lord."

My wife was feeding our son. He seemed to be a hungry boy. That was good. "We have a new knight and squire. He is poor."

She smiled, "And there is nothing wrong with poor." She made to rise.

"Stay; I will see Geoffrey. We still have room but we must give thought to a manor for William and Marguerite."

My wife frowned, "Does that not mean making war on an enemy and will that not bring the wrath of the French upon us?"

"It does and so I must judge the moment well. Fear not I will do my best to avoid the apocalypse."

Geoffrey came into the hall. He had had no problem with finding rooms. "They did not mind sharing and the room is more than adequate, Sir Thomas."

"Tell me Geoffrey, you handle the finances. How many men can I afford to retain?"

"How many have arrived, lord?"

"Twenty-four including a knight."

"Then that is not a problem. I assume that the knight will not need payment?"

"No, but he needs mail, helmet and horses."

"Thanks to your raids we have plenty of those. There is money enough. It is land that we need. Already we have too many houses in the town. There is land, lord, but it belongs to the French or to Anjou."

"You would have me take it?"

"War is expensive lord. Men die and people starve." He shrugged. "I am learning that you are in the mould of Old Sir Leofric. I never knew him but from what my father told me you sound like a similar man. Trust to your judgement. The grape harvest will be a good one. We have never had as much wheat and thanks to your raids we have double the animals we had in Sir Philip's time. It is not a problem."

"And the masons?"

Return of the Knight

"Roger of Meaux and the Council have funded the barbicans. I confess, lord, I pointed out that the building work would benefit them more than us. Trade is going well and they are all rich men. They are not fools, lord, they do not wish to lose you as the lord of the manor and they are confident that we will ride out this particular storm."

That evening we had a larger gathering than normal. Henry fitz Percy and Richard were just pleased to be welcomed. The ladies of Lady Margaret and Lady Marguerite enjoyed the company of the handsome young man. I think he felt uncomfortable in the glare of their gaze. My wife sensed the young man's discomfort and when the sweetmeats had been finished and we drank the heavy wine and ate the cheese she ordered the ladies to bed.

Henry had drunk well but he was not yet drunk. When we had finished the heady wine, he would be. Sir William and I enjoyed talking to him for we learned about England. It had been many years since we had lived there. I had lived outside its borders longer than I had lived within.

"It is a country where men look over their shoulders, lord. King John has set baron against baron. He is like a crow. He picks off the weak and flies away when an eagle or hawk shows itself. Then he undermines those mighty birds."

Sir William said, "He is doing the same here. I fear for Prince Arthur."

"He will not become King?"

"I fear not Henry but I still hope that we can use him to build a rebellion against Lackland."

"You are alone here, lord."

"Yes, Henry and there are other lords who might offer you better prospects."

"I do not need prospects, lord. I need a lord I can follow. When I spoke with Captain Henry I got a good feeling about you and your aunt speaks of you as a new Achilles or Ajax."

I laughed, "I am her only relative. Of course, she thinks well of me."

"It is more than that. Your walls are well laid out and I can see how you could improve them further. I feel lucky that you have given me the opportunity to prove myself. I will work hard and obtain better armour and a horse."

I smiled, "We have those for you already. Tomorrow Fótr will take you to the stables. There are four spare warhorses. Choose one. Geoffrey has mail for you and your squire. I know that Richard is growing but he might as well be protected as best he can be."

"I do not know how to thank you, Sir Thomas."

"Wait until we have to fight our enemies and then thank me."

Sir William said, after the English knight had retired, "Our castle is becoming crowded."

"You wish your own home?"

He gave me a look of absolute surprise, "Yes but how did you know?"

116

Return of the Knight

"You have a family and you share the castle with mine and now strangers. It is natural."

"I thought to ask permission to build a hall south of the river. If I built it to the east it could protect the bridge and we could still retreat to the castle in time of danger."

I shook my head, "That bridge is wooden and it is old. We need one which is protected by our walls. I do not mind you building a hall but it should be across from the town gate. There we could build a new bridge."

"That would require a lot of stone."

"I do not plan the bridge yet. I am looking far into the future but, come spring we will dig the foundations for your hall. This is good."

The next day, while Fótr took them for their horses I met with David of Wales and Edward. "Well? Do they meet our needs?"

David nodded. "We are lucky. There are twelve archers. They are all sound men. We have time to train them in our ways."

My sergeant at arms agreed, "And the men at arms know their business. They lack mail and decent helmets. We have plenty of those. It is a sign that God smiles on us. We now have sixty-five men at arms. I remember the Baltic when we could count our men on two hands."

"Aye and I now have forty-eight archers. That must be the largest number outside of England. I am happy too."

Edward knew better than any the dangers of overcrowded warrior halls. "But we need another warrior hall!"

"Then we shall make one. Take the new men to the woods to the north of us and cut down more trees."

With the extra labour the embrasures and new towers were quickly completed. Jean of Durtal's ditch was finished and we added another ditch on the western side for our new farmers. When the autumn rains came they were not a handicap they were a blessing. The moat and ditches filled.

Our patrols found French scouts to the east of us just after the bone fire of November. They were armed men and they were close to my castle. As such they merited investigation. My men found them twelve miles away and south of the river. I took Sir William, twenty archers and twenty men at arms. We had more men now and I could make a statement to the French. My men were better than the French and they reported back to me within half a day of discovering them. I wasted no time. I mounted a conroi with my two knights, ten men at arms and ten archers. The rest laboured at the walls. We found them close to Le Lude. Le Lude was a small village of ten huts. It had a bridge over the river. There had been a castle there but it had been destroyed in the wars between Count Fulk and Duke Henry. I had thought of taking it over, when the time was right and building a castle there. We did not bother the villagers and they were happy to use our market rather than their own twenty miles to the east.

117

Return of the Knight

My archers surrounded the village and I rode in to catch, unawares, the knight and twenty men at arms. We galloped in quickly. They had not set sentries and were taken by surprise. The knight, an older man looked up in surprise. There was a villager lying on the ground and his mouth was bleeding. A sergeant at arms had blood on his knuckles.

"What is going on here?"

"This is none of your business, Englishman. I do not answer to you. I serve the Comte de Senonche."

I dismounted. I saw David of Wales and my men moving silently towards us with nocked arrows from the other side of the village. All other eyes were on me. "I will ask again, pleasantly, for I would keep the peace but I would have an answer to my question and in a tone which does not offend me."

I strode close to the knight. I had no weapon drawn nor did I wear my helmet. The closer I got the more the knight realised that I was a bigger knight. I saw his eyes flicker around and take in that I had men with me. "This man is suspected of poaching. I was questioning him. It is none of your business."

I reached down and pulled the man to his feet. I vaguely recognised him from our market. He had sold goods from a stall. As I recalled he grew vegetables. I turned to the knight. "Which wood?"

He looked at me in surprise, "I do not understand the question."

"You said he poached. That means he went into a wood to do so." I spread my arm around. "Where is the wood?" I jabbed a finger in the direction of the distant wood to the west. It was closer to my town and south of the river. "You do not mean that wood do you? My wood?"

"No, the wood to the south of Chateau-sur-le-Loir."

I looked at the villager, "You enjoy a challenge, my friend. You ignore a wood which is just four miles away and instead tramp through open countryside for eight miles and poach the land of the Comte de Senonche." He said nothing. "Did you poach? Are you a hunter?"

Taking a step closer to me he spat out a tooth and shook his head, "Lord I did not poach. I do not even own a bow. I tend vegetables and I raise swine."

The knight said, "He lies."

"I think not but I can have a Bible fetched. That would settle the matter."

I could see that the villager was edging away from the sergeant at arms. When he was behind me he said, "Lord I was being punished for selling my goods at your market."

The sergeant at arms began to draw his sword. He was going to silence the villager. The blade was but half way out when two arrows thudded into his back. He adopted a surprised expression and then slumped at my feet. The knight and his men turned around and saw levelled bows.

I turned to the knight, "Is this true?" He hesitated. "You have broken the peace already when your man drew his sword in my presence. If I were to ask the rest of the villagers what would they say?"

"These are French people now! The Comte does not wish them to trade with you."

"You are wrong! This is still Anjou. Your lord stole the castle from William des Roches. The people here have traded at my market and that of Chateau-sur-le-Loir since the time of Count Fulk. Leave now and know that the people of Le Lude enjoy my protection." I pointed to the river. "That river is as far as the Comte has jurisdiction. Tell him so."

The knight nodded. "And you should know, Sir Thomas the renegade and priest killer, that you have now made an enemy of me, Theobald of Bonneval. I will not break the peace but when the peace is broken then I will kill you."

I walked over to his horse and examined his shield. It was a yellow shield with blue fess. "Then I shall watch for you on the battlefield for you are right. The peace will end and then you will rue the day that you made such a boast. Now begone."

The villager bowed as the French left, "Thank you, lord but they may come back."

"What is your name?"

"Jean of Le Lude lord."

"Well Jean I am guessing that you are the head man here." He nodded. "I can tell you that they will be back. The peace can only last until midsummer day next year but fear not. I have an idea." I turned to Sir William. "This is south of the river, William. That high piece of ground overlooks the bridge and the river. Would not this make a good site for a castle and a hall? What say you? Do you wish a manor?"

He did not answer directly. In the twelve years, we had known each other we had become as close as brothers. I could almost read his thoughts. He would be bringing his family and putting them in danger, closer to the French but he would have his own manor. He would have those who would serve him and he would have his own castle. As my men watered their horses he walked to the mound where the old castle had stood. The ditch could still be seen. Scrubby bushes had sprouted from the remains of the palisade.

He walked back to me. "It would need to be built in stone, lord."

"Of course."

"We would not be able to begin construction until Easter."

"And by then the masons should have completed most of the work on the barbicans. I will bring men to help you."

"But we cannot allow these villagers to live without protection. I will send Padraig the Wanderer and my men at arms to build a wooden keep where the castle once stood. They can winter here." Padraig the Wanderer had come with James Broadsword and led William's men at arms.

"That is good. "Jean, you will be protected."

As we rode back I reflected that I had come to this land to seek an opportunity to return to England and yet I was putting down roots that would be hard to break. Was this my destiny? Would I end up as a knight of Anjou rather than an English knight? I had cast the bones. When my ship had docked in this land it had changed my future.

As we crossed the rickety bridge across the Loir I knew that we had to build a better one. I had left the bridge in a poor state of repair as it protected my land from the south. An enemy could not cross it with heavy wagons. If Sir William was going to live south of the river then we needed a secure way to reach him. We also needed one which could be protected by the walls of my town. We sent forty men to help Padraig the Wanderer build the hall and I consulted with Roger of Meaux and the masons about the bridge. The river close to the town was sixty paces wide. The merchants wanted a new bridge as far to the east as we could manage it. Once it was built them we would have a problem sailing further east. They wanted as much space for quays as possible. I pointed out that we would now have frontage on the south side of the river and I saw that they had not even considered that.

"We could build a wall there and protect any buildings you had. There would be men who would garrison the towers there too. Your goods would be as safe as in my town."

Once they realised that they agreed to fund the building of the bridge. They divided the land up south of the river amongst themselves. I reserved one site for a hall. In their eagerness to gain valuable land they began work on both their warehouses and the bridge simultaneously. They decided to make it big enough for one wagon at a time to cross. There they showed the experience of siege warfare. They would restrict any enemies who tried to cross.

Winter, and Christmas in particular, were normally quiet times but that year the outside of my keep was a maelstrom of activity. William made the most of the comfort of my castle and Henry relished the peace and the joy of a family home. Eight more men at arms and four more archers arrived before Captain Henry ceased his voyages. There was no letter this time. However, when I spoke with Ralph of Appleby who was newly arrived I learned something of the process my aunt and her husband used. They spread the word that archers and men at arms were needed to fight in France. She did not specify an enemy. Stockton lay on the main north south road and many travellers passed through it. The innkeepers were more than happy to spread the word. When they arrived then they were housed in the castle. My aunt was a kind woman and Ralph of Appleby told me how all who came were fed and housed. He also added that they were watched. Those who were too old to go to war were given places in the garrison at the hall. Those that she and her husband deemed to be unsuitable were sent away. They were fed first but they were told that they were not going to be considered. The ones who remained were told nothing until they boarded the ship. Captain Henry ensured that none left the ship save to come to me. I could not see how the plan could fail and I now had enough men to garrison two castles.

On Christmas day we gave presents. I had reserved the best present for Henry. Since his arrival he had held a vigil and been shriven by Father Michel. William and I had spoken to him at length about his life up to this point and his hopes for the future. As he stood smiling at the joy in the hall I said, "Come, Henry fitz Percy, I have a present for you."

"But lord, you have done so much for me already! I deserve no more."

"Nonetheless you shall have a gift from me. It is a gift which costs me little yet which is worth the world to you. Kneel so that I may dub you!"

His eyes widened in wonder but before he did so he hesitated, "Lord is this legal? Will I be fighting under false colours?"

"Prince Arthur, Duke of Brittany confirmed that I am the lord of these lands. None has taken the office from me. Father Michel is here to ensure that the Church will be satisfied. When you rise, you will be a knight. A humble knight bachelor but a knight nonetheless." I noticed my wife smiling. She held a wrapped bundle beneath her arm.

He knelt and I touched his shoulders with my sword. It was a simple ceremony but it would not be completed until I spoke the words. As Edward son of Edgar said, it was almost like being a magician. The trick would not work until the magic words were spoken.

"Rise Sir Henry fitz Percy of La Flèche." Fótr stepped forward and handed him his spurs. Fótr had a vested interest in the ceremony for soon he would be knighted too.

Then my wife stepped forward and gave him her parcel, "My ladies and I made this for you."

He unwrapped the tapered standard. It was the coat of arms of the Percy family: a field of azure, adorned with five horizontal fusils conjoined in gold fess. The only difference was that at the widest end was a golden gryphon, my sign.

"I know not what to say. I am now a knight."

"More than that you are a lord with walls to defend." I pointed across the river. "You will command the men who live in the hall on the southern side of the river. Your task will be to guard the bridge when it is complete. My sergeant at arms, Edward son of Edgar and my Captain of Archers, David of Wales, will allocate men to serve you. I am afraid you will have to help in the building of your own hall."

121

"When I came here I had nothing. Now I have all that I could desire. I thank you, lord."

"I fear that, like the rest of us, you will have to fight to hang onto that which we have."

As well as our families my wife had also invited those of my men who were married and had children. Ridley and Anya now had two. Those two apart the rest were babies. They played together and one could not differentiate between commoner baby and noble. They would, hopefully, grow up together. Bonds would be formed so that when they were old enough to become warriors, they would fight together.

Christmas Day was just an interlude. Even on St Stephen's day we were toiling. I helped my men to build the embrasures on my walls. I had little skill but I had strength and they had the skill and the common sense to steer me in the right direction. I was aware that my castle was in disarray but I had to have faith that it would not always be so. We had until June to make ourselves secure for, when the peace ended, then the flood gates would open. What had surprised me was the lack of action from King John. What I did not know was that he was in Poitou where he was dealing harshly with the Lusignan faction who objected to his marriage to Isabella of Angouleme. His absence was a godsend. William des Roches was with him and it seemed that we were being granted the time to prepare for war.

The news of the attack in Poitou also told us that Arthur was with his uncle. That was disturbing. He could learn nothing honourable from John Lackland. I just hoped that William des Roches was honouring his promise to watch over the Duke.

Sir William now of Le Lude, rose before dawn each day and rode to help his men build his castle. He sourced enough local stone for the foundations of the keep. Had this been England then the building would have had to wait until the weather warmed up. Here it rarely froze. Sir William and I had planned a simple design of castle. There would be a keep with a curtain wall, a main gate and a sally port. The garrison would be small; just thirty men in total. Its purpose would be simple. It would protect the bridge and the villagers.

Sir Henry had a different task and a different hall. His hall would have no curtain wall. At least not in the beginning. It would be a simple keep with an entry at the first-floor level. The ground floor would be for the horses. There would be a bridge from the first floor to the gatehouse across the bridge. Sir Henry would defend the bridge. His garrison would be even smaller than Sir William's, it would be twenty men.

My new defences would not be finished by the time the peace was ended but Sir William would have a wooden wall with a fighting platform and a half-built keep. Sir Henry would have a half-built keep, a half-built bridge and the beginnings of two towers. The only defence which would be complete would be my castle. The six new wooden towers for archers were complete. The embrasures were in place. The barbicans at the two ends of the town were well on their way to completion and when we had the spring rains then the new moat would fill with water and an attacker would have two bridges, two moats and two gatehouses to negotiate and even then, they would only have access to my town. The castle was a further set of defences away.

What I found hard was the lack of news and intelligence. When ships docked we questioned their crews to discover what was happening in the outside world. By then it was old news. My friend in Angers was busy fighting for the King and so we patrolled and we built. My people toiled so that we had goods to sell and to trade. Our twice-weekly market now drew in even more people. The incident at Le Lude had not deterred the French and the Angevins, it had encouraged them. I was seen now as someone who would protect their rights. When Lady Marguerite became pregnant once more we all took it as a sign that God smiled on us. As April blossomed so did hope.

A New Castle

Chapter 12

The peace was not broken suddenly. It was not as though King Philip suddenly brought his army to squash us like a summer fly. It was insidious. War came gradually. Sir William now had patrols riding east and north from his lands. It meant the building work slowed but we both knew he needed the patrols. His men saw more evidence of French activity. They were improving the roads west. More banners were seen flying from the French castles. Chateau-sur-le-Loir grew a tented village. My men also noticed more activity to the north east. The south and the west were quiet. King John was still busy in Poitou.

Another ship arrived with men from England. There were twenty this time. That was about as many as could be carried on the small cog. Twelve archers and eight men at arms were a welcome addition. I divided them between Sir William and my castle. Until Sir Henry's bastion was built and the bridge completed he had no need of them.

This time there was a letter.

You know who you are and I hope you know that I think of you every day! Each night you are in my prayers.

I was disappointed to hear that Arthur had lost all support in Normandy and Anjou. He has none in England. My grandfather would be turning in his grave at his treatment. Even now the people of Stockton speak of the Warlord with great reverence. When he ruled this valley, it was a haven.

I still seek knights who would serve with you. There was one. I will not mention his name. He fell foul of the Sheriff of York. He objected to some people being ejected from their homes to build a tax house for the King. He lost his lands. He was being pursued when he came to speak with us and would not stay for fear of putting our homes in jeopardy. I told him of you and he said he would try to join you. He had his son, a squire and ten men with him. Ask him his story. If it tallies with what I have told you then he can be trusted.

I am delighted that you have a son! The family will live on. I pray that one day he will see his great aunt. Keep safe.

124

We keep a place for you and your family here. Our home is your home and always will be.

Xxx

I was intrigued. If King John was acting in such a high-handed manner then it would not be long before the barons had had enough. When a baron was thrown from his land for having an opinion then things had come to a critical state. The fact that John was in Poitou would only worsen the situation.

I rode to Le Lude with ten of my men. I wanted to see the progress on my new castle. As we rode I was aware that the land between the two castles had no obstructions. We could travel there easily. The river was high but that was normal for this time of year. I was happy to see that the fact that they all waved at us was a good thing. We were not hated. That was a start. When I reached the castle, I was pleased to see that there was both a wall and a gate. I could see the keep rising behind the wooden walls. Sir William was stripped to the waist and Johann was helping him. Already they were beginning the second floor and the treadmill crane was lifting the blocks into place.

When he saw me, William climbed down the ladder. "It is going well, lord."

"It is. You have enough men here but you are exposed. I want you to build a signal fire and have a man ready at all times. If an attack comes then light the fire and I will bring horsemen."

"I will, lord." He pointed south and east, "We have a good view from here. I can see why the French pulled it down. With the river protecting the east and the north then the only way they can approach it is from the south and they would be seen some way away."

"When will the keep be finished?"

"By harvest we will be able to defend it and by this time next year, we will have walls that they will struggle to overcome. I will have my family here and I will ensure that the enemy bleed their lives on its walls."

"And your patrols?"

"The French are growing in numbers but they do not appear ready to strike."

"I will keep a well-armed patrol ready to respond should you be attacked. It is not yet June. I think that King Philip is pious enough to abide by the agreement. Every day is valuable to us." I rode back along the north bank of the river. With Sir William at Le Lude the French might try the north bank as a way of avoiding my new defences. Once we passed the bridge I saw that the ground we had made boggy last year was still impassable. They would come by Le Lude. I needed to be ready.

I rode over the new bridge over the moat. The water around the barbican was rising. It was not yet a hazard but it would be. I ducked my head beneath the barbican and clattered across the second bridge. I felt satisfied. There was a healthy buzz in the town as I rode through. It was market day and it felt vibrant. Even more people had come. The fact that King John and the Seneschal of Anjou were in Poitou and the King of France was still in Flanders meant that more people felt that they could come to trade with us. That might stop when the two kings turned their eye on me.

I dismounted and handed my reins to Fótr. He would see to Skuld. I handed him my helmet and I walked through my town. Walking through the square always made me feel that I was close to my people. When I reached the quay, I saw how many ships were being unloaded and loaded. I rarely came here and so I was impressed. I was a warrior and knew not about coin but each ship that arrived brought money to my people and to my coffers. The bridge still required the middle span. I walked down the quay to look at the opposite bank. I did so twice and Roger of Meaux, who was overseeing the bridge, approached me.

"What is it, lord? You have walked up and down as though seeking fault. What have we done that is wrong?"

"Nothing. It is just that I notice that the land is flat across from the town."

"Aye, lord and what of it?"

"If we dug a ditch there," I pointed to the west end of the new development, "and there to the east then the bastion and your warehouses would have the protection of water."

It was as though scales had been lifted from his eyes. He nodded. "And the bridge is not to serve the south but merely to serve the town. That is brilliant my lord!"

As much as I appreciated the compliment I was still worried about the threat of France. We had beaten off one attack but they would have learned from that. We had more men but the French had an inexhaustible supply. Geoffrey had used my money wisely. Even so until we had a greater income we could not afford more men. We would have to fight the French with what we had.

They came at the start of July. We had been ready from the end of May for an attack. We had kept riders in the field but the French had not attacked. I now believe they thought to outwit me. They thought to keep me waiting for an attack and then relax my vigilance. That would not happen.

Sir Henry's bastion was almost complete. The bridge was finished and the towers at the south side of the river could be reinforced by Sir Henry. Sir William had two floors to his keep. He still needed a third but his donjon overlooked his walls. The attack came and we were ready. When the beacon was lit and the thick black smoke rose in the sky I took my men and rode south along the river. I had forty men ready with another twenty in reserve. Our task was simple: we would go to the aid of Sir William. I had twenty-two men at arms and eighteen archers. The ones I took were the best. I rode at the fore with

Return of the Knight

David and Edward. We had enough experience between us to make the decisions which would decide the battle.

The French had attacked from the south. I could see the gonfanon on their spears. That was good for the gate was to the north and faced the bridge. More importantly the land there was open farmland and would suit my horsemen.

"David of Wales, take your horsemen inside the castle. We will upset the French a little and then join you." My archers needed no urging. They worked best when behind a wall.

Some of my men at arms had grabbed spears. I had not. Fótr did not carry a standard but his gonfanon was my gryphon. The French would know who attacked them. The enemy had not reached the walls and I saw why. They were mainly on foot. There were over a hundred of them. They advanced behind crossbowmen. The crossbows were protected by men who advanced with a pavise. Each crossbow had a pavise. The twenty crossbows released alternatively allowing a steadier rate of bolts than was normal but it made for a slow and laborious approach. There were horsemen. Six knights and their squires and four mounted men at arms were behind the hundred men marching on foot. The French saw us. It must have been about the same time as my archers reached the walls. Their plunging arrows negated the effect of the pavise.

The French sounded a horn and the horsemen charged towards us. The men on foot could not turn because they needed the protection of the crossbows. Some of those at the rear of the column did turn. The horsemen would be unsupported. Perhaps they thought that, as knights and squires, they were superior to men at arms. They were going to learn the hard way the truth of that. Although it was farmland it was far from flat and a boot to boot charge was difficult. As we neared them I did not recognise any of the shields. I wondered if these were some of the men who had sought masters at Le Goulet.

Pulling my shield up a little higher I drew my sword. The uneven field made the lances of the French rise and fall alarmingly. Their horses could not keep a steady gait. I saw one squire's horse find a hollow and the young Frenchman barely held onto his cantle. There were not many of us and the collision was a series of cracks rather than the crash of two longer lines. The knight who had charged me punched too early. I saw his lance coming for me and I pulled Skuld a little to my right. We would be meeting sword to lance. The lance came across my body. As I swung my sword the lance cracked and broke in two leaving the knight with the shorter end. My sword smacked across his chest. He dropped his broken lance and his arm came up. I had hurt him. He wheeled away.

I turned and saw that Fótr was having an unequal battle with a knight who had an axe. Already splinters were flying from my squire's shield. I charged Skuld towards him. He saw me coming and tried to turn. Fótr kept striking with

127

his sword and that distracted the knight. Standing in my stirrups I brought my sword from on high and, as the knight defended himself with his shield I struck his helmet on its top. It was a powerful blow and it dented the helmet. The axe fell from the knight's fingers but he was saved by his horse. In trying to turn from me he had given his mount an escape route and the beast galloped away. I think that the knight was unconscious and held in place by his cantle.

Three knights and four squires remained. James was lying on the ground but the rest of my men at arms were still whole and still mounted. The knights and squires who remained galloped off.

"Fótr, see to James! The rest of your, reform! One long line!"

The French on foot outnumbered us and they had turned their lines so that they had two sides of a square. One faced us and one faced the partly built castle. The pavise were facing the castle. Once my men were in a line we began to cover the three hundred paces to the French. I realised that there was no rattle of bolts. My archers had ended the threat of the crossbows. We did not gallop across the open field. It was a steady and measured approach. When Sir William led ten mounted men from the castle it seemed to be the signal for flight. Without their leaders the men on foot fled. They ran. Then we put spurs to our horses.

I saw Edward son of Edgar bring his sword from on high to take the top of the skull of the fleeing Frenchman before him. Henry Youngblood still had his spear and he rammed it through the spine of the man at arms who tried to avoid death by lying on the ground. A sergeant at arms, hearing my hooves turned to face me. Skuld responded to my knees and swerved so that we avoided the swinging longsword. I used a backhand flick. My sword sliced into his neck. Killing men and avoiding dead bodies allowed more than half of the French to escape.

"Hold!"

I reined in. No more of my men had been hurt. Sir William trotted his horse over to me. I took off my helmet, "The signal fire worked."

"It did, Sir Thomas, but had they come at night it would have been a different matter. Although the fire would have blazed brightly they would be able to get a lot closer to us before we knew of the danger."

"I doubt that they will do that. It is almost impossible to do so quietly and moving a large number of men in the dark invites disaster. Men can get lost and, in the dark, it is hard to distinguish friend from foe. But they will come again. The next time they will bring more horsemen. They will know of the signal fire. Did you lose any?"

"One of my men was wounded with a bolt. Your timely arrival put paid to their attack. However, I need more archers. David of Wales and your archers made the difference and they slaughtered the crossbows."

Return of the Knight

"I fear that archers are a commodity rarer than gold in this land. I will ask David to select another five from my garrison to augment yours."

Edward rose up. "We have two wounded men as prisoners, lord. Do you want their throats slitting?"

I shook my head, "War is bad enough without escalating the bloodshed. Have their wounds bound and then brought to me."

"Aye lord."

I dismounted as did Sir William. I saw that we had gained another four horses. The dead knights and men at arms were being stripped of mail and weapons. I saw that James was on his feet but Fótr had bandaged his arm. He had been wounded. As we walked back to the castle I asked, "How much longer before you have your wall walk and fighting platform finished?"

"We will be collecting the harvest before that is complete. I do not want to rush it. When that is finished then I bring my family here. I want them to be safe."

We were nearing his ditch. I saw that his men had deepened it but there were no traps within. "If you seed that with stakes and then join it to the river you will have a good defence from the south."

"I had thought of that but the keep is unfinished." He gave me a rueful smile. "Being the lord of the manor is not as easy as you make it look, lord. You have decisions to make and priorities to balance."

"I would divide your workforce. Half work on the keep while the other half join the ditch to the river. It will not take long."

"But then we would not be able to cross the ditch south of us. There would be no bridge."

"And you do not need one yet." I pointed to the pavise which lay scattered around. "Have your farmers join them. They will make a temporary bridge. They will support a man and not a horse.

Edward and Ridley the Giant brought over the two wounded men at arms. One had to be supported by Ridley. He had a bad cut to his leg. The other had his arm in a sling and a bandage around his head.

"Where will your knights have run to?"

Grateful that their lives had been spared they could not wait to tell me all. "Montoire sur le Loir, lord. The Comte de Senonche has given the manor to Baron Gilles de Sosigny. "

"Did he fall here today?"

"No lord. He was the one whose lance you broke."

I turned to Sir William. "They have come a long way to raid you." I turned back to the two wounded men. "When did you leave your castle?"

"Two days since, lord. We camped at Chateau-sur-le-Loir."

"Then return and tell your master that he attacks my manors at his peril. I brought just a small number of men this day. If I brought all of them then not a man would have survived. We will burn your dead for you. The carrion will not feast on them."

The one with the wounded leg nodded, "Thank you lord for they were good men. I fear my days of war are gone. This wound is a bad one. Your man has saved my leg but not my livelihood." They turned and headed east.

My men collected the bodies. My archers took great delight in using the crossbows for kindling. As I led my men home the sky was filled with black smoke and the smell of burning flesh. War had returned to the valley of the Loir.

The attack acted as a spur. My men worked twice as hard. I sent more archers to Le Lude and they increased the workers there. I sent more men to help Sir Henry build his bastion and the rest of us rode abroad. We would discourage our foes by showing our vigilance. I did not ride forth every day. On the days I was not riding I helped James Broadsword to improve our defences even more and Roger of Meaux and his men to build the bridge. The warehouses on the south bank would soon be needed.

The summer was proving to be a kind one in terms of weather and the crops as well as the grape harvest promised to be good ones. I knew nothing of such things but Geoffrey, my steward did and it was he who kept me informed. As we did not pay taxes to the Duke of Brittany nor John Lackland, my townsfolk paid one tenth of their earnings to my steward. As I had farmers who worked fields for me it meant I was becoming rich. The surplus would not be needed yet but, as more men joined me, it would.

The bridge was completed at the end of August. It coincided with the return of the '**Swan of Stockton**'. Another fifteen men joined us. This time there were just three men at arms and the rest were archers. There was no letter but Captain Henry came ashore to speak with me. "The lady sent no letter. She did not have time. We barely got these men away from Stockton. I fear that the Bishop of Durham is colluding with the Sherriff of York. They began a move to clear the forests of what they termed brigands and bandits. The men you have now left families in the valley, lord. The lady wonders if there is room for them here."

"Of course there is, but is she safe?"

He hesitated. "At the moment lord."

"Then tell her that as soon as there is danger she should come here. I will protect her. She has done more than enough for us."

"I do not think that she will do that, lord, for she is the only hope for those in need who live within the old Cleveland. If she leaves they will be persecuted."

I nodded, "Then bring the families when next you return." I handed him a purse of coins. "Here is for your trouble."

"I do not need this lord."

Return of the Knight

"You serve me well and I ensure that my people are rewarded. Tell other captains that there is good trade to be had in my town. It is that trade which will keep us safe."

He nodded, "King John has subdued the men of Poitou lord but I heard that the Pope is unhappy with his actions."

I did not see how that would help me but I was glad that someone else opposed King John.

As September approached I took to riding further afield. I rode west until I discovered garrisoned castles and I rode east to Chateau-sur-le-Loir. One night I had a dream which disturbed me. I saw Prince Arthur. He was in a castle and he was weeping. I woke in a cold sweat. What did the dream mean? It seemed such a long time since I had seen him. I had not forgotten him but I had put him from my mind. I needed to have better intelligence about Le Mans. That was the nearest stronghold to my castle and when King John tired of my insolence he would come south to punish me.

I headed north with Fótr, Edward and Ridley the Giant. I wanted to get as close as I could to Le Mans. I did not know if King John had returned to England or his Norman stronghold. The best way to discover where he was would be to see if there were patrols from Le Mans. He had taken most of the garrison with him to Poitou and the north had been quiet all year.

Edward kept looking over his shoulder. "What is the matter Edward? We are just fifteen miles from our home, and we have passed no one."

"I know my lord, but I like it not when we have no archers with us. A war bow is very comforting, and our archers have noses like dogs. They can smell an enemy."

"I have no intention of fighting anyone this day, Edward. At the first sign of trouble we turn around and head home for we shall have discovered what we need."

We rode the old Roman road which was wide and straight. The ditches along the sides needed attention but the surface was still a good one. King Henry had understood that good roads meant horsemen could travel swiftly from one place to another. The straight roads meant that we saw the combat taking place half a mile ahead. We had crested the rise after we had heard the clash of steel.

Edward son of Edgar said, "This would be where we turned around and rode home then eh lord?"

I had spied a shield I recognised. It was the shield of the de Ferrers family: vairy or with gules stood out. One thing I had learned in the east was the name for the devices on the shields of knights. I did not know who the men were fighting but the enemy of my enemy was my friend. "Let us first send the men with the red and gold shields hence eh? Then we will go home."

Return of the Knight

We spurred our horses. We were so few in number that we would be neither seen nor noticed until it was too late. This was a mêlée. There were twenty or so horsemen involved. I saw that some were knights. Three men lay on the ground and there were four horses wandering forlornly in the nearby fields. I drew my sword and hefted my shield. I did not recognise the shields of the men who were fighting the de Ferrers. That meant nothing. Even if they were French I would fight alongside them for the de Ferrers were King John's favourites.

One of the knights with red and yellow shield saw us when we were thirty paces from them. I was recognised for I heard him shout, "It is The Gryphon!" I knew my enemies named me thus after my device. The knight and his squire rode at us and two men at arms disengaged to join them.

We rode towards each other, the knight and I, sword to sword. Novices often just try to block an enemy sword. A veteran tries to strike a blow. We were both veterans. He swung at my helmet and I swept my sword across his chest. My sword hit first. The effect was to slow down his strike. He hit my helmet but I barely felt it. Fótr had improved his skills with a sword and he lunged beneath the squire's outstretched sword. De Ferrers' squire's sword scraped off his helmet. Fótr's blade found flesh. It came away bloody and the squire dropped his own sword, jerked his head around and galloped off in the direction of Le Mans. As I had expected Edward and Ridley were too good for the men at arms. Both lay dying in ever widening pools of blood. The knight was hurt and seeing that he was isolated he followed his squire. We could have caught him but the beleaguered travellers were in danger of being overwhelmed.

We spurred our horses and I caught a knight squarely in the middle of his back. My sword ripped through surcoat, mail and gambeson. A long wound snaked down his back. He fell from his horse. Ridley wielded a long axe and he took the head of another man at arms. When Edward's sword came through the chest of a squire I heard a voice shout, "Enough! Back to the castle!"

I saw that the knight we had come to rescue had been knocked from his saddle. A squire and a young boy of no more than eleven summers stood ready to defend their lord's body. There were five men at arms left. They looked at the four of us. They had no idea whose side we were on.

One of them said, "I thank you, lord, for coming to our aid but I know you not and thus far Normandy has proved to be a nest of vipers." He spoke accented Norman. I guessed he was English.

I spoke in English, "I am Sir Thomas of La Flèche and my land begins just five miles hence. Who are you?"

The knight raised his head. He said weakly, "Then our quest is ended. We came to seek you out. I am Richard of East Harlsey and this is my son. Lady Ruth sent us. It has cost me five men but…" he fell unconscious.

132

Return of the Knight

"Edward, see to him. Ridley, Fótr, collect the horses, mail and weapons. Put Sir Richard's men on horses. We must leave quickly. Those men will return and this time they will have more horsemen."

I dismounted and went to Edward. The knight's squire and son looked concerned. "Do not worry, Edward has been tending to men's wounds for many years. How is he?"

Edward did not look up. "He has a wound to his arm and to his leg. He will need stitching but here is not the place." He looked up at the knight's son. "What is your name?"

"Dick."

"Well you can be your father's healer. His leg is not serious but his arm is. See how I have tied this cord around his upper arm?" The boy nodded. "It will stop the bleeding but you need to release the cord and then tighten it every half a mile. Your squire can lead your father's horse and you can ride behind him. Can you do that?"

"Will he live?"

Edward grinned and ruffled the boy's hair, "Of course he will. I have my reputation to consider."

The hard part was lifting the unconscious knight onto his horse. Dick was small enough to sit on the cantle and keep his father upright.

I mounted. "You five watch our rear and bring the horses. Edward, Ridley take the van. Fótr you and I will ride on either side of Sir Richard."

I was desperate to hear their story but it was not fair on the boy nor the squire to ask yet. Sir Richard was the one who would know all. We had left the dead men where they lay. Two knights had been killed. When we had taken their helmets, I had seen that they were young knights. Sir Richard had slain one and his squire the other. King John might have left us alone before now but he would not ignore this latest slight. My ride to the north might be costlier than I thought.

I examined the knight, his son and his squire as we rode. The knight and squire both had good mail but it was not well cared for. I saw that many of the links had been damaged and there was evidence of rust. The journey from England was a long one. It was also expensive. Their horses were thinner than they should have been. It was no wonder the fight had been so one-sided. A weak horse is not the platform to fight overwhelming numbers.

We reached my castle after dark. Had we been pursued we would have been caught. The horses of our new companions were too weak to travel faster than a walk. Sir Richard woke halfway along the road and that made our life easier, still too weak to answer questions coherently, I left that for the safety of my castle.

133

Chapter 13

Father Michel whisked Sir Richard off to his cell to stitch him. His squire and son accompanied him. The five men at arms went with my men to the warrior hall.

"Is this the knight your aunt spoke of?" Concern was written all over my wife's face.

I nodded, "I am guessing so for the numbers fit that which I was told."

"It was lucky that you rode north today. Had you not…"

"I know. It was the dream which made me go there."

"I will go and see cook. She will have made plenty but the three of them look as though they need fattening up."

I went to the flagon of wine and poured myself a healthy goblet. It was the red wine made by Albert Grenville. If I wished to drink white wine it would be Roger of Meaux but, in truth, I preferred the heavy wine made by Albert. One of the servants, Henri, brought in a platter with bread, cheese and strips of ham.

"Thank you, Henri. Better bring in another four goblets. And I think that they will need some water for them to wash."

"Yes, my lord."

Fótr returned at the same time as Henri, "Are the horses being tended to?"

"Yes lord. They have been given grain. Sir Richard will not be able to ride that horse for a month at least. I know not how they have survived this long."

"It has been a hard journey and that is no mistake."

Just then Dick and Ralph, Sir Richard's squire returned, "The priest said we were in the way, lord. He sent us away."

I smiled, "He prefers to work alone. He knows his business and your father is in safe hands. Wash and then help yourself to bread, ham and cheese. Fótr, pour our guests some wine."

Ralph, the squire, said, after Henri had dried his hands for him, "We never thanked you properly, my lord, but I know that had you not arrived when you did then we would have been dead men."

"God guided my horse this day. Come and sit. This is good wine."

Dick said, "We only drink ale, lord."

I laughed, "That was in England. Now you are in wine country. Drink it for it will make you feel better." He drank and I saw his eyes widen. "How old are you, Dick?"

"I have seen ten summers."

"You look older."

"Yes, lord. I am big for my age."

Return of the Knight

As much as I wanted to know their story it would not be right to question them without their father. "And you Ralph, how long have you been a squire?"

"I have seen seventeen summers, lord, and I have served my uncle for the last six years."

"And where is your father?"

"When King John was King Richard's regent he had my father arrested for treason. It was a lie. I was with Sir Richard then and I could do nothing to save my father. It is a regret I will take to my grave. My father was loyal to King Richard but England is now a country without laws and without justice. He was executed and his lands taken from my family."

Without hearing the rest of the story, I now began to understand why Sir Richard had sought me out. Dick and Ralph drank in silence. My questions had reminded them of their past. Ralph ended the silence. "This is a fine castle lord. When we did not enter the keep directly I wondered. It seems so inconvenient but now I see that you have made it a safer place to defend."

Fótr nodded, "Sir Thomas has made many improvements since we first came. We managed to survive a siege!"

That initiated an animated conversation between the three of them. I just sat back and listened. Fótr had missed Johann and Richard. Since the other two squires had left my castle he had been lonely. This was good.

My wife returned. Dick and Ralph stood and bowed, "Do not stand on my account but I can see that you have both been well brought up. Your mothers would be proud of you."

Ralph looked at Dick, "Our mothers are dead, my lady. Mine died of a broken heart when my father was executed and my aunt died of the coughing sickness three years since. We have missed them."

My wife had a kind heart and she walked over to the two of them and wrapped her arms around them, "While you are here I shall be as an aunt to you. I can never replace your mothers but there are times when young men need a woman to speak to. Is that not right, Sir Thomas?"

She was clever. I smiled, "It is and I know that better than any for it was my aunt who sent you here to me."

Father Michel came in helping Sir Richard. His arm was in a sling. His son ran to him but Sir Richard waved him away, "I have a slight wound to my leg. It will not incapacitate me!"

Father Michel shook his head, "My lord this knight needs bed rest. I have stitched his arm. If he exerts himself then he might burst the stitches."

I nodded, "Sir Richard, while you are my guest you will heed the advice of my physician. Sit and have a goblet of wine."

He looked at me and frowned. Then he smiled, "Forgive me my lord. I am not used to suffering wounds. It annoys me. I apologise, my lady. I am not normally this boorish but we have had a hard journey to reach here and it has cost me five men." He looked around, "Where are my men?"

"Peace Sir Richard. They are in the warrior hall and they are being tended to. They will eat well and drink well. They will sleep and they will begin to recover." Seeing that he now had wine, I raised my goblet, "Prince Arthur and death to King John!"

"Prince Arthur and death to King John!"

After he had emptied the goblet he said, "I think I have found the right place, lord."

Henri came in, "My lord, we are ready with the food."

"Then bring it in. Come, Sir Richard, you shall sit between my wife and I. Lady Marguerite will sit between your son and squire. Tonight, we will make life as pleasant as possible."

We did not speak at first for the three of them fell upon the food as only men who have been on short rations can do. When he did speak Sir Richard apologised to my wife. "I am sorry we are so silent, Lady Margaret. The food is most welcome and has taken away my manners. I cannot remember the last time we ate so well."

"Do not apologise, Sir Richard, I take it as a compliment. I remember when we had hard times in the Baltic. It is good to see your son and squire with such healthy appetites. There will be time for talking when you are replete."

The wine helped and when the empty platters were cleared away I said, "And now, Sir Richard, your story for I am intrigued. My aunt said that you lost your lands when you objected to the Sherriff. That seems harsh."

He gave a rueful smile, "Objected might be the wrong word." He leaned back. "After my wife died, I concentrated on my manor and the people who lived there. I let the world go by and I ignored the wrongs that were done by King John. He was Prince John then. My brother's unwarranted death made me leave the comfort of my home and I decided to take on the injustice that lay close to home. The Sherriff of York was another of John's cronies. When he demolished the homes of twenty families to build a new tax house and left them with no means to support themselves it was too much."

"You objected."

"As I said, it was slightly more than that. I rode into his guild hall with my horse whip and I whipped him. Four of his men tried to stop me and I slew them. I was declared outlaw. It was the last straw but I was foolish. I let my temper get the better of me. We fled north. I had heard that the lord of the manor in Stockton still provided justice. That was where I met your aunt and she told me of this place. The Sherriff's men were on my trail and I could not put her in jeopardy. We slipped south across the river and headed through the moors. I knew that the monks of Meaux Abbey used ships to transport their wool to France and the Low Countries. I knew the Abbot. He was the brother of my brother's wife. He gave us passage to Bruggas. We then made our way through Flanders and France. As soon as we reached Normandy we found danger. Someone recognised my livery and we were attacked north of Rouen. I lost two men in that fight. We fled south. I did not know the land and when we reached Le Mans we were found again. We tried to outrun our enemies but our horses were spent. We did not rest them enough after the sea voyage and they have had short rations."

"Fear not, your beasts are being cared for."

"I have much to thank you for."

"Now you are here, what would you?"

"I would serve you, Sir Thomas."

"Yet you are much older than I am. Is that possible?"

"I may have seen more years but that does not mean I have more experience. I have fought the Scots when they raided and I have kept my men well trained. You are the hero of Arsuf. You fought in the Baltic Crusade. I would serve you, if you would have me."

"Of course. I now lead three knights. When first I came here I was alone. Now I am in the company of honourable knights."

As Sir William and Sir Henry were in their own halls there was room enough for the three new guests. I insisted that Sir Richard remained in the keep until Father Michel was happy with his recovery and I took his son and squire to visit with his men at arms and horses. When they reported back that all was well Sir Richard was able to relax a little more and obey orders. Leaving the three of them in my keep I took a strong patrol north. I led forty men. I could not believe that the death of de Ferrers' men had not resulted in pursuit. That could only mean one thing, they intended to punish me and my town.

Having archers who could ride faster and further than mailed men I was able to send our scouts to discover where the enemy lay. My archers knew how to hide and they met with us fifteen miles from my castle. "Lord, there is a large conroi heading down the road. Half are mounted men and we counted the banners of twenty knights."

"Any archers? Crossbows?"

"They have twenty crossbows, lord."

"Any war machines or baggage?"

"No, lord."

"Then this is a chevauchée. They mean to punish me by taking from my people."

We were still in my land and I knew of a site which was perfect to meet them. The road rose steadily towards a wood. Although the trees were well back from the road they afforded shelter for my archers. We headed for it and my archers dismounted and spread themselves in the woods.

Return of the Knight

Edward said, "Should we send back for more men, lord?"

"No, we hurt them and send them back to Le Mans. It will not end the threat but it will give us more time to finish Le Lude and the bastion. It will allow my people to gather their crops and make their wine. We wait and let them attack us."

"Aye my lord."

We dismounted too. The horses grazed on the grass which lay close to the road. Then we spied the approaching banners. They would see us too. I saw the banners stop. I could not make out individual banners and I do not think they would be able to identify ours. The fact that there was just one banner would give them confidence.

They began to move again and we mounted. I kept my helmet by my saddle. I would don it at the last minute. I turned in my saddle. "Two lines of ten. Fótr, unfurl my banner and keep it flying. Signal as though you are summoning other riders."

My men laughed at the ruse. None of us had lances or spears. I could see, as the knights approached us that they did. However, they would have to attack uphill. Surprisingly they stopped just four hundred paces from us. I wondered if they knew that I had archers waiting in the woods. Two of their knights took off their helmets and rode towards us with their palms uppermost.

"They want to talk. Edward, come with me."

I nudged Skuld forward. I saw that the two knights both bore the de Ferrers' livery. Both were my age and they had similar features. We stopped. The elder of the two spoke, "I am Henry de Ferrers and this is my cousin Richard. You are Sir Thomas of La Flèche?" I nodded, saying nothing. Yesterday you slew our cousin also called Henry."

"I saved a knight who was being attacked yesterday. I know not the name of the man I slew but he had a gold and red shield." I waited. What was this truce's purpose?

"You struck him in the back and that is dishonourable."

I suddenly realised that this knight was angry. I took a stab in the dark. "You were the knight I struck. It was your squire Fótr killed. You fled the field and you feel guilty because your cousin died."

The other knight, Richard de Ferrers, spoke. "It was my squire who died and it was I who left the field. I would have satisfaction."

"You would have what?"

"A combat to the death. You were lucky yesterday. God will judge your actions. He will guide my arm and you will die."

Edward laughed, "Lord, the man is a fool. Let us ride back up the hill and let them bleed upon it."

138

Return of the Knight

Henry de Ferrers turned and pointed at Edward, "I do not speak with commoners. If Sir Thomas is base enough to mix with curs like you then that is his business. Be silent."

Edward gave him a cold smile. He was a very dangerous man. "My lord, I will remember this insult and I tell you this. Your family will have no need of ransom for you will die at my hands."

I knew that Edward meant it but the knight did not. He continued, "Well, Sir Thomas, what say you to my cousin's offer?"

"Here?" They nodded. "Then it will be with swords for I brought no lance."

"So be it."

I turned Skuld and headed back up the hill. "You have no need to do this, my lord. Our archers will slaughter them."

"I am a knight, Edward, and I have no choice. The man is good. I saw that yesterday. I will have to be better."

My men had no idea what had been said. Edward explained it to them. "His lordship is going to have a combat to the death."

I lifted my helmet, "And no matter what the outcome they will attack us so be ready."

I drew my sword and pulled up my shield. I turned Skuld and began to walk down the slope. I had no intention of charging him. I wanted the control of my horse and the advantage of height. Would he strike at my helmet as he had done the previous day or would he try to trick me? I saw him spur his horse. It was a war horse and was bigger than Skuld. Skuld was nimbler. I reined back. When I spurred Skuld I wanted him to move like quicksilver. Richard de Ferrers was eager to atone for his mistake and he spurred his horse. The slope was not steep but the war horse was exerting itself. It was an unnecessary waste of energy and effort. I saw him raise his sword and move it to the side when he was ten paces from me. He was coming at my sword side. I suddenly spurred Skuld and he leapt forward. I pulled the reins to the right. We would be shield to shield. I had taken him by surprise. He tried to do two things at once. He attempted to pull his labouring horse's head around and to swing his sword across his horse's head. He managed the latter but I had expected that and my shield was ready. I stood in my stirrups and brought my sword over and struck him on the helmet. He attempted to bring his shield up but his left hand had been jerking his horse around and he failed to block the blow.

I allowed Skuld to continue to turn around the rear of the warhorse. He could see that he would never match the turn and so he forced his horse's head to the right. I swung my sword above his horse's ears. I swung my sword again. Richard de Ferrers had just managed to reverse his own sword but the block had little power and my sword hit him in the middle. I could see that there was a trickle of blood coming from beneath his helmet. My first blow had wounded him.

Return of the Knight

"Yield, Sir Richard, you are wounded."

"To the death!"

Our horses were stationary. This would be a battle won by the one with the quickest reactions. My blow to his head had dulled him. My strike to his stomach had winded him. I stood in my stirrups and brought my shield across my middle. As he tried to do the same I used the pommel of my sword to hit him in the helmet. His head jerked back and I punched with my shield. He tumbled from the saddle. As his body rolled over its rump the horse bolted and passed me. My men cheered but the knight lay still. I took off my helmet. That was a sign that, for me, the combat was over.

Sir Henry galloped up and threw himself from his saddle. He took off his cousin's helmet. I could see that I had dented his head with my first blow and there was a great deal of blood. Sir Henry raised his head and said, "He is dead! He died at the hands of a priest killer!" Turning he shouted, "Charge! No quarter!"

I had been expecting that. I galloped, not back but down the hill. I took my right foot from my stirrup and kicked him hard in the face. He fell in a heap. Picking up their leader would delay their attack. Turning Skuld I rode back up the slope. I heard Edward shout, "Form line!"

When I reached my men, I turned Skuld into the gap they left for me. I heard Fótr say, behind me, "The knight's war horse decided to join us, my lord. He is grazing just behind us."

Sir Henry had been helped to his feet. His men, however, had continued to charge up the hill towards us. There were forty jostling horsemen. If we had had time I would have dismounted. We did not have that precious luxury. Suddenly arrows flew from our flanks as our hidden archers sent arrows at less than forty paces range. With the arrows we used there was no armour yet made which would stop them. David of Wales and my men targeted the ones at the front. Inevitably some horses were hit. That drove others into the ditches. They were not as deep as when they had been built but they were still an obstacle. I saw one horse break a leg as it fell and throw its knight to the ground. It was chaos.

The arrows flew constantly and the barrier of bodies grew. Although each arrow hit either man or horse they were not all killing strikes. Wounded horses thrashed and kicked out blindly before galloping down the hill through the advancing men who were on foot. The men who fell staggered to safety too. A voice shouted, "Dismount and fight on foot!" It was not Henry de Ferrers. Someone else had taken charge.

A line of knights and men at arms formed a shield wall and began to advance the last thirty paces. They had to climb over bodies to do so. Arrows thinned their ranks. It was the time for boldness and for us to use the advantage of height and horse.

Return of the Knight

"Charge!" I spurred Skuld. My command gave me a slight lead over my men and I brought my sword from behind me and over my head. The man at arms lifted his shield to protect himself from Skuld's snapping jaws and did not see the strike which descended upon his helmet. I reined in Skuld. There was no point in riding to the pile of bodies. We had to hurt the men before us. We had to make them fear advancing. A spear was thrust up at me. I blocked the blow with my shield and then Ridley the Giant brought his axe to hack through the shoulder of the man at arms. David and his archers concentrated their arrows on the men clambering over the dead animals and men. When the knight who was leading the attack was felled by Edward the rest took to their heels.

"Back to the rise."

I saw that three of my men had been wounded. This could not last much longer. I turned Skuld when I reached the top of the rise and surveyed the scene below me. Whatever had been planned by the de Ferrer family would not now happen. We were too few to hold the field. I shouted, "David of Wales. It is time to fall back!"

A Welsh voice shouted. "We will follow, lord."

As we turned Edward said, "I am betting they would have had full purses lord."

"You may be right but this day we will content ourselves with our lives and a warhorse. We have the answer I sought. There are forces in Le Mans who wish us harm. We have not stopped them but they will be discouraged. We have bought ourselves a little time." We reached home safely. They were not foolish enough to follow us to the Gryphon's den.

The bridge across the river was completed as the leaves began to fall. Sir Richard recovered and I took him on a tour of my tiny island of freedom. I was surprised and pleased with the efforts made by Sir William at Le Lude. His wife and family would be able to move in by Christmas. I knew that Lady Marguerite wished their second child to be born in their new home. The keep was complete but the living quarters needed work and the fighting platform was incomplete. Sir William was putting embrasures in place.

As William took Sir Richard and myself around his defences I saw Jean of Le Lude. He hurried over to us and knuckled his forehead. "I came to thank you, Sir Thomas. We are now prosperous once more. Our fields are fertilised by your men's horses and the walls of the castle are reassuring. This will be a good Christmas."

Sir Richard said, "You pay no taxes?"

I smiled, "William des Roches had not asked for any. Perhaps he fears my answer."

Sir William said, "I think that the seneschal is an honourable man, my lord. I have seen little evidence of a treacherous or vindictive nature."

Return of the Knight

"I think you are right and therein lies my hope for Prince Arthur. So long as William des Roches remains as seneschal then Prince Arthur will be safe."

"And when John returns to England, what then, Sir Thomas?"

"I looked at Sir Richard. "I am not certain what you mean."

"Will Prince Arthur go with him? If the young Duke has tied himself to his uncle will his uncle let him out of his sight? When I was in England there was talk of the Prince and his sister, Eleanor being the only hope against John's tyranny. I cannot believe that King John will let them be free."

I had not thought of that. "And if Prince Arthur does return to England with his uncle then that will truly end all opposition to John here in Anjou and Brittany." As we rode back to my castle I had much to ponder.

The autumn rains were welcome if only because it meant that there would be little likelihood of an attack from either the French or the men of Le Mans. It also completed our moats. Although the two gatehouses and barbicans still needed finishing they were a deterrent to an enemy. They were manned by men who could raise the bridges in case of attack and our town would be protected.

On the south side of the river Sir Henry had not been idle. He had completed his bastion and he had taken it upon himself to dig a moat around the southern settlement. Backed by a palisade it would deter an attacker. Since his arrival he had grown in stature. His story was similar to Sir Richard and the two of them had friends in common. Dick spent a great deal of his time in the bastion. He got on well with Henry's squire. My wife was pleased for the sadness we had seen in the knight's son when he first arrived had gone. It was replaced by something else, hope.

Captain Henry had not returned for some time but another English ship, from Bristol, did call to buy some wine. It was from Captain Jack that we had confirmation of King John's marriage to Isabella of Angoulême. At the time we dismissed it as being unimportant. Later we learned that it was like a stone being thrown into a pond. Once begun the ripples would not stop.

Lady Marguerite gave birth to a daughter, Matilda. It was a time of great joy. As my wife said, "It seems that God has given us a present this Christmas." She was right and there was much joy in my castle as we all came together to celebrate the winter feast.

My son was now able to take more in. He could sit without support and crawled so well that the servants spent more time trying to stop him from hurting himself than actually serving us. When I could I carried him with me and walked my walls with him. I chattered to him, like a magpie. My wife smiled for I used the same words I would use when talking to another knight. I was not sure how much he understood but it made me feel closer to him.

One cold December morning I stood on the wall walk of my keep. I held my son in my arms. He was swaddled against the cold wind and I had my cloak around him. "One day, Alfred, you will be master here. You will command the men of my castle. I hope that you will fight, alongside me, against King John to restore the fortunes of the rightful heir to the throne, Prince Arthur. I cannot promise you that it will be an easy fight but it is the right fight."

A quiet voice behind me said, "I reckon, lord, that young Master Alfred will be looking out from the walls of Stockton castle."

I turned, "Perhaps Edward but at the moment we cannot even evict John from these lands. How will we do so in England?"

My Sergeant at Arms came a little closer. "We have an interesting mix in the warrior hall now, lord. The new men who came with Sir Richard and the others tell us of England. It is not just the common men who are sick of King John's rule. The barons are too. Just as the King has taken away the ordinary man's rights so the barons have lost their rights. And this King plays favourites." He shook his head, "That is never the way to rule. That is why men serve you, lord. You are fair." He pointed to the bastion across the river. "Sir Henry came here with nothing and now he is master of a hall. The men you offer a home to all know that you share. That is rare. King John is a bad king. It is as simple as that."

I saw that my son was listening to Edward's words. He was taking it all in. He was also looking a little paler and I took him back into the relative warmth of the castle.

La Flèche

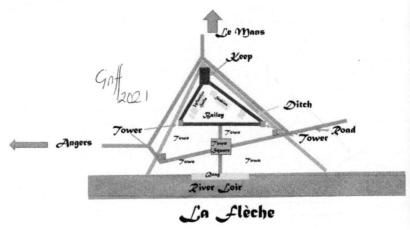

La Flèche

French Raids

Chapter 14

Our defences were ready by the middle of February which also coincided with the *'Swan of Stockton'* docking. There was no letter and no men with her. Captain Henry told me that he had had to avoid both Stockton and Herterpol for the Bishop of Durham had learned of his connection to me.

"I am sorry, lord, but I am barred from those ports. I have asked other captains to visit Stockton but the lady, well, she is cautious. She will not risk lives trusting someone who may be false. We will have to make other arrangements to bring the families of the last men I brought."

"You have served me well, Captain Henry. If, on your travels, you discover others who tire of John then bring them here. I will make it worth your while."

"I do have news though, lord. Prince Arthur has fled the court of King John."

The bad news Captain Henry had delivered was now replaced by joy. "He is back in Brittany?"

"No Sir Thomas, he has fled to the court of King Philip. It is rumoured that he is betrothed to King Philip's six-year-old daughter, Marie of France."

My spirits had soared, briefly and now they plummeted. If he was tied to King Philip then his lands would become French. King Philip was greedy and grasping. He was like King John but he was French. That was worse!

I summoned my knights to a meeting at my castle to tell them the news. It coincided with the completion of the living quarters at Le Lude. It meant that Sir William could take his family home. Matilda was a healthy child and could be moved without fear. There was no priest at Le Lude. Marguerite had asked Father Michel to find a priest for the manor. He had not been hopeful, "The Bishop does not approve of Sir Thomas, my lady. I am barely tolerated. It is only that I am old that I am allowed to continue as priest. I will do my best."

I told them all my news. Surprisingly they did not look concerned. Sir Richard asked, "What does it mean for us, Sir Thomas? I can see that it is unfortunate that the Prince has made such an unfortunate decision but we carry on the fight against King John do we not?"

"Of course, but it now means that William des Roches is freed from his obligation to watch over the Prince. He is a capable commander. If he chose to fight against us then we would be hard pressed to defeat him. We have suffered no attacks from the south. If William des Roches closed the river at Angers we could be starved into surrender."

Fótr asked, "But would he do that, lord? He could have done so before."

"Until recently Arthur was with King John. Now the Duke of Brittany is with the King of France. It changes everything. We will now need to keep a close watch on the south too." I looked to Sir Henry. "Your ditch may need to become a moat and you might have to build a wall."

The young knight did not seem put out at all. He rubbed his hands together, "Excellent. My men and I enjoy a challenge. Fear not, Sir Thomas, an enemy would struggle to pass my bastion!"

Sir Richard laughed, "By St George but we are a merry crew. There are but four of us and yet we are all lion hearts!"

I had gathered them to give them bad news and yet they took it as good news. Four days after Sir William had departed we had more news. An English ship docked. She was the *'Bronnen'* out of Bristol. I was summoned by the sentry from the river gate, Richard Red Leg. "I am sorry to disturb you, lord but the captain would speak with you. I did not recognise him." I looked towards the quay. There was a small cog tied up.

I remembered that Captain Henry had said he would ask other ships to call. I nodded to Richard, "You did right. I will speak with him. Return to the wall. Keep watch."

"Aye lord!"

The captain was a squat man and when he spoke I detected a west country accent. "You are Sir Thomas, my lord?"

"I am."

He took out a letter. It was sealed with red wax. I knew who it was from. He handed it over. I was going to take it and read it later but the captain said, "Lord, if you would read it now."

You know who you are and I hope you know that I think of you every day! Each night you are in my prayers.

I must warn you that the land is worse now than ever before. There are spies who watch everything. Poor Captain Henry barely escaped with his ship when last he called. I fear he will not call again. Captain Will seems like a man who is willing to help. He told my lady that he would help but it would be at a price. I did not meet him but one of my ladies did. He docked at Herterpol. I asked him to pick up the latest volunteers from the sands where the seals bask. He did so but he asked for forty gold pieces. We have not such an amount. He is expecting you to pay that amount.

I am uncertain when I will be able to write to you again. I will send a letter whenever I can, if only to let you know that we are alive and still enjoy our freedom.

We pray for you and your family each day. Our home is your home and always will be.

Xxx

"Who gave you this letter?"

"A woman, lord. If you have read it then you know that I am due payment."

I nodded. "I will give you your payment, Captain Will, but I do not like such demands being made."

He shrugged, "Then do not pay me and I shall sail to Angers with my cargo and deliver them to the Seneschal there. Perhaps he will reward me."

I began to become angry. "You think to come to my town and to make threats against me?" I waved my hand around me. "You are surrounded by my men. If I so chose then I could impound your ship and take the cargo."

For the first time he looked fearful. "But you are alone! I could cast off and set sail!"

I raised my hand and shouted, "Richard Red Leg!" Four bows appeared over the gate and they were all aimed at the captain. "In my town I am never alone." He was chastened and so I softened my tone. "We have got off on the wrong foot. There is great profit for you here."

"How so?"

"If you bring more cargo such as you have in your hold then I will reward you on each visit. Secondly there are no port taxes here and we make wine. I am certain that you could sell our wine and make a much greater profit than forty gold pieces. What say you?"

"You will pay me for this cargo?"

"I will but it will not be forty gold pieces. That is not the price for cargo. That is extortion."

He nodded, "Whatever you think is fair."

Richard Red Leg had joined me, "Richard you can stand down the archers and then ask Fótr to bring my purse."

"Yes lord." He glared at Captain Will, "And you, my friend, came within a whisker of dying. You are lucky!"

The captain said as Richard departed, "I took a great risk in picking up those men. The Bishop of Durham has forbidden all captains who use his port from trading with you."

I nodded. "And what of Hwitebi, could you not use that port?"

"It is small but I suppose we could."

"Then I will try to arrange something. The cargo?"

He nodded and shouted, "Guthrum!" A mountain of a sailor nodded and opened a hatch. Men's heads appeared, blinking against the light.

"Have they been kept below decks all this time?"

"Just since we passed Nantes, lord. I did not wish them to be seen."

I shook my head. I could see how lucky I had been to have Captain Henry. I said to the men, "Welcome to my town. If you would go ashore we will make you welcome. More welcome than on this vessel at any rate."

Fótr arrived and handed me the purse just as the last of the men had walked, somewhat unsteadily down the gangplank. "See to those men. They need food and drink. Speak with them."

"Aye lord."

I handed over ten gold pieces to the captain. "If you speak with any of the merchants there they will sell you cargo. Our wine is highly prized."

I left the ship. I was not sure that I wished to do business with the man but I had to tie him to me so that he would not inform on my aunt to the Bishop of Durham. If she was already under suspicion then the captain's testimony might be her death warrant.

When Fótr returned to the hall he brought disturbing news. "Sir Thomas, they are not men at arms who have been sent. They are young men whose families have been imprisoned or killed. They were all outlaws."

"They have skills in weapons?"

"I am not certain. Only two have short swords. The rest have daggers. I think two said that they could use a bow. I asked Edward, James and David to speak with them. They had a hard voyage. I do not think the captain treated them well."

Then things were getting worse in England. I went to my hall and wrote a letter for my aunt. I would have to give it to Captain Henry the next time he called. If Hwitebi was safe then that would be the port we used from now on. By the time I had finished Edward and James Broadsword had finished interviewing the men and he and David of Wales presented themselves.

"They are raw clay, my lord. None can ride. They have no training as warriors. A few can use a bow but what they do have is a hatred for King John and a desire to fight back. We will train them. They are all young. None has seen more than twenty summers. One is little older than Sir Richard's son, Dick."

I nodded, "Good. I leave them in your hands then. I am uncertain when or indeed if we will receive more."

Our new extended patrols were wearing. We had four knights to lead them and I used Edward too but they took their toll on our horses. They were, however, worthwhile. As spring turned into summer we saw the usual signs of men preparing for raids. I had thought that Prince Arthur's position with King Philip might have resulted in less attacks on us but Chateau-sur-le-Loir began to fill up with banners and standards. They would come again and we would have to be ready for them. They knew about the signal fire and I expected a different tactic.

It was Griff Jameson who gave me the answer. He had been raised in the area and knew it well. "Sir Thomas, it is my belief that they will use the woods north of the bridge over the Loir to attack Le Lude. The woods have been much thinned and horses can get through. It would be just a thousand paces from the edge of the woods to the bridge."

I looked at David of Wales. He nodded, "I think that Griff is right, my lord. It would be simple enough to have twenty of my archers in the woods. We could hunt. The time would not be wasted. If they do not come we will have game to feed us."

"Even so you would be isolated if the French came in numbers."

"We would enter the castle and await you. As soon as we saw them one would ride to the castle and light the fire."

"Then do so. Choose the best twenty archers for the task."

I made sure that James Broadsword had enough men to defend the castle and the bastion. "Aye lord. I have enough. I have the older warriors and the twelve new lads are keen enough. I would not like to put them in the open field but behind a wall they could be effective."

All told we would have four knights and squires, eighty men at arms, sixty of whom were mounted, and sixty archers. It was many more than the last time de Senonche had attacked us and the French would be in for a shock. I decided I would use Dragon rather than Skuld. Dragon was a younger horse and if the French came they would do as they had done the last time, they would come on big warhorses. I now had three knights to lead and they would all be riding war horses. Three of my men at arms also had warhorses. Edward rode the one captured from de Ferrers. If we fought their horsemen, then it would be on a more even basis.

It was two years since the meeting at Le Goulet. I wondered if the Comte de Senonche had chosen that date deliberately. Whatever the reason, when I saw the smoke rising in the east I knew that they had come and we went to the stables to gather our horses and lead them to the square. My people knew that we were going to war and I saw the men gathering their arms and preparing to go to the fighting platforms. None thought that we would lose but if an attack was coming from the east then it paid to be prepared and be ready to defend against a second attack.

Once mounted we headed east. We did not use the same route we had before. I was gambling that Griff had been right and they were attacking over the bridge. It would make sense. The farms lay to the north of the river. If the French wished to hurt us they would attack there. My archers rode ahead of us. We had sixty mounted men. Sir William was at Le Lude already. I rode flanked by Sir Richard and Sir Henry. Neither knight had much experience of war and, as we rode, I told them how we would fight.

"We ride boot to boot. You two should stay by my side. Edward and Ridley the Giant will flank you two. You can rely on them. We only use our lances and spears for the initial attack. Even if your weapon remains whole discard it. Our aim is to break up their attack. Fótr carries the horn. If he sounds it twice and then continues to repeat the call you retreat."

"Will he not use the standard?"

"Sir Richard, he will be behind us. You will not see it."

When we were just two miles from the bridge Thomas son of Tom rode towards us. He had been with Griff and David, "Lord they are come in great numbers. We counted fifty banners. We have ambushed their scouts and slowed them down. David of Wales sent our horses into the castle. He said to tell you that they will fall back inside the castle." He looked up at the sun. "They will be inside by now, lord."

"Join the other archers. Remind Cedric Warbow that you guard our left flank."

As he rode off I said, "Fifty banners mean that they could have three or four hundred men. There will be fifty knights for us to fight. Do not worry about ransom. You survive and if that means killing then do so. This is no tourney."

The road passed very close to the river and we swept south towards the bridge. I saw the French. They were pouring from the woods. David and his archers were on the south bank of the river pouring arrows into the advancing French.

"Form line!"

We would charge in line. The line would be forty men wide. There would be a second rank of twenty men, including the squires. My archers had galloped off to the left and were preparing to rain death upon the French. They had horse holders. Cedric Warbow was no fool. If they were threatened they would mount and ford the river. Archers could do that. Mailed men could not.

The French horse had stopped. There was little point in advancing to the bridge until their crossbows and men on foot had taken it. The men who advanced towards the bridge were on foot and marched behind shields. My archers aimed at the legs of the men. Sir William's archers, inside the walls were adding their arrows to the storm of death. Inevitably the shielded snake crept closer to the bridge. There would come a point where they would cross and then David of Wales and my men would have to take shelter in the castle. There were too few of them to withstand an attack. Even as we hurried to their aid I saw Hamlin the Archer struck by a bolt. As the French gained the bridge I saw David of Wales wave his arm and they hurried to the safety of the castle. They had done all that I had asked and slowed down the attack.

The French knights and mounted men at arms were still filtering through the woods and then forming up. We were less than four hundred paces from them and my other archers, led by Cedric Warbow, were now in position and sending their arrows towards the French.

"We charge them! Keep together!"

It might have seemed like madness to Sir Richard. This was the first time he had gone to war with me but it was a risk worth taking. If we hit them while they were still forming up we could break the back of their attack. We could not defeat them; there were too many but we could hurt them so that they did not have enough men to take Le Lude. Until I had more men not losing would count as a victory.

I saw the French reacting to our attack. Their leader had a shield with a fleur de lys in the corner. He was related to King Philip. I saw the Comte de Senonche too. Would he fight? They saw how few men we had and the Comte waved his men forward. Thirty men on horses had emerged from the woods. There were another twenty men at arms on foot. It was a mistake for they were in no order at all.

I lowered my spear when I was just forty paces from them. I rode at the knight with the fleur de lys. He had a lance and he charged at me. He had courage. His horse wore a caparison. The knight was wealthy. I rested my spear on Dragon's neck. The French knight would strike first and I braced myself for the blow. Next to me Sir Henry would have no foe to fight for there was a gap. When we were twenty paces apart I pulled my spear back. I would slide it across my cantle. The wood would support my spear and I would have a cleaner strike. The French knight was aiming at my chest. As he punched, I leaned into my shield. The head of the lance shattered and it felt as though I had been kicked by a horse. I kept my saddle and lunged at his thigh. My spear head tore through his chausse and into his leg. It continued through to stab his horse. The head of the spear broke off pinning the leg to the horse. I let go of the broken spear and drew my sword. A knight was hurrying to the aid of the knight I had hurt. He tried to punch with his lance but I was able to avoid it for he did not have control over the weapon. I swung my sword across his unguarded middle. My blade was sharp and it came away streaked with blood.

A man at arms ran at me. He held a pole axe. The weapon could hurt me and my horse. Jerking the head of Dragon to the right I took the blow on my shield. The shield began to crack. I stood in my stirrups and hacked through the man's neck. We had done enough. I saw that more men were coming. I shouted, knowing that my squire would be behind me, "Fótr, sound fall back!" The horn sounded twice and then twice again. I pulled Dragon's head around and slashed with my sword. My blind swing hit the shield of a mounted man at arms and afforded me the time to retire.

I saw that my men had obeyed and were galloping towards Cedric Warbow and his archers. While we were fighting they were impotent. Now they could release with impunity. Their arrows soared over our heads. I heard cries as their arrows hit horses and men. I also saw empty saddles. Some men had fallen. I reined in next to Sir Henry. His spear was shattered, his sword was bloody and his helmet had a dent yet he was grinning. Sir Richard rode up and I saw that he too had a notched and bloody sword.

"Form line. Cedric Warbow, slaughter them." I took off my helmet. The cool air felt good.

"Aye lord!"

This was what my archers did best. Releasing from behind a line of horses their arrows would plunge down and decimate the French. They had the bridge but with a full garrison and nineteen extra archers they would have to suffer casualties to get any closer.

Sir Richard said, "We just wait?"

"Let our horses recover and allow our archers do what they do best: kill. If they threaten us we charge them again but I think they will look for a way out of this dilemma."

The Comte de Senonche had struck me, when I had met him, as a man best suited to politics and intrigue. Planning conspiracies and coups was more his forte than commanding on a battlefield. This was the third time I had fought him and I saw that he came to fight with one plan; when it went awry he was incapable of another. I had thwarted him twice before. I could read his mind. I had outwitted him and he could not see a way out of his predicament. I watched as he marshalled his remaining horsemen. He still had over eighty horsemen including thirty knights. He put them into a double line of forty men. He outnumbered us.

The French were slow to organize and I shouted, "We wait. Cedric, when they charge I want you to send as many arrows over our horses as you can."

"Aye lord."

"When they are fifty paces from us we charge. We stay boot to boot. We ride in one line. Squires, you will be our reserve."

I saw the relief on Sir Henry and Sir Richard's faces. Their squires were not yet ready to face mailed foes. We donned our helmets and my world narrowed to the slits through which I peered. Timing would be all. The French lumbered towards us. They would be hampered by the bodies of their dead. None lay before us. I intended to hit them as late as possible when our archers had weakened them.

I saw the effect of our arrows as horses fell. The caparisons the horses wore did not deflect the arrows which plunged down and through them. The missiles rarely killed the beasts but they maddened them. They bucked and reared. They turned to snap at the nearest man or horse in their fury at the pain. Knights and men at arms were struck. Few were killed but the arrows would incapacitate them. They had a very loose line. It was time. "Charge!"

Our horses would not be able to gallop but a wall of horseflesh would hit a line which was fragile at best. Cedric's archers sent their arrows towards the rear of the French. I swung my sword at a man at arms who had arrows in his shield and his shoulder. He tried to raise his shield but my sword bit through to the bone. His shield dropped and he pulled his reins around to flee. Sir Henry finished him off. The crack of our swords on the French mail and shields and the shouts and cries of the dying were deafening. I took a blow from a sword on my shield and Dragon's head whipped around to bite at the French horse. As the horse reared I lunged and my sword struck the man at arms under his arm. When I saw the tip emerge from his neck I ripped it out. He fell, dead. The French needed no trumpet or horn. The survivors turned and fled. I looked around. This time we had lost none.

We backed our horses back to our archers. I removed my helmet. We would wait once more but I was almost certain that the attack was over. The French knew how skilful my men were. As soon as darkness fell then the men on the bridge would be slaughtered by men at arms and archers who could use knives well. This time the horn did sound and the men on the bridge fell back. The retreat cost them another four men. They filtered back through the woods.

"Cedric, mount and follow them discreetly. Make sure they head back to Chateau-sur-le-Loir."

"Aye lord."

"Edward, strip the dead and recover the wounded."

We held the field and I would take that as a victory. More French had left than we had killed but we had hurt them. We had bought more time. As I looked around I saw that I had lost men at arms. They were hard to replace. We would bury our dead and improve our defences. We would find more men to walk our walls and to fight our enemies. Some day King Philip would bring his army to squash this gnat which irritated him but that was another day and would be another battle.

We stayed at Le Lude for the rest of the day and the night. We had much to do. We were about to burn the bodies when riders approached as the sun was setting. They were squires and they each led a horse. My archers had them covered with their bows but I did not sense any danger.

"What is it that you wish?"

The leading squire spoke. "Our lords died and we would take their bodies back for burial." He hesitated, "Their bodies have not been spoiled, lord, have they?"

153

"We are not savages. The wounds they bear were suffered in the battle. Take them. We will burn the bodies of the common men." I realised they were still waiting. "Was there something else?"

"The squires who fell?"

"Take those too but I fear you will not have enough horses with you for the dead."

They draped two bodies on each horse and it was a sad sight as they rode along the road with men and boys who had begun the day full of life and now lay dead. We made a pyre with the shields and bodies. As we crossed over the bridge to the castle the flames rising in the sky told the land to the north of us that we had laid down a marker. This was our land.

Chapter 15

Sir Henry and Sir Richard now had more riches. The mail and the coin carried by the dead more than compensated for the lack of ransom. My archers had recovered the animals they had hunted while waiting for the French. We would eat well. As we headed back to my home, the next day, there was cheerful banter amongst my men. We had mourned our dead when we had eaten; they would not be forgotten, no dead warrior was ever forgotten, but we would not dwell on their deaths. I still heard the sadness in the voice of the French squire who had come for his master's body. I prayed Fótr would never have to perform such a duty.

We had captured horses. Some had been left with Sir William. The rest were stabled. Sir Henry had built a stable at the bastion and we put the new mounts there. The spare weapons and mail were cleaned and stored in the cellar of my keep. When new men arrived, they could be fitted out as warriors.

Life settled back into a peaceful routine until July. We patrolled and we were vigilant. My married warriors enjoyed their families and my unmarried ones courted the young girls of the town. Life was normal. Despite being surrounded on all sides by our enemies, life went on much as it always had in this sleepy part of Anjou. In July that changed. Hamlin the Archer said, "Lord, a hooded man came to the town gate. He said he would speak with you. The sentry tried to persuade him to enter but he said he would not."

"And where is he now?"

There was an avenue of trees just two hundred paces from the west gate. They would not afford protectionto an attacker but they gave pleasant shade for those who liked to fish along the river in the summer. Hamlin pointed. I could see the horse and the rider.

"I will go and speak with him."

"My lord! He could be an assassin."

I smiled, "Hamlin, you will be in the gate tower will you not? He is one man and if he tries anything then you could slay him with your bow. However, I think if this was a killer he would pick a better place for an attack."

I was mailed and I had my sword. I was not worried but I was curious. The man wanted his identity hiding from me. The hooded man kept his hands in plain view. He was no killer. As I approached I saw that he had a good palfrey. This was no common man. I saw that his boots were made of fine leather. He wore spurs and the scabbard of his sword was well decorated. He waited until I was close before he stepped behind a tree and lowered his hood. It was Guy, the squire of William des Roches.

155

Return of the Knight

"My lord, I apologise for this but the Seneschal did not want it known that he was communicating with you. He has enemies who would bring him down."

The man was full of surprises and intrigue. "And what is it that he wishes?"

"He wishes to meet with you."

"Why?"

"There is a delicate task and only you can be trusted with it."

I looked into his face for any deception but I saw none. "I am the enemy of his master. The Seneschal has hundreds of knights and yet I am the one he needs. I am intrigued. Where is this meeting to take place, Angers?"

"No, lord, the Seneschal waits just five miles down the road in the woods to the north of Bazouges sur le Loir."

I knew then that this must be important for him to risk coming so close to my castle. While I debated what to do I noticed that Guy was better dressed. I pointed to his spurs, "You have been knighted?"

He smiled, "Aye lord, I was getting a little old to be a squire but his lordship had to send someone that you knew." He paused, "And, hopefully, someone you would believe."

I nodded, "Someone I would trust." He nodded. "Now that you are a knight I can ask you this; will I be safe when I meet with the Seneschal? Do you give your word?"

He nodded, "I swear my lord, on my life, that you will come to no harm from this meeting."

"Then wait here while I get my horse." I strode back to the gatehouse. I saw that Hamlin had summoned Sir Richard, Fótr, Edward, David of Wales and James Broadsword. I could not help but smile at their concern. "Fótr go and saddle Skuld and your horse. I want a plain cloak. We go in disguise. Edward, I need four men."

"Aye lord!" They both departed. The others looked at me expectantly. "The Seneschal wishes to meet with me. He is waiting in the woods north of Bazouges. David of Wales, I have been told I will be safe but just to make sure I am I wish you to take ten archers and ride to the woods. Stay hidden and watch. At the first sign of treachery…"

"Aye lord."

Sir Richard shook his head, "This seems an unnecessary danger and risk, Sir Thomas. What have you to gain from this meeting?"

"If I do not attend then I will never know, will I? Sometimes you have to take a risk Besides William des Roches seems to me to be the most honourable of John Lackland's men. He could have attacked us many times but he has chosen not to. I cannot see why he needs me for this task but I will go. It will be a pleasant ride by the river."

James Broadsword nodded, "I will have the garrison stand to, lord. If this is a trick to lure you from the castle then we will be ready."

156

Return of the Knight

James was right to be cautious. Sir Guy had said I would come to no harm. He had said nothing about my town. The six of us met Sir Guy and rode the road west through the woods and by the river. Bazouges sur le Loir was well known to me. My patrols often passed through it. There was no castle now. It had been destroyed during the time of the wars between Count Fulk and King Henry. Its people used my market. It had been in my mind to do as I had at Le Lude and build a castle there. It was a good site and would protect us from the west.

Edward had chosen Ridley, Robert and Henry Youngblood to come with us. They were the largest men in my retinue and all of them were proven killers. I saw the murderous looks Edward gave to Sir Guy as we rode. Until we were back in my castle their vigilance would not be relaxed.

William des Roches had also brought a handful of men with him. There were just five men at arms waiting in the woods. They were all dressed for hunting and I saw a deer being gutted. I felt more at ease. I dismounted and handed my reins to Fótr. "Out for a day's hunting my lord?"

"When we return to Angers there will be no suspicion. I take a great risk in riding here today."

"And yet you did."

He put an arm around my shoulder. I saw my men stiffen. I laughed, "Relax. We are going to talk in private. I am safe."

William smiled, "Your men are loyal. That speaks well of you." We sat on a felled tree. "First I will congratulate you on your defeat of the French. That was well done. Your attack on the de Ferrers retinue was less wise."

"They were attacking a knight and his men on the road. I was protecting them."

"The de Ferrers clan are a bad lot but the King favours them. You know that the King of France has summoned him to Paris to answer for his treatment of the Lusignans?"

"I did not. Will he go?"

The Seneschal laughed, "Of course not. Now that Prince Arthur is with the French King it is a trap."

"And why do you tell me?"

"Because, Sir Thomas, you are a clever man and you know that knowledge is power. I have come to ask you for a favour." I cocked an eye at him. "It is not for me. In fact, I am risking the King's anger by asking you to do this." I nodded for I was intrigued. "Prince Arthur's mother and sister, Eleanor, are at Seiches-sur le Loir. If King John knew where they were then he would take them as hostages. My honour dictates I cannot allow that. The only place where they will be safe is at Mirebeau with Queen Eleanor. Even King John would not risk taking them from her."

"And what would you have me do?"

"Escort them to Mirebeau."

"Are you mad? I would have to pass Tours and Chinon. It is almost eighty miles. It is impossible! Why me?"

He smiled, "A number of reasons. Firstly, you are loyal to Prince Arthur and you are the only hope for his mother and sister. Secondly, I cannot do it for it would be the end of my time as Seneschal and, as you know, I do not make war on you. My replacement might decide to eradicate the annoyance. Thirdly, Duchess Constance asked for you."

"She asked for me? The last time we spoke it was as though I was the dirt beneath her feet!"

"She has come to reassess her opinion, Sir Thomas. She trusts you. She trusts me too which is why she came to us."

I nodded. I could not refuse. When I had sworn to help Prince Arthur, that had included his whole family but it would be a hard journey filled with risks. "How many in the party are there?" I remembered when I had rescued my wife. She had not been the problem. Her ladies had been.

"There are four other ladies and six servants. They have horses and they can all ride. At the moment they are safe in the priory at Seiches-sur le Loir but there are many spies. It will not be long before someone discovers their identity and tells King John or, worse, the de Ferrers."

"And our journey? Where do we stay? If we stay at inns then we will be discovered before we have travelled seven leagues."

"There are two priories on the way. The ladies will be welcomed there. We have sent word to say that two ladies of high position may wish to visit and they should be prepared to have rooms made ready. The Empress Matilda endowed them both. They are beholden to her. They know that ladies who are related to Eleanor of Aquitaine will be arriving and that they need accommodation. You and your men will have to camp in the grounds. We gave them no names and we did not give them a day."

I turned, "I will be at Seiches-sur le Loir by dawn tomorrow. If I do this Seneschal, then you will owe me."

"Understood and I will repay you. I will not be at the priory. Sir Guy will be there. He will go with you and get you across the Loire."

"Does that put you in jeopardy, lord?"

"No for if it is discovered then I shall chastise my overzealous knight for taking the ladies to the dowager Queen. He is prepared for such a reprimand."

I clasped his arm. "Then I will see Sir Guy on the morrow." I turned and shouted, "David of Wales, we are safe!"

A voice from the forest made the Seneschal's party turn, "Aye lord."

I mounted my horse and we rode back to my castle. That was the game which William des Roches would be able to play. He could put any blame on his newly knighted man. I wondered why he was doing this. There had to be more to it but I could not fathom the reason. So long as it thwarted King John then I was happy. I already knew the boon I would ask in return. I said nothing on the journey back for I was making plans. I had to choose the men I would take. I could not take too many. I did not wish to attract attention. Nor did I want the quest to be known. I trusted my people but ships came and went and loose lips might jeopardise our chances. It was not just that we would have to get to Mirebeau, we would have to return too.

When we reached my hall, I sent for Sir Richard, David of Wales, James Broadsword, Fótr and Edward. My wife was about to leave us and I said, "I pray you stay for this may concern you too." Intrigued, she sat. "Firstly, what I say must go no further than this room." They nodded. I told them what we had been asked to do. With the exception of my wife their faces showed that they thought it a foolish idea.

My wife smiled and put her hand on mine, "You are a true knight, husband." She turned to the others, "It is dangerous, yes, but it is the right thing to do. You are the men who can do this."

I squeezed her hand. Her words had helped. "Edward, I need ten men to come with us. They must be experienced and good horsemen. Phillippe of Poitou and Michael of Anjou should be among them. Do not bring Ridley. If he is with us then they will know I am too. Those two know the land through which we will be travelling. David of Wales, I need ten archers. Griff, Tom and Harry should be among them. They also come from this land. Fótr you will be with me too. Sir Richard I leave you and James to watch my land. I want none to know I have gone. Wear my surcoat when you ride on patrol. It should be as though I am still here. If word gets to de Ferrers or the French then all of us will be in danger. We have to get back once we have delivered our charges. I intend to slip out well before dawn. We use plain cloaks."

Once they knew my mind they were happy and they left happier than when I had made the announcement. My wife said, "You will be careful, husband. You not only have Alfred but soon he will have a brother or sister."

"You are with child?"

"I think so but I was going to wait until I was certain."

I hugged her, "It is you who need to be careful. I am just going to escort some ladies."

She laughed, "And remember what happened the last time? You and your men barely escaped with your lives."

"That was Estonia. This is Poitou. It is less dangerous."

"For others, perhaps but you are a hated man." She shook her head, "And yet I cannot understand why you are viewed so. You do nothing for yourself and all is for others." She disengaged herself from me, "Now go. You have much to organise as do I."

Return of the Knight

I went to the stables. Edward was selecting the sumpters to carry our supplies, "Lord what about the ladies? We cannot camp."

"We will camp but they will be staying in priories. It is the journey back which I fear more. The priories may well be honoured to have such guests but they are loose lipped and will tell all once we have passed. We will keep our route home a secret from all. Make sure there are spare spears. Food is not an issue. We can go hungry for a couple of days if we have to but we will need grain for the horses."

We rose in the middle of the night. The guards at the two gates had been sworn to secrecy and we left silently, walking our horses. We did not mount until we were well clear of the walls and then we headed west. It was a quiet road to Seiches-sur le Loir. There were no gates or walls at Bazouges to hinder our passage. If the villagers thought anything of mounted men riding through their village, they were wise enough to stay indoors.

We heard the bells tolling at the priory as we approached. The nuns would be up early and at prayers. Sir Guy and his squire, Robert, awaited us at the gate.

"Are they ready?"

He nodded. "They joined the nuns at prayer. The servants have the horses ready."

"Good, I am anxious to ride. And the route?"

"We will avoid Tours. It is too close to the border with France and the garrison there are wary of strangers. I know the castellan at Saumur." He smiled, "He is my brother. If I am to be a traitor to King John it is best I keep it within the family."

I was pleased, when the ladies emerged, to see that they were dressed for riding. They were cloaked and booted. I would not have recognised Prince Arthur's mother. Her hood came over her face and the clothes were not the fine ones I had seen her with hitherto. His sister looked like the Prince. She was the elder and she was very pretty. I could see why she was named Eleanor, Fair Maid of Brittany.

As they emerged, I said, "Edward you are to ride with the Duchess. If danger threatens then take her reins and protect her. Fótr you do the same with the Lady Eleanor."

The Maid smiled, "I am a good rider, Sir Thomas."

"Good, that will make Fótr's job much easier but he will be like your shadow until we see the walls of Mirebeau."

The Duchess laughed, "You cannot argue with him, my child, he is a law unto himself, but we are in safe hands now."

We had sixteen miles until we reached the Loire. My river was a stream compared with the mighty Loire. The fortresses of Tours, Chinon and Saumur protected it. Sir Guy might get us across but getting back would be a different

160

matter. With my archers ahead with Sir Guy and his squire and my men at arms at the rear with the baggage I rode ahead of Edward and the Duchess and Fótr and Eleanor.

To make conversation I spoke with the Duchess. Edward would be uncomfortable with such a lady. "I was surprised at your son and his decision, my lady."

"As was I. He was ever headstrong. But he was right to fear John. That man is evil. I know that King Philip is greedy and grasping but he does what he does for his country and I admire that. King John does what he does for himself." We rode a little way in silence. "I was wrong about you, Sir Thomas. I knew you had slain the Bishop of Durham and I thought you, too, were evil and that it would be you who would lead my son astray. It was why I opposed you."

"And what changed your mind? I have not changed."

"I spoke with William des Roches and he told me why you acted as you did and how you had done penance with a crusade. When people began to flock to your castle for sanctuary I knew I had misjudged you. You were the only one to stand by my son. You tried to rescue him and put your own life at risk. I am sorry. We have been badly used by those from England. The Earl of Chester abducted me, you know, on the orders of John!"

"Will you be safe in Poitou?"

"It was either there or Rome and I could not see us managing that journey!"

We settled into an easy silence and I heard Fótr and Eleanor speaking. "You are not English then?"

"No, I am from Sweden. My family were slaughtered and Sir Thomas was kind enough to take me as his squire. I am sorry that my family are dead but I could not be happier with my lord and master. I have a good life."

"I envy you."

"You? But you are almost a queen!"

She laughed. It was a tinkling laugh, like a mountain stream bubbling over rocks. "I am a prize cow! A heifer!"

Her mother snapped, "Eleanor!"

"It is true, mother and you know it. King John would have me married off to a fat Flemish warrior if I stayed in Angers. He would have an alliance. You are lucky, Fótr, you have choices. I have none. Tell me more about your home in Sweden."

They chatted like two young people out for a pleasant ride rather than those who were fleeing for their lives. We made good time and we reached the mighty fortress of Saumur just an hour after the gates were opened. We arrived before they had begun the market. The presence of Sir Guy meant that we were allowed free passage across the bridges and the island. We were seen but were we identified? Sir Guy's brother could slow pursuit but there were other ways across the Loire. However, the most serious obstacle had been overcome.

Once we reached the southern bank of the Loire Sir Guy and his squire left us. "I will stay here at Saumur. If you come back this way I might be able to help you."

I nodded, "But you would prefer it if I found another way back which did not complicate life for you, your brother and the Seneschal."

He laughed, "You are a wise man, my lord. Go with God."

I had my archer scouts a little closer to us. Although there was plenty of daylight we could not afford to ride our horses into the ground. I was also concerned with the ladies. They were not used to thirty-mile rides. We rode for another three hours until we reached the Priory of the Order of St Therese. Although it was a nunnery they had male priests who tended the gardens and dealt with outsiders. Sir Guy had warned me.

Edward helped the Duchess from her horse. From the pained look on her face it had been some time since she had ridden as far. I heard her say to Edward as he helped her towards the gates, "Had we not been with you then you would have ridden further."

Edward smiled, "Aye, your ladyship but our backsides are more used to a saddle than yours!"

I shook my head, "Edward!"

"Sorry my lord."

The Duchess laughed, "It is refreshing to hear honesty. I am used to false sentiments and lies. Do not change man at arms. All the way here your eyes have never left me or my horse. Had danger come then you would have dealt with it."

I saw that Fótr, too, had kept a close watch on Eleanor. He helped her from the saddle and took her arm and led her to the gate.

David of Wales said, "We are making camp in the sheep meadow lord."

"Good. Duchess, we will need an early start on the morrow."

She grimaced, "Another day in the saddle!"

"Perhaps two but we will try to do it tomorrow. We can rest our horses at Mirebeau before we return north."

One of the priests, a lean older man with a cropped beard, said, "We cut some grass the other day, lord. We can have it fetched."

"Thank you. That is most kind."

He turned and shouted something. He was used to giving orders. Two servants rushed off to a large building at the bottom of the sheep meadow. Fótr returned, as did Edward. "Thank you both. That was well done. We covered more miles today than I expected. The rest will do the horses good."

Edward nodded, "The lady is tougher than she looks, lord."

As we sat around our camp fire and ate the food brought by the servants from the priory Fótr said, "It is unjust, lord. Lady Eleanor will be married off to someone she has never even seen. How can that be right?"

Return of the Knight

"Her brother is betrothed to a six-year girl. That is even worse is it not?"

David of Wales had finished his food and was lying looking up at the sun which was lowering in the west. "Master Fótr they move in different worlds to us. You are lucky to have Sir Thomas as a lord. I cannot see him marrying you off to anyone."

Fótr looked around at me, "Why would you do that lord?"

"Rest easy I would not but there are knights who try to arrange marriages for their knights and squires. One day you, like William will choose a wife. I hope you are as lucky as he. Sir Henry will need a wife too. When you have a wife then you have children and more knights. There is an order to this."

I took a walk around the priory as the sun set. It was partly to make myself acquainted with the place and also to check the security. We would have sentries watching and guards patrolling but until I had delivered my charges safely I would be wary. As I was nearing the main gate I saw the priest who had been so helpful. I made conversation.

"What do you do here brother?"

"I am not a brother, lord. I was a knight but after the Holy Land I tired of fighting. I became a priest who serves the ladies. I like the life. I came here seven nights' since. I was heading north but the nuns were kind enough to offer me a position. They thought I had skills I could use." He smiled, "The other priests are well meaning but you know yourself, lord that you need order in life."

"Were you a Templar or Hospitaller?"

He gave me a surprised look, "How did you know I was in either of them, lord?"

"Something about the way you carry yourself. And the two orders are priests both. Were you at Arsuf?"

"I was, lord, and I saw you there. You were young and you were brave. If you do not mind me saying so you were reckless."

"When we are young we are all a little reckless are we not?"

"Aye lord and I fear that your day tomorrow will be hard. The Priory to which you ride is twenty miles from here. The ladies all looked a little weary."

"They are. Good night. I am pleased that you have found peace."

I went back to our camp. It was a pleasant night to be sleeping out beneath the stars and I soon fell asleep. I was awoken in the middle of the night by Phillippe of Poitou, "Lord, one of the priests has taken a horse and ridden north. He laid out Michael with a cudgel!"

Even as I asked the question I knew the answer, "Which priest?"

"The one with the cropped beard who was so helpful."

I cursed myself. He had not answered my question. That had been deliberate. He had been a Templar and they were involved in a plot with King Philip! Whether I wanted it or not we would now have to do the journey in one.

Return of the Knight

We could not afford another night in a priory. I recalled his words, *'The Priory to which you ride is twenty miles from here'*. He knew where we were going. I did not go back to sleep. Instead I made sure that he had done nothing to harm the horses. Michael was recovering; he was being attended to by Edward. The blow had just laid him out. He was angry more than anything, "A bloody priest, lord!"

"A Templar."

"Templar?" I saw the surprise on his face.

"Aye. I should have known that something was wrong but I was taken in by his robes. I will not make that mistake a second time. Tomorrow we ride hard and we ride fast. Edward, you and Fótr must ensure that, no matter what happens to us, the two women get to Mirebeau."

"Aye lord."

"And David, have two of your archers ride half a mile behind us. They can warn us of any pursuit. The priest made one mistake. He told me that he knew we were staying at a second priory. That is where he will send men to catch us. We will ride hard."

I told the Duchess when she rose. She was angry and berated the Prioress. The poor woman quailed before the verbal assault. I said nothing to the Duchess of my plans while we were in the priory. I did not know if there were more agents. As soon as we were on the road. I told her.

"We ride as far as we can. We stop to rest the horses. I realise it will be hard for you, my lady, but it will be harder if you are caught. If we are attacked then Edward and Fótr will ensure you reach Mirebeau."

"And my ladies?"

"I cannot promise. I do not think our pursuers would harm them. They wish to capture you and to kill me."

"Who is it? The French? I saw Templars with King Philip."

"It could well be or they could be playing both sides. In my experience the Templars do not respect countries and kings; they are more concerned with their order."

As we headed south, I wondered at the happenstance of a Templar being at the Priory. Then I realised it was not. I had no doubt that another would have been at the second Priory. Word of the plan must have leaked out.

The day was filled with tension. I had thought the crossing of the Loire had been the biggest problem. Now I saw that it was not. Every village through which we passed now represented danger. We had already planned on skirting the castles but now we avoided anything with more than a dozen houses. It added to the journey. The horses my men and I rode were good horses. The ones ridden by the ladies and their servants were not. Only the Duchess and her daughter had horses that were as good as ours.

Return of the Knight

The only ones who appeared unconcerned were Fótr and Eleanor. They were of an age and they chattered to each other as though they were out for a pleasant ride in summer. I heard them laughing. Fótr had a fund of stories about the men at arms. He had a natural story telling ability. Perhaps that came from his Viking heritage.

The Duchess commented on it as we stopped to water the horses some fifteen miles from Mirebeau. We had made good time but if we had pushed the horses harder they might have broken. "Your young squire is just what my daughter needed. He is not trying to court her as the knights at court tried. He is just being friendly and making her laugh. She has had an upbringing which would not suit most girls. She has to put on a face and be polite to all. She has to listen to tedious old men trying to impress her and marry her off to some half-witted offspring. My decision to use you and your men was a wise one."

The second priory was off the main road and I merely glanced east as we passed it. If there was another Templar or agent there he would be disappointed. I knew that we would be hotly pursued. Their plan now became clear. The first Templar would find us and bring the French to the second priory. There we would be massacred and the ladies taken prisoner. Therein lay hope. They would ride down the road to the second priory and discover that we were not there.

At Angliers we entered a forest which would take us almost all the way to Mirebeau. We were within ten miles of our destination. I was not complacent. Danger could still strike. The horses and the women were tiring. When that happened mistakes could occur. One advantage of the forest was that it was cooler. The hot sun had made the journey harder. Now the horses rode easier in the cool of the trees. We passed neither house nor village. It was perfect. Then I heard a shout from behind. I turned and saw Mordaf son of Tomas galloping towards me and waving. He was the rear guard.

Without waiting to hear his news I turned to Edward, "You and Fótr ride and ride hard. Take two archers with you and ask David to join me."

"Trouble lord?"

"The way Mordaf is riding, I should say so."

Edward said, "Right, my lady. Let us get the blood flowing eh? We ride as though the devil is after us." He slapped the rump of the Maid's horse and then spurred his own. The four of them headed for the vanguard.

Mordaf reined in, "Riders, lord. There were twenty of them. I think, from their shields that they are French. Gruffyd is watching them." His brother was reliable. The French would have an attack from an unexpected quarter.

Sometimes a knight has to make instant decisions. The trees here had enough room for men and horses to move easily amongst them. My archers would have clear line of sight and be relatively safe from the French. David had eight archers. It was not enough but it would have to do. "Richard Red Leg and

165

Gurth, ride with the women and the servants, get to Mirebeau. It cannot be far. The rest of you we make an ambush here. David organize the archers."

I had seven men at arms. Donning my helmet and unsheathing my sword I led them into the woods

"David of Wales, you initiate the attack. I want them confused."

"Aye lord."

We had just backed our horses so that we were off the road and hidden from view when we heard the thunder of hooves. The French were galloping hard. I was tempted to peer down the road but that would have been a disaster. I had to trust my handful of archers spread out to the north of us. With three on one side and four on the other the French would not know where the arrows came from. The waiting was hard. To have come so close and then fail would be galling and I cursed the Templar. The leading riders began to come into view. I recognised the leading rider. He wore no helmet, and it was the Templar from the Priory. He was wearing mail. A knight rode next to him and then sergeants at arms.

Suddenly arrows fell amongst those at the rear of the column. Their cries and their shouts made the ones at the front stop. I spurred my horse and we burst out amongst the French. We had hidden in the woods to the west and that meant we attacked their sword side. Some of my men had spears. I made for the Templar. His head turned as I raised my sword. He was good. He brought his shield around to block the blow. He could do nothing about my horse. Dragon was a big and powerful war horse. It bit and snapped at the palfrey ridden by the Templar. As he struggled to control his rearing and bucking horse I hacked, back hand across the Templar's unprotected face. My blade ripped through his arming cap and into his cheekbone. The blade carried on into his skull for his horse was pinned by his companion. As I sliced deeper into his skull life left his eyes and he fell from the saddle.

His companion smacked the Templar's horse with the flat of his sword as he rode at me. He too, was a Templar, I saw the token around his neck. My blood was up. I hated treachery. I had disliked the Templars in the Holy Land and, here, in this Christian land, where they were not needed, I despised them. I lunged with my sword. It went beneath his sword which slid alongside my helmet, scoring a line. My blade went up, under his arm and into his body. I pushed harder. Like the other Templar, he rode with just an arming cap. I watched blood spill from his mouth. I twisted and turned the blade. He fell from the saddle.

They were the only two knights and my archers had thinned out the company so much that there were just four sergeants remaining. They turned and fled. I took off my helmet and looked around. Peter son of Richard lay dead as did Michael of Anjou. Phillippe of Poitou was trying to hold in his guts. I threw myself from my saddle.

"Fetch vinegar, bandages and honey!"

My man at arms shook his head, "No lord. It is mortal. Leave me. It is good. I will die in my homeland."

"We will not leave you. The French are fled."

Padraig came over with a skin and said, "Here my friend, have some wine."

Phillippe drank from the skin and nodded for Padraig to remove it. "Lord I have had much honour serving you. I can go to God and face him knowing that I served a true knight. We never did aught that was base and I died saving noble ladies what…" his eyes glazed over and his head lolled to the side. He was dead.

Padraig closed his friend's eyes, "He was a good man."

More of my men had died. I knew that my plan had fooled the Templars. They had thought to catch us at the second priory. We would have been slain while we slept. Now I wanted them to know that I was onto them.

"So were they all. Take the heads of the two knights and plant them here on spears. I would have the French and the Templars know the price they pay for treachery."

Chapter 16

We took our dead with us and the horses and mail from the dead. When I searched the two Templars we found coin but, more importantly, I found a letter. It was getting onto dark and I put the letter in my surcoat. I would read it when we reached Mirebeau. The archers had suffered no losses. All of the sergeants at arms had been Templars. The fact that we had killed sixteen and lost but three spoke well of the skill of my men but the three men lost would be hard to replace. As we rode through the darkening forest I began to second guess myself. Suppose the attack behind us had been a ruse and there were men waiting ahead? The enemy were desperate to get their hands on the two ladies. The Empress Matilda had been such a pawn in the battle for a throne. Eleanor could be Duchess of Brittany and then her brother would no longer be needed. She could be married off to some lord who would be tied to which ever king arranged it. I was still not certain if King John or King Philip was behind this. The letter was burning in my surcoat.

The gates were closed when we arrived. We waited on the drawbridge.

"Who goes there?"

"Sir Thomas of La Flèche." That was all I said.

"Open the gate."

As the gates creaked open we wearily rode through them. Burning brands appeared as we entered the lower ward. I dismounted. A sergeant at arms ran over, "The Duchess told us to watch for you, my lord. She will be pleased that you are safe for she was worried."

"I have three dead men. I would like to lay them in the chapel and then we can bury them in the morning."

"Of course, lord." My men had lifted the three bodies from their horses and stood waiting. "Follow me."

I was left along with the horses. I slipped the arming cap from my head and hung it from my saddle. I went to Dragon. "You did well today, my friend. You saved my life. We rest here for a while."

Just then Fótr and Edward ran over, "Thank God, lord. Edward and I were worried."

I nodded and said to Edward, "We lost three men. They are in the chapel."

Edward's face hardened. These were his men. He had chosen them to accompany us. He recognised their bodies draped over their horses. "Did you get the treacherous bastards, lord?"

"The Templars are dead."

"Good." He smiled at Fótr, "The lad did well, lord. He will be a good knight." He turned and headed towards the chapel.

"The Queen, Countess and the Maid await you in the Great Hall, lord. I will see to Dragon."

I was bloody and I was sweaty. I stank of horse. In a perfect world I would have washed and changed. I was meeting the Queen who, along with her husband, Henry, had presided over the largest Empire since Charlemagne. As the Templar had shown we did not live in a perfect world. I slipped the mail from my hands and removed my cloak before I entered the hall. A servant waited. There was a bowl of water and a cloth. I used the water to wash some of the blood from my surcoat. I wondered, idly, if I should change the blue of my surcoat to red! It would make the blood less easy to see.

"The Queen is waiting, Sir Thomas."

I nodded and he opened the door. The Queen was seated at the head of the table. There was food laid upon it. They had been eating. Even though she was the oldest woman I had ever seen, she was almost eighty, you could still see her beauty. When she had been young she had been described as *perpulchra*, more than beautiful and I could see it now. She had outlived all of her children save John Lackland and Queen Eleanor of Castile. She had held together an Empire after her husband had died. I felt honoured to be in her presence.

I dropped to a knee, "Your majesty."

"Rise, Sir Thomas, and sit by me."

There was a gap between her and the Duchess. The Duchess put her hand on mine, "You did what you said you would. I am indebted to you."

The Maid asked, "Are your men all safe?"

I shook my head, "Three fell but we killed the traitorous Templars."

Queen Eleanor said, "Give Sir Thomas wine. He has need of it. We will talk of this tomorrow. I know warriors. If they dwell on such deaths it makes them both sad and morose."

"Thank you, your majesty. I need this." I lifted the goblet, "To the beautiful ladies."

The Queen laughed, "You are a throwback, my lord. Now men appear chivalrous but they are not. You alone show how a true knight should behave. I knew your grandfather and great grandfather you know. Your great grandfather saved my life on more than one occasion." She shook her head, "As I recall we were pursued through a forest by Geoffrey Duke of Anjou. Your great grandfather saw me safely to Henry. I could never repay him the debt I owed him. And your grandfather was as a northern rock for my husband. He kept the Scots at bay. It is good to see that they have returned in you."

"I fear your son would not agree with that, your majesty."

"My son has made many mistakes, but I fear that I must support him."

169

Return of the Knight

It felt as though the world was falling from beneath my feet. Had my men died in vain?

She saw my face. "I love my grandson, Arthur, as I love my granddaughter Eleanor but Arthur has made his bed with the French. My husband and I disagreed about many things but that was not one. That is why the Duchess and her daughter are here."

"Then John does not seek her."

"King John might seek her but it would be to protect her." I did not believe that but I kept silent. "You do not afford my son his title?"

"No, for he is not the true King. King Richard wished Arthur to be King."

"And on his death bed he recanted."

I shook my head, "That seems a little too convenient for me."

The Queen laughed, "You are as obstinate as the Warlord was! If I were my son I would fear you. You are like the English mastiff. When it gets its teeth into something it does not let go. Let us say that tonight we are all friends. We owe you and your men a great debt. You shall be rewarded." Fótr returned. He bowed and sat next to the Maid. The Queen said, "And now that the young Viking has returned we will eat and I will tell you the tales of your grandfather and great grandfather that you may not have heard. Even if you have then you must indulge me for I am an old woman and talking of the past makes me young again."

She had lost none of her wit and she told a good tale. I had heard most of the stories before but I laughed and I smiled.

"And what of your aunt, Ruth, was it? Does she live still?"

"Yes, your majesty, but she speaks of great hardship in England thanks to your son's tyranny."

"I thought that William Marshal would be as the Warlord and guide the King but it seems not. Still he is the best of the barons in England. You should seek him out, Sir Thomas. I will give you a letter of introduction."

"I have met him already, majesty."

"Then the letter will tell him of your better qualities. Gratitude does not appear to be one of them!"

"Sorry your majesty, it has been a long journey."

"Aye, we shall speak in the morning."

Fótr took me to the room which had been prepared for me. A servant hovered close by. "My lord, the Queen thought you might wish your surcoat to be cleaned."

Fótr helped me to take it off. I removed the sealed letter first. "Thank you." Once in the room I said, "Fótr, bring that light closer. I would read this missive."

As he brought it over he asked, "Where did you get it, lord?"

"It was on the Templar." I had also taken the Templar tokens from around their necks. I used my dagger to slit open the seal. Before I did so I examined it. It was the seal of de Ferrers. Here was a tale!

These knights serve God and they are on a mission from me. I command whoever reads this letter to offer all assistance to them. They will take the Maid of Brittany into my protective custody. Further, if you bring me the head of the traitor, Sir Thomas of La Flèche or any of his men, you will receive gold.
Sir Robert de Ferrers, Lord of Leicester.

I handed it to Fótr to read. He shook his head. "Then it was not the French as we thought."

"No Fótr, I may have misjudged Philip and, perhaps, King John. I fear the de Ferrers family sees an opportunity to gain power through marriage. I am just happy, now that they are safely ensconced in this castle. It would take an army to take it. The one thing de Ferrers does not have is an army capable of taking on the mother of the King. The death of our three men may not have been in vain."

We prepared for bed. Fótr had a pallet by the door. He blew out the candle and, as we lay in the dark said, "Lord, who will decide on the husband for Eleanor, Maid of Brittany?"

I did not answer at first. Fótr had a simple upbringing. His family had lived deep in the forests of Sweden and he had not experienced court. I knew the reason for his question and he was in for a disappointment.

"I fear that would be her mother and also, King John. We have saved her from de Ferrers and the King of France but that means she is delivered into the hands of a cruel and ruthless man. He will decide whom she marries, perhaps even if she marries."

"He cannot deny her a husband, lord!"

"I fear he can. An unmarried Breton heiress is as useful as a dead one. Her hope lies in Arthur. If we can rescue him from the clutches of King Philip and restore him to the Breton Dukedom then who knows. I know what is in your heart, Fótr. Do not get your hopes up. They would be shattered."

He was silent. I do not think he slept much. He and the Maid had become close during the journey. Fate could be cruel.

We buried my men the next day. We buried them in their mail, with sword and helm. The priest who performed the service did not know them but we did. Long after the priest and the ladies had departed we remained there. Each of us had different memories of the three of them but the deaths were a stark reminder to us all of the parlous nature of our lives.

Return of the Knight

The Queen and the Duchess left us alone for the morning but, in the afternoon, we were summoned into their presence. The Queen smiled, "You are in better humour this day, great grandson of the Warlord?"

"I am, your majesty and I apologise for my comments. I will gladly take a letter of introduction to William Marshal."

"Good." She waved a hand and a servant materialized with the letter. It was sealed. She handed it to me. Another servant appeared with a chest. "In here I have two rewards for you. One is coin. If you are anything like your sires that will mean little to you but the other may be of more use." She opened the chest and took out a parchment. "This gives you the manor of Whorlton. It lies close to Northallerton. It belonged to Robert de Meynell. He rebelled against my son Richard and my son gave me the manor. Until you came I had forgotten it. This one is not owned by the Palatinate. Only the King can take it from you and I have written to my son to tell him of my gift to you. So long as you do not rebel against him then you have a home in England. I cannot return Stockton to you but Whorlton has a castle and it is a start."

I bowed. "I thank your majesty."

"And now I will retire. It is the time of day I like to take a nap and all of this excitement has wearied me. Stay here for the Duchess wishes a word."

When the Queen and her entourage left there were just the four of us in the room. The Duchess opened a small chest. "I feel that this is inadequate bearing in mind what you have done but it is a reward for your services." I saw that it was filled with coins.

"Thank you but you need not reward me for I know that life will be hard for the two of you."

She laughed, "Ever the chivalrous knight. Do not worry. We have coin enough."

I nodded and looked around. "I did not show this to the Queen for fear of… well let us say that there may be others close to the Dowager who might work for your enemies."

"The French?"

I handed her the letter, "There are other enemies, my lady, and some are closer to home."

"De Ferrers! I knew he had ambition but…" She looked at me. "What will you do with this letter?"

"I will keep it. It may prove useful. We still have to return to La Flèche. I fear there will be men looking for us."

Eleanor said, somewhat fearfully, "You will return north soon, my lord?"

I nodded. "The longer we stay here the more chance our enemies have to cut us off. I am now three men down. The French seek me, King John hunts me and now, it appears, de Ferrers has Templars looking for me."

"You could stay here! This castle is safe."

Return of the Knight

"I would bring danger and, besides, I have a family and people at home." I looked pointedly at Fótr, "Besides, my lady, the sooner we leave you the sooner you can get on with your life. You are the Maid of Brittany and one day you may be Duchess."

Her hand went to her mouth and she ran from the room. Duchess Constance said, "You are wise, Sir Thomas but I fear you have broken her heart." She looked at Fótr, "If she were an ordinary lady, Fótr, then you and she could be as one. As it is I fear that you are both doomed to pine in vain. Your lord is right. It cannot be."

My squire nodded. In that moment he appeared to have grown a hand span, "But so long as I breathe and she has no husband then I can dream. My ancestors believed in something called, *wyrd*. You would call it Fate. There were three sisters who wove webs to trap men. Since we became Christian we no longer believe in such legends but I am not so certain. My lord discovered me, by accident and I have never regretted following him. When he met his lady, she was betrothed to another yet he married her and they have a family. Until they put you in a grave then you know not what might happen. Tell her that I will not give up."

The Duchess put her hand on his, "If this were my choice to make then I would say be wed and live. For if you did then my daughter would have a life. I am Duchess and it seems I have spent the last ten years clinging onto the title for my son. I will tell her but I fear that your love is doomed."

We waited two days to allow the horses to recover. We had spare horses now. We had captured six and we had the three from our dead comrades. I intended to ride home in one day and change horses. I would not risk an inn or a camp. I feared a knife in the night.

The three ladies came to see us off. Eleanor the Maid was red eyed. Fótr looked at her stoically. The Duchess smiled and kissed us both on the cheek. She handed Edward a beautiful dagger in a finely made scabbard. "Here, my defender, this is for you. You may be born common but there is nobility in your heart."

I could see that Edward was touched.

The Queen said, "I doubt that I will see you again, Sir Knight but you have reminded an old lady of her youth. It is good to know that chivalry still rides."

"And I am honoured to have met you and to have served you. Farewell!"

Fótr put his hands together to help me climb into the saddle. Before he could mount his own horse, the Maid ran to him and kissed him hard on the lips. She said not a word but pressed something into his hand. She turned and walked defiantly back to her mother. Stunned Fótr mounted Flame and I led my men out before anything else untoward happened.

As we left the castle Edward asked, "So, my lord, what is the plan?"

173

Return of the Knight

That was a good question. I had spent half the night trying to wrack my brains for an answer which would get us home. The de Ferrers would now know that their plan had failed and they would seek their letter. They would be hunting me. The arrival of the Duchess and the Maid in Mirebeau would now be common knowledge. The fact that I had taken them there would also be widespread. The French would want the Duchess but they would also want me. King John might not wish harm to the Duchess but he would do all that he could to capture me. I had thwarted him too often for him to allow me to slip through his fingers.

We will head north and cross the rivers Vienne and the Loire where they combine between Saumur and Chinon. It is thirty miles to the rivers. That way we cross in daylight and get some miles north before we are forced to rest."

Robert of La Flèche nodded, "There is a bridge over the Vienne, lord but the Loire is over five hundred paces wide there and it flows swiftly."

"And there is an island. We have spare horses. We put the mail on the spare horses and we swim them across. Our enemies can watch all of the bridges. They cannot watch the whole river." I shrugged, "We can try."

Edward laughed, "Aye sir. It is never dull following your banner."

Chapter 17

When we passed the site of the ambush I saw that the heads and the bodies were gone. There were others out there still hunting us. David and his archers had filtered through the woods and ensured that we were free from ambush. The horses were well rested and we made good time. We swapped horses after fifteen miles. We would swap again when we reached the rivers. We ate when we stopped for the horses. We watered the horses and then ourselves. They were our hope. If they lasted then we would get home. We hit trouble when we neared the bridge over the Vienne. It was not a wide river but the bridge was old and made of wood. Worse, it was guarded. There were just four men there but they wore the livery of Anjou. Sir Guy was not with us and the men knew nothing of us. We sheltered in the trees to decide what to do. Our options were clear. We could wait until dark and either slip over the bridge or, if it was guarded and barred, ford the river. The problem with that was that we would have to cross the more dangerous Loire in the dark. The second was to try to bluff our way across.

I gave orders and sent four archers ahead of us. We rode down towards the bridge. There was no way of disguising our numbers. We had too many horses. But we had cloaks covering our surcoats and we carried no banners. As we rode down the road I saw that were neither towers nor defences at the bridge. There was a small castle at Candes, just a thousand paces from the bridge. I guessed that the sentries came from there. I did not recognise the standard which fluttered from the castle. They would see us and we would need to be across the bridge as quickly as we could.

The four men there stood with crossed spears. They were barring our route. From the castle I heard a horn. We had been seen. I looked at the sergeant at arms, "We would cross this bridge."

"I am sorry my lord but we have orders not to allow any armed men across in either direction." He pointed to the castle. "The baron will be here shortly you may ask him for permission."

I nodded, "Sergeant we will cross and if you try to stop us then you will die. I do not wish to harm you but my business is urgent."

They turned their spears to face me. Suddenly four arrows flew from the side and landed at the men's feet. David of Wales' voice barked, "Drop your weapons and allow his lordship to pass or you have the next arrows in your bodies!"

The sergeant was no fool and the weapons were dropped and the men parted. I waved the men and horses through. "Ride." I leaned down to the sergeant and said, "A wise move. Advise your baron that if he pursues us he does so at his peril."

He caught sight of my surcoat beneath my grey cloak, "You are the Gryphon!" He crossed himself. "Are you a ghost? We thought you dead!"

I heard hooves and David of Wales shouted, "My lord!"

"I am not dead! Pass on my message for your baron's sake!"

I galloped across followed by my archers. The bridge reverberated to the sound of our hooves. Robert had led the men along the south bank of the Loire. He took them half a mile upstream to the place an island split the river unevenly in two. As we approached, I shouted, "Take them across!"

We would now have to risk the river in mail. The first part, which led to the island, was just a hundred paces across and I could see the sand beneath the water for the last forty paces. It was a risk worth taking. We forded the river. The water came up to our horses' necks briefly but then we were on the sand and made the other bank. We reached the shelter of the trees on the island unscathed and we turned to watch the southern river bank. The baron led ten mounted men to the bank. We were well hidden. I saw them looking for us. Eventually they descended the bank. Our hoofprints were clearly visible.

"David. Kill four horses!"

"Aye lord." His archers took aim and the eight arrows flew to kill four of the horses. One was the knight's and a second his squire. Shaking their fists, they all clambered back up the bank.

"Time to take off our mail. David, keep watch while we do so."

The knight would send a message and ask for help. They knew who we were. A rider to Tours might not bring the result they wanted but one to Chinon would. We had to hurry. We helped each other pull off the heavy hauberks and chausse. We tied them onto the spare horses.

"David of Wales, we are ready."

We moved to the other side of the narrow island. The river looked deceptively slow but I knew that it would have a strong current. Fótr was the one I was worried about although Flame, his horse was a good mount, he had never done this before. I said, to them all but my words were especially meant for my squire. "Swim upstream!"

Fótr did not have a spare horse to lead. They were led by men at arms and archers. My archers were used to this. They forded rivers as a matter of course. I led Dragon into the water and pulled him so that he faced north east. We walked the first thirty paces and then the water rose to my chest. I grabbed the cantle and urged him on. He was a strong horse and I found that I was heading north east. He was managing to defeat the current. I clung on and kicked. Ironically the fastest part and the place where the current threatened to take us downstream was the part closest to the sand. There was a deeper channel and I found that Dragon was facing north west. When his feet found the sand, I breathed a sigh of relief. I led him from the water and tied him to a tree. I returned with a length of rope. I knew I had one of the stronger horses. The others might struggle.

The ones who were struggling were the ones leading the spare horses. What saved them was the weight of mail on the backs of the spare horses. It made it harder for the current to pull them downstream. Jack, son of Harold, was carried the furthest downstream. I was about to send one of the archers to seek him when he and the two horses appeared. We were all bedraggled and wet but we had crossed the Loire. We had no dry clothes, but we donned our hauberks. Who knew when we might have to fight? The other bank was hidden by the island and I wondered if the Baron of Candes watched us still.

Our horses had exerted themselves and so we fed them some damp grain and fortified ourselves from our wine skins. We had thirty miles to go and although we were close to home we were now in danger from both King John and the French. The bridge had been our undoing. Had we crossed unseen then we could have laid up in the woods and moved off after dark. That was now impossible. The hunters would be out.

With David of Wales leading we headed north west using trails when we could and if there were no trails then small roads. This time we knew where the castles lay and we avoided them. What we could not avoid were the villages at crossroads nor the farmers working in their fields. I hoped that they would simply ignore us but that was a forlorn hope.

We were less than twenty miles from home when we were found. We were on a little used back road which led to Parcay les Pins. Parcay les Pins had a grander name than it merited. In the middle of a pine forest the four huts were occupied by foresters who made a living in the woods. The timber was sought after for masts. I knew it because we used the wood for our ships.

As we entered the hamlet Jean, the head man, ran up to us, "Sir Thomas, there are men awaiting you on the road to Noyant."

"French or Norman?"

"They are French and there are French awaiting you on the road to Le Lude. The Normans have closed the road to La Flèche."

"How do you know, Jean?"

He smiled, "We know, lord, for we live in the forests. They think they are silent but they are not. They arrived two days since."

I took one of the coins the Duchess had given to me. I slipped it into his hand. "Thank you, Jean, I will not forget my friends."

He looked at me in surprise, "Will you not turn around and find another way home, lord?"

"There are men behind us too. Do not worry. Forewarned is forearmed."

177

Return of the Knight

I turned my horse's head around, "David of Wales, there are men on the Noyant road as well as the road to La Flèche and Le Lude. Find out if we can get past the men at Noyant."

"Aye lord. Griff, Tom, Harry, come with me. You know this land like the back of your hands." He turned to me, "You have four or five miles before you need to make a decision, lord."

"Aye." We made sure our saddles were secure and our weapons ready. We set off north. Once we reached the end of the forest we would be in farmland. We would be in the open and we would be exposed. My archers would use cover to scout out Noyant.

At Briel there was a road which led to Le Lude. I was loath to take it for that would bring me closer to the French at Chateau-sur-le-Loir. If we could pass Noyant then there were four different ways we could reach either La Flèche or Le Lude. We carried on north. We would try to get around the men who waited for us. I looked at the sky; the sun was beginning to set. With eighteen miles to go to safety we would not make it before dark.

"Fótr, stay close to me. We have lost three men at arms. This night you will have to fight as though you are a veteran."

"Aye lord."

We took it steadily as we headed north. With all eyes ahead, we were suddenly surprised by three riders who burst from the small road to our left. It was not a stone road and we had not heard them. Even so we reacted quickly. Edward and Fótr's swords were out in a flash and two riders fell. The third one, however, managed to turn his horse and escape back down the road. I dismounted. None had mail and they rode ponies. That was why we had not heard them. One carried the sign of St. Denis. They were French. They had come from the south west. Had they been in the castle at Candes? If they were then there was collusion between the French and the garrison at Candes for it was still Angevin. Treachery was all around us.

"Should I follow him, lord?"

"No Henry. There is little point. If they are the scouts of a larger force we risk losing men. We will hurry north and hope that David has found a way around the town."

Noyant was bigger than Parcay les Pins but not by much. The main difference was a wooden palisade. It was intended to keep animals in and predators out. There was no castle but if men had occupied it then we would have our route barred.

David and his archers materialised from the side of the road. David's face in the fading light was grim. "There are thirty men waiting there, lord. Only ten are mounted but there are two knights and men at arms."

"Could we force our way through?"

Return of the Knight

He shook his head. "We would lose men. They have barred the road and they keep watch."

Had we not been surprised by the three riders then I would have risked sending men in with knives to slit throats. The deaths of the two men had ended that idea. I pointed to the north west. "We dismount and we lead our horses around Noyant. We take the road to La Flèche. Muffle your armour. David of Wales you lead. Robert of La Flèche, bring up the rear."

David said, "In the dark our bows will not be effective, lord."

"I know. Once we have passed Noyant there are no more castles and no towns. We only have to avoid farms."

We set off west heading across open fields. We were heading into the setting sun. The men at Noyant would be watching the road. As we walked I listened for the sounds of horses and men from our left. All the time I was thinking that I now had a price on my head. That might explain the alliance of Angevin traitors and the French. This was the borderlands. A lord had to be flexible to survive.

We each followed the horse in front. I was behind John Wayfarer and Fótr walked behind me. I was aware that we were turning more to the north. The sun had almost gone down but there was a faint line of pink light to my left. David of Wales had a natural instinct and knew the direction he was travelling by means I did not understand. I trusted him.

It seemed an age before John Wayfarer stopped and David came back to me. "The road is ahead. I have checked and it is clear. By my guess we are two miles north of Noyant. We can mount."

"Good. Pass the word, mount."

I climbed into the saddle. I had not walked as far for a long time. We had been on the road for barely a mile when we heard a commotion to the south of us. I did not panic. We kept our gait at a steady walk. I did not want thundering hooves to alert our enemies that we had slipped their trap.

It was only when Robert of La Flèche passed a message to me that we were being pursued that I ordered my men to gallop. It was a race. I spurred Dragon and pulled next to David of Wales. Edward joined me.

"There are men waiting at La Flèche. We have to find somewhere to fight those who pursue us."

"They outnumber us."

I did not answer Edward. It was obvious that we would be outnumbered. David of Wales said, "The forest south of La Flèche is just seven miles from the castle. If we held there one man might get through to the castle."

"One man?"

"Griff Jameson. He knows this land better than any and he is a good warrior. He could bring help. Sir Richard and Sir Henry cannot know that our enemies wait for us."

179

Return of the Knight

It was not much of a plan but it was a plan. I turned in my saddle and shouted, "Griff Jameson."

He galloped up to me, "Aye lord."

"We are going to hold up in the forest south of La Flèche. I want you to sneak through the enemy lines and bring help from the castle. Can you do it?"

Even though we were riding hard he still grinned and nodded, "Sneak through a bunch of dozy Frenchmen? In my sleep lord."

"Good then bring them to the sound of the battle and let us hope we are still alive when you reach us." As he disappeared I shouted, "As we only have a short way to go let us ride hard and prepare a welcome for these Frenchmen!"

Even in the dark we could see the forest looming up ahead of us. We hunted there. It was familiar to us. The road to Le Lude passed along its northern edge. Even as we rode I was planning where to stop. The road twisted and turned. Two miles in there was a slight slope. It was not much but we had felled trees at the top and it meant there was a slightly more open space for us. More importantly we had not yet removed all of the logs. We were allowing them to season before using them for building. We would be able to make a defence. David must have read my mind for he reined in as our horses began to breathe heavier after the exertion of the slope. "Here is a good place and I fear the horses have done enough, lord."

"You are right! Stop here. Hobble the horses. Archers put the horses where we can reach them easily. Men at arms make the logs into a wall. Build it where the road is narrow. Here is where we make our stand."

I heard Padraig the Wanderer say, "Just when I get a bit of coin together and think about taking a wife we have half the French army after us!"

Edward laughed, "You have not enough coin yet to induce a woman to take on an ugly bugger like you!"

The banter was a good sign. I laid down my cloak. I needed space to swing my sword. My blade had been sharpened at Mirebeau and was perfect. As the logs were dragged into place I heard the thunder of hooves. We were less than six miles from home and yet we might as well have been on the other side of the world. With enemies before and behind, we were trapped. I took off my helmet. I would need to use all of my senses. Fótr looked at me, "Take off your helmet. The arming cap will have to suffice."

We had nine archers. The light was too poor for accuracy at distance but they could shower the narrow road with arrows. We would be in darkness until the sun came up and, by then the battle would have been decided. It all depended on Griff. He would be almost at the castle now. It would take Sir Richard some time to rouse and mount the men and more than an hour to reach us. We needed to hold them off for almost two hours.

"David when you can hit them then release."

Return of the Knight

"Aye lord. Right lads, we will send our arrows when they are two hundred paces from us. Nice and steady."

We waited and listened to the drumming of the hooves as they approached us. We could not make out faces but we saw the mass of horses. I was not sure how far away they were until David of Wales shouted, "Draw! Release!" After that the archers worked at their own pace. The nine of us with swords and shields stood behind the logs. We would have to wait. If any of the French were brave enough or foolish enough to try to jump the log barrier then we could be in trouble. I put that unpleasant thought from my mind.

The arrows struck. Even as horses whinnied and men fell from saddles more arrows were in the air and then more.

A French voice shouted, "Ambush! Look to the trees!"

They could not see us and thought that we flanked them. They would soon realise their mistake but as long as there was such confusion men would die; their men! Four riderless horses came to the log barricade and stopped. That told the French where we were and the French voice shouted, "Fall back and dismount!"

"Now they will try to flank us."

David of Wales said, "Mordaf and Gruffyd take Will and John, go to the left. The rest with me." As he passed me he said, "We will stop them flanking, lord, but they will come at you."

"I know!" Turning to my men I said, "We have to trust David of Wales. They will not flank us. We stop them getting over the barrier. If they climb they cannot use their swords. We do not climb! We are not squirrels. We kill!"

They did not come straight away. I am not clear if they meant to make us worry or they were just being very cautious but it seemed an age before I heard movement. A scream from my right told me that the archers had made their first kill. Trying to outwit my archers in a forest was like trying to get the better of a wolf in its den! I was dimly aware that, in the east, the sky looked marginally lighter. False dawn. I saw a movement. It was the French and they were advancing. They had their helmets on. It would limit their vision. The eye holes were bad enough in daylight but in the dark, they were a positive hindrance. There were more cries from left and right. I heard arrows as they flew through the dark. My archers would be sending them from ten paces distance. The men they struck would die.

I heard a wail and then a French voice shouted, "Get back in the woods, you cowards! There are a handful of these bandits, no more." Numbers were hard to estimate but they had filled the road. That meant seven men abreast. When they saw the logs, a knight, I guessed it was a knight, shouted, "Charge!"

They ran at the logs. They were built to chest height. They could have used their weapons over the top but they were eager to close with us and they tried to climb. The first knight grasped the top of the logs and put his foot on the bottom one. I lunged with my sword and it entered his right shoulder. He fell backwards and struck one of his men who was climbing. Padraig had a long sword and he brought it across the side of the head of a man at arms. The man fell. Another used the body of the dead man to help him to climb and he made the top log. Edward swung his sword and it sliced through both legs. Pumping blood he fell.

More men tried to use the dead to climb onto the logs or to use them as a fighting platform. That played into our hands. We had nine swords we could bring to bear and they had only seven. Added to that the light was improving and we could see them. We were still shadows. When another five had fallen a voice from the rear shouted, "Fall back! The sun is rising. We will await the Comte."

I turned to Fótr. "Take four men and fetch the horses."

As he went Edward said, "We will run? This is a good place to defend."

"Not when dawn breaks and there will be reinforcements. Our horses are rested and they have a barrier to overcome. Go and fetch Mordaf."

As he left I whistled and David of Wales shouted, "Aye lord?"

"Did you hear?"

"We will pull back."

Of course, just as we could hear the French so they could hear us but Fótr and my men arrived with the horses and we mounted.

"After them." The French would be following!

The road continued to twist and turn through the trees. I was tempted to abandon the horses we had brought but they contained not only the treasure but the Templar letter and the rights to my new manor. I would not let them go easily. Noise travels a long way at night. We had been battling in the woods for some time. Someone close by must have heard the sound of combat. My archers were ahead and the sky was light enough to make out that the trees were ending. Suddenly Gruffyd ap Thomas who was in the lead held up his hand and reined in. That told me all I needed to know.

Donning my helmet, I shouted, "Fótr, stay with the horses. Archers to the rear! Men at arms to me!"

David of Wales called out "Enemy horse ahead lord." Already he and his archers were moving back through my men at arms. Until they were dismounted and their bows readied then they were in the greatest danger.

I had seven men with me. I spurred Dragon. I could see a banner. De Comte had spread his knights out. Therein lay the tiniest glimmer of hope. I could see that they outnumbered us but if I could take the leading knight and the head of the snake then the others might lose heart.

I shouted, "La Flèche and the Maid of Brittany!" My men at arms had been taken by the young girl and the obvious love between her and Fótr. It would put heart into their fight and strength in their tired arms. I pulled my shield up. The

Return of the Knight

French were in the same loose formation as we were. My powerful war horse would bring me into combat first. Our castle was just a few miles away. I should have known that the French would have camped close to the edge of the wood where they could remain hidden and prevent me from reaching the safety of my river and my walls. Hindsight was always perfect. The thought that I was so close to my wife and family steeled me.

The light was the thin grey light of dawn but it was enough. The knight I would strike was also riding a war horse. I did not recognise the blue and yellow design. Perhaps it was another sword for hire. I hoped he had been paid in advance for if he captured me he would have earned it. I had already made up my mind which side I would strike. I would feint as though I was going for his shield side and use Dragon's speed to take me to the left. The road was descending to the Loir and while it might not be much of a gradient it be would enough to aid me.

I saw his sword come across his cantle as he prepared to stand in his stirrups and strike at my head. We were barely four paces apart when I switched Dragonto the left. I brought my sword hard across his chest. My heart was filled with thoughts of my castle and my family. It was a crushing blow. He tumbled from the saddle. I jerked Dragon's head to the left. His squire sat petrified in his saddle. I punched his shoulder hard with my shield and he fell backwards. We were outnumbered and, as I continued my turn I saw that Fótr and my archers were beleaguered by the men who were following. My men at arms were all engaged. I slid my sword into the side of the man fighting Edward and as he fell from the saddle shouted, "Back to the archers. Fótr is in danger!"

"Aye lord." David and the archers were using the horses as a barricade but soon they would be overwhelmed, there were but nine of them. The four men at arms who had ridden around the circled horses did not expect us to return. There was no finesse to our attack. We simply charged our war horses into them. I used shield, sword and Dragon's teeth to knock them from their saddles. Dragon was tiring. I could see more men heading for my archers. If I had a few more men we might have held them but I could see that we had too few.

Suddenly, behind me, I heard a horn. It sounded three times and then three times again. It was Sir Richard and Sir Henry. Turning to Edward I shouted, "We have help! I have run enough! Let us charge!"

My archers saw us coming and moved aside the horses. As we passed through I saw two bodies lying there. The horses parted on the other side and the two of us burst through and headed towards the surprised French. They had been on the verge of breaking through and now two madmen were attacking them. The French were on foot. I brought my sword from behind me and ripped up through the hauberk of the man at arms who was too slow to bring his shield around. I pulled back on the reins to allow Dragon to smash his hooves down on a second. A man at arms ran at me with an axe. An arrow plucked him from

183

the air and then, suddenly Sir Richard and Sir Henry were next to me. Dragon was spent but I laid about me with my sword until the French finally broke and fled down the road. Eager to atone for their tardy arrival my two knights chased them down the road.

I took off my helmet and turned. Edward, son of Edgar was still there. He and his horse were covered in blood. I could see that his sword was notched but he lived. I took off my mail mitten and held my arm out. "Edward, that was nobly done. This trip has opened my eyes to many things. When we return home, you will begin training. I would have you a knight."

"Me lord? I am the son of a hawker!"

"The Duchess saw it in you. Edward son of Edgar, you have nobility which is in you if not your blood." We turned around and rode back to the circle of horses. Three of the captured horses lay dead. I saw that John Wayfarer and Harry Archerson, two of my archers lay dead. Fótr was having his wounds tended to by David of Wales. "Lord your squire is a true warrior. He fought like a lion!"

"As did you all."

I looked up and saw Henry Youngblood leading two horses. Draped over them were the bodies of Jack son of Harold and Gurth Sven's son. My men had been faithful unto death. We had survived but at a terrible and irreplaceable cost.

It was noon by the time we entered my castle. It had taken time to chase the French away from the forest. We took our dead, the captured horses and the mail and the weapons from the dead. Sir Richard was abject in his apology, "My lord I am sorry we were late. In our haste to leave I did not send out scouts and we were ambushed not far from the castle. By the time we had dealt with them we had lost time and…"

"These things happen, Richard. You must learn from them. Here a single mistake can be costly." I pointed to the four cloak draped bodies. "We will talk more when these are buried and we are safe within our walls. There is much treachery around us and much honour too. I would dwell on the honour and not the treachery."

My townspeople all gathered to watch us enter my town. We dismounted and took first the four bodies of the men who had left with me and now lay dead. My tiny conroi left our horses for others to care for and we went directly to my chapel. My wife and Father Michel awaited us. Neither said a word but Father Michel opened the door and went to the altar. We laid the bodies before the altar and then we all knelt in prayer. It was a stark reminder that this was our fate. One day all of us would lie here.

Father Michel said, after some time, "My lord, leave the dead with me. We will prepare them for burial. There are many who would attend for these men were popular."

Return of the Knight

I stepped out into the light and my wife threw her arms around me, "Welcome home. The knight has returned and all is well."

"Aye love and my home feels even more special now!"

Epilogue

When we reached our home Fótr came to me and showed me and my wife what Eleanor Fair Maid of Brittany had given him. It was half a heart made of gold. "All the way home, lord, I have wondered what this meant."

My wife said, "The Maid gave this to you?"

"She did, my lady."

Margaret squeezed her hand around Fótr's hand. "Then she has the other half. It means her heart is yours. No matter what happens she will be true to you."

"Then I have hope?"

I shook my head, "The world would have to be turned upside down for that to happen but you can dream and I am pleased that she gave it to you."

Edward son of Edgar began his training. He moved into the castle and Sir Richard undertook the task of making him a knight. The treasure we had been given was spread amongst the survivors. They were all rich men. Any one of them could have left my service and returned wherever they wished. The fact that they chose not to I took as a compliment. Now that my wife knew of Fótr and the Maid she spent a long time with him. She spoke to him of love as only a woman can do. It took time but, gradually he healed.

I told Sir Richard of my new manor. He nodded, "It is not the richest of manors but it can be defended easily. As the crow flies it is a few miles from my old home. Does this mean you return home, lord?"

"No, Sir Richard, but it does mean that now I have a home to which I can return."

A month after my return Richard Red Leg summoned me to the west town gate again. "Lord that knight is returned. The Seneschal's man."

I nodded and, taking Fótr with me, went to meet him. Sir Guy nodded, "You did well, lord. The Seneschal would like to see you." I made to return for my horse. "No lord, he is in the woods yonder."

As we walked, I said, "Is he becoming brave or am I trusted now?"

"Do you not know, lord that the Seneschal trusts you and your word more than any other. He knows that you are honourable."

When I reached him William des Roches shook my hand. "Sir Thomas I am more grateful than you can know."

There was something in his voice which alerted my curiosity. "What has happened?"

"Prince Arthur believes that his mother and sister were kidnapped. He and the French are gathering an army to ride to Mirebeau. They intend to take the Dowager Queen. Had you not taken them there then the French King might have his hands on them. They are safe within Mirebeau."

"And you have a traitor too. De Ferrers is in league with the Templars. He sought the Maid too."

"The King will never believe such treachery. You have proof?"

"I have a letter."

"Then keep it safe for that is your security. Guard it well."

"And you Seneschal, you continue to serve this faithless king who will ignore such behaviour from his knights?"

"Sir Thomas, I do all that I do for this land and for England. I will not stand by and see tyranny. Here there is none. So far, our people have been treated well. When time allows then I will return to England to speak with William Marshal for therein lies our hope."

"Then all is well."

He nodded, "And now, your reward. Gold?"

I shook my head. I had had much time to think this through. "Bazouges sur le Loir; I would have that manor and I would build a castle there."

"You do not ask for much! King John would not allow it."

"I do not ask King John I ask William des Roches the seneschal of Angers and Tours. You know that I will not take advantage, but I would have my home protected. I have knights now."

"Then you have it."

"And two priests!"

"Two priests? A strange request. Why?"

"My knights would have churches in their manors as would I. We know we have God on our side. We would like his priests too."

"Very well." He clasped my arm, "You are an enigma Sir Thomas but I am glad that you live in this land. Where others fight for what they can take you fight for that which you believe. You truly are a chivalrous and honourable knight!" He clasped my arm. I had learned that my first impressions of this knight had been misguided.

I left him and returned to my castle. We were not finished but I had survived and we now had two allies. That was more than I had had when I had returned from the Baltic. Who knew what the future held?

The End

Glossary

Chevauchée- a raid by mounted men
Garth- a garth was a farm. Not to be confused with the name Garth
Groat- English coin worth four silver pennies
Luciaria-Lucerne (Switzerland)
Mêlée- a medieval fight between knights
Nissa- Nice (Provence)
Vair- a heraldic term
Wulfestun- Wolviston (Durham)

Historical Notes

Prince Arthur

"After King John had captured Arthur and kept him alive in prison for some time, at length, in the castle of Rouen, after dinner on the Thursday before Easter, when he was drunk and possessed by the devil ['ebrius et daemonio plenus'], he slew him with his own hand, and tying a heavy stone to the body cast it into the Seine. It was discovered by a fisherman in his net, and being dragged to the bank and recognized, was taken for secret burial, in fear of the tyrant, to the priory of Bec called Notre Dame de Pres."

Margam annals

Eleanor Fair Maid of Brittany

I did not know the story of Eleanor until I began researching this book. Hers is a sad story. Eventually King John captured her and imprisoned her in a castle: although the exact location is uncertain. Some said Corfe and then Bristol. When King John died his heir, Henry III continued to have her incarcerated. Her burial and her final resting place are unknown. There is a story there.

William des Roches

In May 1199, King Philip of France met with William des Roches at Le Mans and together they attacked the border fortress of Ballon, the fortress was surrendered by Geoffrey de Brûlon, the castellan, but not before being demolished. A quarrel ensued between King Philip and William over the lordship of the site. William was adamant that Ballon belonged rightfully to Duke Arthur, while King Philip wished to retain it as his own.

In June 1199, King John of England launched a massive attack into Northern Maine from Argentan. On 13 September he was successful in repulsing King Philip from the fortress of Lavardin which protected the route from Le Mans to Tours. Arthur's supporters were forced to come to terms with John, and William met with the English king at Bourg-le-Roi, a fortress of the pro-John viscounts of Beaumont-en-Maine on or about 18 September. John convinced William that Arthur of Brittany was being used solely as a tool of Capetian strategy and managed to convince him to switch sides. With this, John promised him the seneschalship of Anjou. During the night, John's incumbent seneschal, Viscount Aimery, took Arthur and Constance and fled the court. They fled first to Angers, then to the court of King Philip. King John officially designated William seneschal of Anjou in December 1199 and entered Angers triumphantly on 24 June 1200.

Griff Hosker,
December 2017

Other books by Griff Hosker

If you enjoyed reading this book, then why not read another one by the author?

Ancient History

The Sword of Cartimandua Series
(Germania and Britannia 50 A.D. – 128 A.D.)
Ulpius Felix- Roman Warrior (prequel)
The Sword of Cartimandua
The Horse Warriors
Invasion Caledonia
Roman Retreat
Revolt of the Red Witch
Druid's Gold
Trajan's Hunters
The Last Frontier
Hero of Rome
Roman Hawk
Roman Treachery
Roman Wall
Roman Courage

The Wolf Warrior series
(Britain in the late 6th Century)
Saxon Dawn
Saxon Revenge
Saxon England
Saxon Blood
Saxon Slayer
Saxon Slaughter
Saxon Bane
Saxon Fall: Rise of the Warlord
Saxon Throne
Saxon Sword

Medieval History

The Dragon Heart Series
Viking Slave
Viking Warrior
Viking Jarl
Viking Kingdom
Viking Wolf
Viking War
Viking Sword
Viking Wrath
Viking Raid
Viking Legend
Viking Vengeance
Viking Dragon
Viking Treasure
Viking Enemy
Viking Witch
Viking Blood
Viking Weregeld
Viking Storm
Viking Warband
Viking Shadow
Viking Legacy
Viking Clan
Viking Bravery

The Norman Genesis Series
Hrolf the Viking
Horseman
The Battle for a Home
Revenge of the Franks
The Land of the Northmen
Ragnvald Hrolfsson
Brothers in Blood
Lord of Rouen
Drekar in the Seine
Duke of Normandy
The Duke and the King

Danelaw

Return of the Knight
(England and Denmark in the 11th Century)
Dragon Sword
Oathsword (October 2021)

New World Series
Blood on the Blade
Across the Seas
The Savage Wilderness
The Bear and the Wolf
Erik The Navigator

The Vengeance Trail

The Reconquista Chronicles
Castilian Knight
El Campeador
The Lord of Valencia

The Aelfraed Series
(Britain and Byzantium 1050 A.D. - 1085 A.D.)
Housecarl
Outlaw
Varangian

**The Anarchy Series England
1120-1180**
English Knight
Knight of the Empress
Northern Knight
Baron of the North
Earl
King Henry's Champion
The King is Dead
Warlord of the North
Enemy at the Gate
The Fallen Crown
Warlord's War
Kingmaker
Henry II
Crusader
The Welsh Marches
Irish War

Return of the Knight
Poisonous Plots
The Princes' Revolt
Earl Marshal

Border Knight
1182-1300
Sword for Hire
Return of the Knight
Baron's War
Magna Carta
Welsh Wars
Henry III
The Bloody Border
Baron's Crusade
Sentinel of the North
War in the West
Debt of Honour

Sir John Hawkwood Series
France and Italy 1339- 1387
Crécy: The Age of the Archer
Man At Arms
The White Company

Lord Edward's Archer
Lord Edward's Archer
King in Waiting
An Archer's Crusade
Targets of Treachery (August 2021)

Struggle for a Crown
1360- 1485
Blood on the Crown
To Murder A King
The Throne
King Henry IV
The Road to Agincourt
St Crispin's Day

Tales from the Sword

Conquistador

Return of the Knight
England and America in the 16th Century
Conquistador (Novemberr 2021)

Modern History

The Napoleonic Horseman Series
Chasseur à Cheval
Napoleon's Guard
British Light Dragoon
Soldier Spy
1808: The Road to Coruña
Talavera
The Lines of Torres Vedras
Bloody Badajoz
The Road to France
Waterloo
The Lucky Jack American Civil War series
Rebel Raiders
Confederate Rangers
The Road to Gettysburg

The British Ace Series
1914
1915 Fokker Scourge
1916 Angels over the Somme
1917 Eagles Fall
1918 We will remember them
From Arctic Snow to Desert Sand
Wings over Persia

Combined Operations series
1940-1945
Commando
Raider
Behind Enemy Lines
Dieppe
Toehold in Europe
Sword Beach
Breakout
The Battle for Antwerp
King Tiger
Beyond the Rhine
194

Return of the Knight
Korea
Korean Winter

Other Books
Great Granny's Ghost (Aimed at 9-14-year-old young people)

For more information on all of the books then please visit the author's website at www.griffhosker.com where there is a link to contact him or visit his Facebook page: GriffHosker at Sword Books

Printed in Great Britain
by Amazon

83164597R00112